JUNK

JUNK

Michael Goodwin

iUniverse, Inc.
New York Lincoln Shanghai

JUNK

iUniverse, Inc.

For information address:
iUniverse, Inc.
2021 Pine Lake Road, Suite 100
Lincoln, NE 68512
www.iuniverse.com

ISBN: 0-595-27682-2 (pbk)
ISBN: 0-595-74945-3 (cloth)

Printed in the United States of America

Everybody I knew was in the bond business, so I supposed it could support one more single man.

—THE GREAT GATSBY

Contents

Chapter 1: Big Deal 1
Chapter 2: Anything to Anyone, Anytime, Anywhere 9
Chapter 3: A Tall Order 16
Chapter 4: Just Do It 22
Chapter 5: Account Development 28
Chapter 6: Dream Street 36
Chapter 7: Pops 43
Chapter 8: When the Whip Comes Down 52
Chapter 9: Doubt and Redoubt 59
Chapter 10: Gung Hay Fat Choy 65
Chapter 11: Oh Happy Day 73
Chapter 12: Fortune's Fool 81
Chapter 13: Defenestration 89
Chapter 14: This Importunate World 94
Chapter 15: Hapless 102
Chapter 16: Hightailin' 111
Chapter 17: Yellow Dog Blues 121
Chapter 18: Back at the Factory 131

Chapter 19: Blood 135
Chapter 20: Red Nut 144
Chapter 21: One of the Boys 156
Chapter 22: Deus Ex Machina 168
Chapter 23: One Year Later 180

CHAPTER 1

BIG DEAL

MARTIN STALLWORTH COULDN'T GET THE SONG out of his head, not matter how hard he tried. His dorky business school roommate used to wake him every Monday morning to the stereo blasting out *I don't like Mondays…Tell me why I don't like Mondays…*This early Monday found Martin, as usual, scudding across the cavernous sixty-five thousand square foot trading floor of Whorman Skeller & Company, touted as the world's largest without supporting floor-to-ceiling columns. The roommate was long gone but it was still Monday morning, and the same old tune danced in his head.

Most impressive about the trading floor was the fifty-foot high atrium ceiling and huge air ducts, held in place by giant tensile chords dramatically criss-crossing the roof's exposed support system. A clerestory had been designed to allow just enough light to enter, giving the floor an airy feeling without creating glare against the two thousand computer screens arrayed on rows of desks spanning across the expanse of teal carpeting.

It was that time again, and a muffled murmur suddenly filled the cavern as traders, salespeople and office personnel came ambling in, seemingly going nowhere, but each one following a well-worn, specific path to a cubicle, keyboard and screen. Most amazing was the perfectly tuned acoustic engineering. Even when the floor was at fever pitch with frantic market activity, the noise level never rose above a muffled murmur, thanks to the state-of-the-art acoustic system that emanated an electronic drone while wrapping all sounds within a mantle of incoming "white noise" from above.

Martin quickly glanced at the huge digital clocks on the far wall displaying up-to-the-second time in major financial centers around the world. New York: 7.12.32 He would have to hurry to make the routine Monday morning, High-yield Research and Trading Meeting at 7.15.00. Usually the first salesman at the meeting, he believed it was important to start the week off on the right foot, and that meant being alert, prepared and ready. He would even get there early enough to have read The Wall Street Journal, front to back, before the meeting. But at the moment he was angry for being so slow getting dressed. Now there was no time to grab the usual cup of coffee at one of the four commissary stations on the trading floor. *I wanna shoot the whole day down, down, down...*he muttered.

Martin briskly strode another thirty feet, made a left turn and scurried past rows of carrels to one of the conference rooms that lined both sides of the trading floor. Already assembled inside the conference room was most of the team at Whorman Skeller responsible for the issuance, trading and distribution of high-yield bonds, or "junk bonds," affectionately called ever since Mike Milken went to jail.

Martin took a seat at the conference table where the other six high-yield salespeople sat. Although bond salespeople are often castigated as being paid way more than they deserve, the sales force was granted the token prominence of table—seating while the research geeks were consigned to chairs along the wall. The traders stood at the head of the table, all the better to glower at the sales team.

Martin glanced about as he sat down, hoping to see Mihra—the cute Pakistani research assistant. Not that Martin had the hots for Mihra, an infatuation that he was not prepared to admit. Also he was comforted by the presence of another person of color in a room filled with white people, given he was the only African-American in the thirty-person, high-yield department. Such discomfort was something else he would not admit to, not today, not tomorrow.

Martin sat next to Lyle Shiner, who made a grunting sound in response to Martin's mumbled good morning. Martin guessed that Lyle was lost in some sort of self-serving reverie. *Probably day-dreaming about something that had occurred the preceding Saturday night—or in the wee hours of Sunday morning,* Martin thought. He knew he would hear soon enough about it, whatever it was. For some reason, Shiner made sure every Monday morning that Martin was doubly informed about the sordid details of another Shiner-debauched weekend. Martin guessed that Lyle used him as an audience because Shiner thought Martin's office demeanor was strait-laced, upstanding, a goody-two-shoes.

The past Monday morning, Lyle had regaled Martin with the story of how he had met a "mystery lady." The tale was typical of Lyle—another Saturday night, fulsome carousing involving all manner of intoxicants, including a shot of Absinthe, the old fashion kind that Toulouse-Lautrec drank every night. The story was further heightened by reference to a six-foot blonde "ex-model," lady fair, pushing the brew at an after-hours club somewhere in the cobblestone confines of the meatpacking district.

"Anyway, I'll never forget her, a stranger in the night—

"Two ships passing on uncharted waters—

"My mystery lady," Shiner said, his Bensonhurst inflection undermining any effort at romantic expression. She had exited her cab just as he had stepped from his in front of the Tribeca loft building.

"Mystery lady?" Martin said. "Waxing a bit lyrical, aren't you, Lyle ol' boy?"

Shiner then confessed this lady was no more mysterious than a short, middle age woman, whose attractions were, at most, modest and whose dyed blonde hair would retain a permanent curl for at least another week. Judging by the plaid overcoat with fake fur collar, Shiner had instantly appraised her as a Wal-Mart floozy striving towards some sort of Sears's respectability.

Lyle had then cut to the chase and related how, within fifteen minutes of their "bumping into each other," he had found himself banging into her spread legs as she straddled the cash-dispensing machine in the ATM cubicle across the street from his apartment. He told how she had grinned at him with that screwy boozy leer of hers. "Hey, you're kinda cute, baby," she managed to declaim between loud moans and caterwauling. He relished telling Martin how he had grabbed the corners of the cash machine so as to put more torque into his manic pumping. Watching the whole time were two Scandinavian gals, tourist chicks who decided to save some hotel expense and lay their sleeping bags down in the small, warm and cozy ATM cubicle.

"And I bet you smiled and winked at them, didn't you?" Martin had asked.

"Let's just say I did," he answered. "That makes it all the more better."

Martin wondered how Lyle would top that one this week.

Seated across the table from Martin and Lyle was Libby Sullivan, Lyle's exact opposite. "Typical bond salesman" was the way Libby, a bond saleswoman, would have summed up Lyle—unprincipled and unintelligent, quick with a joke and a light of your smoke, all bluster and bullshit. More reliant he was on New York Knicks tickets than knowledge when it came to selling bonds. "You wouldn't know a good idea unless it was sucking your cock," Libby had once shouted at Lyle, causing an outburst of howls in the high-yield sales pit. Libby saw herself as the thinking man's—make that thinking woman's—bond salesperson. She could ingest reams of research and regurgitate it all back at you, colored of course by her own insightful insight. Her Vassar education endowed her, in her mind at least, with an analytical ability that few on the sell side—or on the buy side for that matter—could claim. A lot of Seven Sisters women graduate with the ambition to make the world a better place. Libby's life's goal was not so lofty. Her aim was more modest—transform the junk bond business into something resembling a graduate studies seminar.

Martin didn't mind Libby. He didn't dislike her, anyway, as did Lyle. She acted nice. Oh, so nice. Perhaps, too nice. Martin sometimes felt that Libby condescended to him because he was black. So when he first joined the high-yield group, she acted like she had just found a pet to care for. That was why he could never get too comfortable with her.

At 7:15 precisely, Terry Barker, the head trader on the high-yield desk, brought the meeting to order. "All right, who in the research department wants to start? And let's not have any babbling, guys. Keep your piece to three minutes or less—solid stuff, to the point." Martin glumly noted to himself that Terry was being his usual, diplomatic self.

Martin saw saleswoman Lori Putterman gazing at Terry, running her fingers across the white-gold embroidery on her discounted Cartier watch. Martin guessed that it wasn't just Terry's shiny black hair and dark eyes that attracted her but his rough style. Martin could almost hear her sigh, "Oh, if only Terry were Jewish..."

Arnie Markum was the first research analyst to take the podium, discussing briefly events and developments in his specific sector, telecommunications. Arnie was a real motor mouth and Martin sensed that Terry was itching at the chance to grapple-hook him once his spiel went beyond three minutes. Terry didn't particularly like Arnie as he was always acting too much like Woody Allen, whom Terry didn't like either. He didn't particularly like any of the research analysts or any of the salespeople, for that matter, or anyone, come to think of it, Martin realized.

"What's new in the telecommunications sector, you ask?" Arnie rhetorically hammered. "You hear about these 'smart phones'? They're so smart they can do my kid's trigonometry homework!"

As Arnie was being pelted with a fusillade of rolling eyes, into the room burst Dick Moore. He was the titular head of Whorman Skeller's high-yield group, though nobody was sure exactly what he did. Dick Moore had been born and reared among a large Catholic family in a fishing town just north of Boston. His father trapped lobster while selling insurance on the side, and the rather pedestrian background still didn't stop him from putting on the air of a pedigreed Connecticut WASP. Dartmouth educated, he was a member of the New Canaan Country Club, the Stanwich Country Club in Greenwich, the New York Yacht Club, and last and least in his estimation, the New Canaan Trinity Episcopal Church. His redeeming quality was a wicked, jocular sense of humor, marred too often by wrath directed at underlings. During those moments, his face with its long chin and straight nose would contort into a vicious scowl/sneer, all the while behind his wire-framed spectacles his eyes were menacing.

"All right, everyone, listen up," Dick Moore said, a bit breathless from trotting from the trading desk to the conference room. "Christmas is coming early. I just got off the phone with our next client while beating my brains and busting my ass to get you jokers our next deal. Reeled in a real cahuna this time, baby. Huge deal. A lot of dough in it." Martin stirred in his seat, knowing that a new issue bond deal would mean a big meal ticket for him and the other salespeople. Salespeople made their money, not from trading bonds in the secondary market for a quarter of a point but from new-issue deals that had sales credit for as much as three points (three percent) of the issued total. Deals were the mother lode.

"How big, you mullets wanna know, I'm sure," Moore continued. "Five hundy. Five hundred million dollar deal! How you like them apples, my little butterflies?"

Someone among the sales group whistled, while Lyle muttered, "Fuckin' A!" under his breath.

"You chowder heads all love me now?" Moore asked with self-satisfied glee as he surveyed the group.

Skeets Daniel, at fifty-eight the senior bond salesman among the group and thus the only one who could get away with giving it back to Moore, said in his Southern drawl, "We always loved you, daddy."

"As in sugar daddy, right?" Moore responded with a laugh.

"Pray tell, Kimosabe, what kind of company are we talking about here?" Skeets said.

"Birds, baby. Space birds. Satellites. A company named Lodestar that plans to put sixty-five satellites into orbit for a global telecommunication system."

"Giddy up, go!" Arnie blurted out. As the telecommunications analyst, he would be covering this deal, which would mean tons of work but also a huge bonus at the end of the year.

"Giddy up, go?" Moore mocked as he sneered at Arnie, now slinking down into his chair. "You just make sure you have a sales memo ready for these knuckleheads, Arnie. Make it simple so it can sink through their thick skulls." Head lowered, Martin bit his lip, barely able to stand Moore's insults.

"The prospectuses will be out tomorrow, guys. Everybody better read it thoroughly because this deal is extremely important not only to this desk but also to Whorman Skeller—period. So use what little imagination you have to picture a guillotine on the trading floor and your head in it if you don't move this deal out smartly." A pause and then Moore asked if anyone had any questions.

Martin stared at his notepad. He once again considered himself lucky that he had joined Whorman Skeller six months before Moore because, otherwise, a WASP poseur like Moore would never have hired a black guy to be salesman—maybe an assistant to an assistant to a research analyst or some similar token job, but not an out-front face position in sales.

No one braved the guillotine with a question, and Moore finished by saying, "Okay, well, I've done it again. I've climbed to the top of the mountain and slayed a ten-point buck and dragged it back down so that all you could eat. No, no, don't thank me. Just sell the fuckin' bonds." With that, Moore spun around on the heels of his Italian alligator-skinned slippers and departed, Terry Barker, as always, following closely the shadow of Moore's ass.

After the research analysts left the meeting, the sales group remained seated at the table. A kind of schizophrenia infused the collective psyches as the Lodestar deal presented both the possibility of an enormous bonus if they got the deal done and getting canned if they didn't.

"Okay, guys, crunch time!" said Wooly Finnegan, the sales manager, as he walked to the head of the conference table. "That asshole, Moore," he muttered under his breath but loud enough so everyone could hear, "does he think he's God or what? One of these days, I'm gonna..." Wooly didn't finish the sentence but pulled his attention back to the business at hand.

Finnegan got the name Wooly from the thick, raven hair he sported right out of the womb. "Lord Jesus, you gave birth to a monkey, Gracie!" Wooly's father had said to Mrs. Finnegan as the Doc held Wooly upside down by his feet. Wooly had three passions in life: boxing, golf and drinking beer. The order depended upon occasion and weather. While attending Villanova, Wooly had been a star on the boxing team, back in the days when boxing was a regular varsity sport at many universities. Although now fifty and his woolly head more gray than Irish black, he worked and sparred three nights a week at the Downtown Athletic Club gym. Wooly was cocky to a fault and ended every other sentence with a threat to knock somebody's block off. Nonetheless, people liked working for Wooly because he was basically a straight shooter with a heart bigger than he was willing to show on his sleeve.

"How much time is Moore going to give us to get this deal done?" Hap Boggs asked. Hap hulked over the table, knitting his eyebrows with a high-level intensity, the same facial expression he had at the line of scrimmage when he was a guard at Boston College and Doug Flutie called the snaps.

"Two weeks," Wooly answered. "Two weeks and not a day more. At the end of two weeks we'll have it put away or else Moore will have all of us put away."

"But it's a half-billion dollar deal, Wooly," Martin protested.

"I know that, Marty. And it's also not the simplest deal in the world, either. A communications satellite company! Gimme a break!"

"And the market technical's are abhorrent," Libby chimed in, a few raised heads over the word *abhorrent.* "Nobody's buying anything since Russia defaulted. Nobody—"

"Yeah, we all know that. Everybody but that dimwit Dick Moore," Skeets added.

"Hey, speaking of Russia," Lyle said. "You hear the latest joke? What's the difference between a Russian bond and a Russian bond trader?"

Lori, who had always thought Lyle was cute, was the only one who responded. "What, Lyle?" she asked.

"The Russian bond trader matures!" he answered.

"This is no time for jokes, Lyle," Libby said sternly. "Jobs are on the line."

"Take it easy, Lib. I'll sell enough of these bonds for both of us."

"Oh, how will I ever be able to repay you," she responded sarcastically.

Lyle didn't answer, only snickered, as if to say, "I'm sure I'll think of something.

"Cut it out, you two," Skeets said.

"Look, guys, this is an important deal, Wooly said. "Moore was right for a change when he said this was critical to Whorman Skeller. We do a lot of biz with companies in the defense sector. You know, mergers and acquisitions, bond and equity underwriting, the whole shebang. Well, no one has come right out and said it but whispers say the Defense Department is going to be the main client for the Lodestar system. Supposedly for missile defense, something way beyond my pay grade."

"Now this is really getting intriguing," Lori said.

"The point is," Wooly continued, "if we don't get the deal done, then Lodestar doesn't have the funds to start building their network, and the Defense Department gets their knickers all in a twist because they don't have an integral part of the Star Wars defense in place. And next thing you know, the suits in the military start directing contractors towards other firms besides Whorman Skeller for bond issues and IPOs. Then there goes tens of millions of dollars in fees to the firm. And guess who gets the blame, guess who's made to look like assholes in this whole mess?" Wooly raised his hand and pointed his finger at each salesperson at the table. "That's who.

"To get this deal done we're going to need a real intense road show. We're going everywhere. No stone left unturned. Boston, Minneapolis, Chicago, Kansas City, LA, and maybe even a few places we've never been before.

"Look, I know this market sucks right now. The mutual funds are throwing paper out the window and the insurance companies are waiting for prices to get lower before they buy. Everyone's wetting his or her diapers, given that the whole fucking global finance system is melting down. But we need to get around that, somehow. We have to do whatever it takes to get accounts to buy this deal. Whatever it takes." Wooly paused to rub his eye sockets, the pressure already showing.

"Okay, marching orders are in place. Let's get crackin'!"

"When the goin' gets weird, the weird go pro," Lyle said, quoting Hunter S. Thompson, as everybody rose from the table. As they filed out the room, no one made a sound except Skeets, who mournfully whistled a weak version of Taps.

CHAPTER 2

ANYTHING TO ANYONE, ANYTIME, ANYWHERE

RUSSELL KIINKAID STOOD AT THE PODIUM, holding the slide projector control in one hand, his face barely visible against the light cast by the projector. Kinkaid was the Founder, Chairman and CEO of Lodestar. He was presently wrapping up the hour-long slide show presentation that would sell Lodestar to the investor community. This was the first time he had made the presentation himself, from beginning to end. For the dress rehearsal, his audience consisted of most of the members of Whorman Skeller's high-yield department. Not only did this dry run give Kinkaid the chance to smooth over any rough spots in the presentation but allowed the sales force an opportunity to learn something about the deal they would be selling. Of course, everything one needed to know was contained in the preliminary prospectuses ("red herrings" or "reds" as they were called since the cover had a red border), but none of the salespeople except Libby took the trouble to read the one hundred and twenty pages. So this practice road show and the sales memo that Arnie had put together would be all the sales group would know about Lodestar.

"And so Lodestar takes another giant leap for mankind in the on-going telecommunications revolution," Kinkaid said, his squeaky voice rising with the hyperbole. "With this one instrument," he said, holding up something that no one could really see in the room's twilight, "our customer will be able to fax anything to anyone, anytime, anywhere."

At that moment the last slide slid across the screen, showing a blow-up of what Kinkaid had held in his hand and Lodestar's blue rubric-letters slogan in full view: ANYTHING TO ANYONE, ANYTIME, ANYWHERE!

At that instant, someone switched on the overhead lights, revealing the bad dental work on Kinkaid's front grill as he smiled benignly at the group assembled in yet another Whorman Skeller conference meeting. Hap Boggs' conspicuous yawn did not deter Kinkaid's smile in the slightest.

Russell Kinkaid was an upper class Brit, at least in clothes and manner. He wore a blue, chalk-striped, double-breasted suit, one of those tailor-made paradoxes that seemed both snug and loose. His shirt, hand-made in Singapore by undernourished waifs, was sea green, his tie, a tasteful silk composition of muted jade stripes. The ensemble was one of those mismatched confusions that English sophisticates think only they can pull off with the panache of a David Niven on vacation. But just to make sure everyone knew he had an American entrepreneurial bent, he wore his mouse brown hair, color rinsed monthly, long over his collar. "I am a financial artist," he wanted his locks to say, telling everyone that he had attended Oxford yet failing to specify that his alma mater was, rather, Oxforshire College, a small village affair about twenty miles from the famed university. But even immodest Oxforshire College had been too much for Mr. Kinkaid's patience or intellect, and after fleeing or flunking out, however you way wish to put it, he had stumbled upon a job selling satellite dishes door-to-door. A decade and a lot of pluck, moxie and chutzpah later, he was on the verge of launching a sixty-five-satellite system that would cost upwards of two billion dollars.

Arnie Markum, analyst on the deal and acting more or less as MC of the presentation, approached the podium, leaned his head in front of Kincaid and spoke into the microphone, even though his natural voice would have carried just as well in the small room. "Russell will now entertain any questions from the audience."

"Yeah, question for Mr. Kinkaid," Skeets Daniel said in his Tennessee drawl while simultaneously raising his hand. "Who the hell is gonna buy this thing?"

Giggles popped up like daises throughout the room. Martin put a hand over his mouth to cover his grin and leaned forward. Regardless of the situation, he knew he could always count on Skeets for whatever was uncalled for.

Kinkaid raised his hands palms up, jiggled his head and squinted his eyes in puzzlement. "What do you mean by that?" He still retained his smile.

"Well, I mean, this thing's gonna cost, what, somethin' like eight grand, five bucks a minute when you use it? Hell, I can buy a fax machine down on Canal Street for less than a thousand. So, I'm askin', who's gonna pay that kinda money to send a fax?"

Kinkaid harrumphed. "You, dear, sir, are missing the point. Unlike any fax machine in the world, it is truly portable. Wireless. Lodestar has pioneered a major technological breakthrough in designing the system."

"So what?" Hap Boggs blurted out. He wanted to join in the fun now that Skeets had drawn first blood. "One of the slides shows a print ad that you're going to use in promoting this thing," he continued, his Boston accent making ad sound like *odd*. "And the ad shows some Eskimo up in the Antarctic—"

"That's down in Antarctic," Libby interjected, shaking her head. "Antarctic is the South Pole, and Arctic is the North Pole."

"The Arctic is where Santa Claus lives, Hap," Lyle added. "You know, with the elves who make all the toys you get every Christmas." Lyle leered at Hap, his eyes wired and weird, like they were attached to electric sockets.

"Okay, whatever, North Pole, South Pole, who gives a rat's ass. The thing is, you show this guy sitting on an iceberg someplace faxing a love letter to his Eskimo squaw or somebody." Hap then paused and looked at Kinkaid, now wide-eyed. "I mean, what's that all about? If you're counting on all the people who live at the South Pole to buy this thing then I'm here to tell you that you ain't got an ice cube's chance in hell."

Everyone in the room went silent, including Kinkaid, astounded by Hap's stupidity. Kinkaid drew a deep breath and shut his eyes, hoping the Cro-Magnon with dark hair straight down over his sloping brow would be gone at next instant.

Libby made a rescue attempt. "On page forty-five of the prospectus there is independent marketing data which supports the revenue projections in the pro-forma financials. I suggest everyone read accordingly." Libby smiled smugly at Kinkaid who smiled equally smugly back.

"But those phones are so ugly," Lori said. "Why do they have to be so big and bulky? I couldn't imagine pulling one of those things out in, like, say, Le Cirque."

Kinkaid pressed his lips together, face strained. "This is a fax machine, not a fashion accessory as are most of those obnoxious pocket phones that obnoxious people are always obnoxiously pulling out in restaurants and movie theaters."

"Could you at least come up with some more attractive colors?" she said. "That phone looks like some military gadget for attacking Iraq."

"It's not a phone," Kinkaid shouted, slamming his fist down on the lectern. "It's a portable fax machine. And we have intentionally made the design and appearance very basic, very minimalist in order to emphasize the practicality of our product. Am I making myself clear?"

"Geeeez—Excuse me for asking..." Lori uttered *sotto voce* as she turned her head away from Kinkaid to share a comic grimace with her colleagues at the table.

Martin raised his hand. "Mr. Kinkaid, can you give us more details as to why the pro forma projections in the red don't show Lodestar making a profit until 2006?"

Wooly gave a sigh of relief that one of his salespeople had finally asked a decent question, while Lori, Lyle and Hap emitted a collective "What?!" at this bit of insight. "No profit until the year 2006?" Hap uttered, further evincing his alarm by placing a hand on top of his head and crying out, "You're kidding, right?" Not having read either Arnie's sales memo or the red, they had no idea what a roll of the dice this deal really was, and from the get-go.

Kincaid took the question as the opportunity to ramble on about the enormous cost and time the enterprise would consume. Satellites had to be built and launched at a cost of several hundred million dollars. Central receiving stations, called gateways, would have to be set up in twenty-five different countries around the globe, requiring hundreds of millions of dollars more in costs alone. (He neglected to mention the several millions of dollars in bribes to government representatives of those respective countries.) Equipment distributors to retail the fax machines had to be established in each country, notwithstanding parochial peculiarities relating to language and customs, business legalities and marketing infrastructure—almost insurmountable right there. Then there was the global marketing and promotion, requiring one hundred and six million dollars before the network was even launched. Of course the fax machines had to be manufactured by outside suppliers and Kinkaid didn't even want to get into the hitches and headaches that would entail.

Within ten minutes of Kinkaid's last breath litany of obstacles obstructing the fulfillment of *The Great Vision,* every sales person in the room was aghast. Despair descended over the sales group's outlook like black paint running down a windowpane. Lyle Shiner then took the opportunity to smear on one more coat.

"I was flipping through this red here," Lyle said as held the document up for all to see and then disrespectfully tossed it onto the table, "and way in the back there's something called OUTSTANDING LEGAL ISSUES. I'm perusing these outstanding legal issues, then, and I see that you have been charged for sexual harassment by one—" Lyle reached for the red and opened it to the page which he had marked with a paper clip. "—one Ethel Martinez. A secretary, right?

"Hey, look, don't get me wrong. I'm not one to cast stones. I even admire a guy whose blood runs hot, who's got some apple-size pontoons, know what I mean?" If Lyle had been standing, he would have most certainly grabbed his crotch for emphasis. "But this doesn't do much to help me sell this deal. Can you explain yourself, Russell, my man?"

Libby struggled to suppress a violent gasp. She was upset that the man for whom she was attempting to raise half a billion dollars was accused of sexual harassment, a sin that would consign its perpetrator within the innermost circle of hell, if a Vassar graduate were benighted enough to believe in sin and hell, and everything that went with it. But she was even more upset that Lyle had managed to discover something that she had missed. Hap meanwhile had not only placed his hand on top of his head but was now tightly clutching at his coarse hair in anguish.

Kinkaid took a deep breath, sighed heavily and then said, "My lawyers have advised me that I can make no comment about this case since it has entered litigation. I will tell you, however, that Ms. Martinez is a harlot who is trying to extort money from me, and in no uncertain terms."

Wooly knew it was time to throw a lifesaver that Kinkaid could poke his drowning head through. "Russell, we know that the Defense Department is involved in the Lodestar project. I know too that much of their involvement is classified, but what can you tell us about it, in generalities if you will."

"Excellent question," Kinkaid said with relief as he wiped the visible sweat from his brow. Normally the hanky sprouted from his suit coat's breast pocket as a decoration only, never to be used, but Kinkaid deemed the beads of sweat on his forehead as something of an emergency.

He proceeded to explain that the Department of Defense had taken a keen interest in the satellite technology that Lodestar had developed. He wasn't at liberty to say for what purpose they might use this proprietary technology but it was safe to say that it wasn't for faxing documents. The bottom line was that the Defense Department had entered into long-term contracts to use the Lodestar network, contracts which would require payments from the federal government to Lodestar that would cover a significant portion, thirty-six percent to be exact, of the new bond issue's debt service. Not insignificant.

Wooly crossed his arms, leaned back in his chair and looked up and made sure that this detail escaped no salesperson's attention. On that positive note, Arnie brought the presentation to an end as Russell Kinkaid and his entourage had to get to Kennedy Airport to catch a flight to Buenos Aires.

The sales force was the last to file out of the conference room. "We're dead, we're goners," Lyle muttered aloud. "We'll never sell this deal."

"The guy is a walkin', talkin' sexual harassment perp, a blackguard," Libby hissed, the venomous spit glistening on her lower lip.

"Huh, funny he didn't look like he had any Negro in him," Hap said as he lumbered onto the trading floor. He looked at his homey, Martin, for confirmation of Kinkaid's ethnicity but Martin, as usual, simply ignored Hap.

"You couldn't pay me to take one of those gadgets," Lori said as the group reached their row of seats. "He dresses like a fashion plate but doesn't have enough sense to put some aesthetics into his phone. What a schlemiel!"

Martin sat down in his chair and began to think how he would sell a company that wouldn't show a profit for six years, if then. Then he overheard Skeets on the phone, talking to a client.

"Now, listen hear, Johnny, I got a deal for you that's sweeter than bourbon bread puddin'. Got the backing of the U. S. fuckin' federal government!" Martin noted how he said gov'ment and figured he was talking to one of his accounts down South. "Unconditional guarantee, you got it. And I ain't talkin' some pitiful interest rate like six percent. No, siree. Double it, man—Talkin' twelve percent or better.

"Like the little birdie says, cheap, cheap, cheap. No deal's too tough if the yield's enough. That's right. No, this is not some sucker deal with a big schmuck premium.

"What's the company do? Well, it's a satellite company, space birds, and telecommunications. Pioneered some major technological breakthrough that I couldn't even begin to explain. It's all in the red that I'm overnightin' to you. Proprietary stuff, you know.

"Look, all I can tell you is the damn Defense Department has entered into some long term contracts to use this stuff. What more do I need to say? When can we come down to see you with the road show?" Skeets turned and winked at Martin. By this time, the rest of the sales group was also eavesdropping on Skeet's pitch.

"I don't know if we can get to you that soon, bubba. We've got everybody and their cousin wantin' to see this mutha.

"I'm tellin' you this deal is hotter than a three-balled billy goat in a pepper patch! Biggest doggone roadshow I've ever seen. But look, I'll circle the date and see if we can somehow squeeze you in for a one-on-one presentation.

"It's gonna be tough, but, you know me, I'll give it the old college try.

"Well, so what if I didn't go to college? You're gonna lap this one up, honey. Okay, okay. Don't be too good now. A little trouble never hurt anyone. Let's do a little tarp fishin' at Walker's Cay come springtime. Huh?

"Say hello to your lovely better half, Melba, for me. Yeah, you too. Adios, amigo. Yeah, bye—"

"Let's bond!" Lyle shouted, taking Skeet's lead. He immediately picked up the direct line to his best account and began regurgitating Skeet's lines but with a coating of his own signature slime that some accounts found so perversely entertaining.

By the time, Wooly got to his desk in the sales pit, he witnessed every salesperson on the phone, chatting up the Lodestar deal, hawking it like their jobs depended on it, each of them in their own way turning the sow's ear into a silk purse. He gazed up to the apex of the cathedral-high ceiling and winked at the big Celtic Lord in the sky.

Chapter 3

A Tall Order

MARTIN SAT IN THE LOBBY OF THE NEWARK, NEW Jersey offices of Standard Atlantic Funds (SAF), a mutual fund company that Martin had only recently began covering. He was planning to meet Owen Brosky, the principal manager of SAF's huge high-yield fund. In terms of assets, SAF was his biggest account, so he was particularly eager to make a good first impression. Martin had scheduled the Lodestar road show to come to SAF's offices for the presentation, knowing enough about Brosky to know that he would not deign to attend a group presentation and a rubber-salmon luncheon in some dim hotel banquet room. Such private presentations were known in the business as "one-on-ones" and were a way of paying tribute to the biggest players on the high-yield buy-side.

Since Russell Kinkaid and the rest of the crew would not be arriving for another hour, Martin wanted to introduce himself to Brosky and get some QFT (Quality Face Time).

After waiting fifteen minutes, Martin was approached by a gentleman who asked if he were Martin Stallworth. Martin answered, yes, and the man introduced himself as Owen Brosky. As Martin rose to shake Brosky's hand, he wondered why Brosky would have thought he was anyone else other than Martin Stallworth, given that he was the only person in the lobby other than the receptionist.

Martin thought he detected a moment of bewilderment in Brosky's eyes, then realized Brosky didn't know he was black. Brosky had to ask such a question even though Martin had dressed in a quintessential Wall Street gray suit with chalk pinstripes and a Prussian blue shirt with starched white collar and French cuffs.

Never seen a nigger bond salesman, Martin wanted to say but instead offered, "It's a pleasure to meet you, Owen, after hearing a lot of great things about you." Martin almost winced at his own obsequiousness.

"I doubt that, Mr. Stallworth. I don't have many friends on Wall Street because I make it clear that I don't need or want any more 'pals.' Too many guys like you think that if you become my buddy that entitles you to rip me off."

Martin's smile stayed on his face even though his eyes frowned. Well, howdy-doody to you too, Mr. Brosky. He had just confirmed all the great things that Martin had heard about him, such as how he was a grump, curmudgeon and asshole, who thought all bond brokers to be glorified carnival hucksters. "C'mon back to my office," he said to Martin over his shoulder as he turned and walked away. Martin got the impression that Brosky viewed his visit as an annoyance, and that he planned to dispatch him as quickly as possible. But one never knew—

Everybody on the Street believed that Brosky's disdain for brokers stemmed from the fifty percent losses that his fund had sustained during the junk market meltdown in the early '90s, losses that had caused him to negotiate a nervous breakdown. Naturally, Brosky had blamed Wall Street brokers for the debacle, and as Martin strolled behind Brosky, he remembered how Skeets was always saying to him, "That's our number one job, bubba—takin' the blame for everybody else's fuck-ups."

Owen Brosky was a small man, about five-six, pasty-white round face with a perpetual tomato-red shaving rash visible on his neck. His 5:00 shadow at 11:30 in the morning indicated he probably had to rake a razor pretty hard across a scabrous face to get a clean shave, and his dark hair receded enough to reveal a scalp bubbling with oil forty-five minutes out of the morning shower.

They meandered through a labyrinth of office cubicles that reminded Martin of mini cells in a beehive, except this honey barn was eerily quiet. Befitting a man of his stature, Brosky's rather large office was at the far end of the floor, private with solid oak double-doors, well carpeted, and replete with mahogany, top-of-the-line Thomasville furniture, including a twelve-seat conference table, soundproof acoustics and sporting a huge, floor-to-ceiling, double-pane window with a neat view beyond of Newark's trouble-and-strife. The blue marble vase on the desk came from northern Italy and housed two large white roses, replaced daily and delivered on time by the local flower shop.

"Nice view," Martin said with some calculation, as he looked out the window behind Brosky's swivel chair at the lovely view of grubby, downtown Newark. Brosky grunted, as if to say, "Yeah, right..."

"Ever take in any Devils games in the Meadowlands, Owen?" Martin asked, anxious to break the ice with a little chitchat.

"No. Don't follow hockey, basketball either," Owen said.

Who said anything about basketball, for chrissakes? Martin thought. "Too bad—" he said, deciding to forego the palaver and get straight to business. "Did you get the red on Lodestar?"

"Yeah," Brosky said quickly.

"Well, whadya think?"

Brosky raised his hands off the desk in animated fashion as an irritated look crossed his face. "Does it matter what I think? If I told you guys I really liked it, then you'd try and cram the deal at eleven and half percent instead of twelve, which is where a weak sister ought to price. Don't you think?"

"So you think it's a weak deal?"

"Who wouldn't? The company's got no assets, no chance of making money for years. It's a venture capital deal, for chrissakes!"

"But you mentioned twelve percent. I take it you have interest?"

"I'll let you know where my interest is when I'm ready, okay," Brosky answered testily.

"Fine," Martin suavely replied, "but *I'll let you know* that we took several large orders after the New York luncheon yesterday." Martin was now resorting to blatant lies in order to prod Trosky.

Brosky tilted his head back and considered Martin. "Oh, really? How was the attendance?"

Martin wasn't sure but he thought fifteen accounts or so had attended the luncheon and presentation at the Four Seasons Hotel, a decent turnout. "Sparse considering, about twenty-five, I'd say," he answered.

"That many, huh? Not bad."

"You have to understand, Owen, that these Defense Department contracts really give comfort to a lot of people. The revenue stream covers approximately a third of the debt service of the bonds until maturity. So there's a lot more to this issue than in a standard venture capital deal, to say the least. Then there's—"

"Yeah, yeah, I know," Brosky blurted out, cutting Martin short.

Martin viewed Brosky's irritation as a good sign, indicating he had interest in the deal despite his efforts to pooh-pooh it. Brosky was obviously annoyed there was so much interest in Lodestar away from him and that such interest might prevent him from getting the yield he wanted.

Martin sensed that Brosky was on the ropes. He figured it was time to quit jabbing and go for the glass jaw. "Let's cut to it, Owen," he said with a little more vigor in his voice. "Interest in the deal at twelve percent?"

Brosky squirmed in his chair, turned and looked out the window.

"'Cause if you have interest at twelve percent, then the best thing you can do right now is give me an order at that level."

"Why would I do that right now before I've even seen the road show," Brosky said, swiveling back hard in his chair to face Martin, the tone of his voice not quite as supercilious as before.

"Make the order subject to your seeing the roadshow and doing your due diligence. The point is, Owen, putting an order in now makes your voice heard as far as the pricing goes, gives you some say, some leverage, a little control. Otherwise, you wait until the last minute when the deal's been pretty much placed and whatever you want at that point doesn't matter diddly-squat" (an expression picked up from his Georgia granny, the same one who had convinced his parents to name him Martin Luther, after the great King).

Brosky picked up a ballpoint pen and studied it as if seeing it for the first time. After several seconds he finally said, "Tell you what. Put me down then for twenty-five million," he said, glaring at Martin, "but at twelve percent and not a basis point less. You got me, Martin?"

"Yes, sir," Martin said, doing his best to restrain from leaning over the desk and planting a big wet sloppy kiss on Brosky's greasy forehead. Especially noted was how Brosky had, for the first time, called him by his first name. He was making some real progress.

Later that day, as Martin was walking from the Whorman Skeller Building toward the subway stop on his way home, he spotted Mihra walking a few yards ahead of him.

"Hey," he called out. "You working a half day?"

She turned and smiled. "Guess it's a rare sight to see a research analyst leaving work before nine o'clock, huh?" She stood and waited for him.

"You know all salesmen are lined up in three-point stances at 4:59." Martin said this even though he was known to stay at his desk until seven o'clock or later, studying research or reading reds as the cleaning people worked around him.

"C'mon and I'll get on the Lex with you," she said as they walked into the tile-walled subway entrance and hurried through the turnstile just as the train rolled into the station, brakes hissing and squeaking.

Martin held open the closing subway doors so that Mihra could squeeze into the crowded car with him. They grabbed the overhead metal bars as the train rushed on. Martin couldn't avoid rubbing up against Mihra and that made him pleasantly nervous.

"How did it go today?" she asked.

Martin told her about the Lodestar order he had pried out of Brosky, restraining himself so as not to seem like he was trying to impress her, which of course was exactly what he was trying to do. "I played the guy like a flute!" he declared triumphantly.

"Okay, Martin, don't let your head swell to the size of a watermelon," she teased.

"Ease up on the pain—Don't be making watermelon references to a black man," he replied, taking mock offense.

"Okay, then, the size of a basketball."

"There you go again, basketball. Another stereotype."

"Oh, quit it," she said with a laugh.

"Speaking of which, you should have seen Brosky's face when he realized the guy he'd been talking to on the phone every day for the past six months had skin as dark as the ace of spades."

"I think it's more toffee-colored, is it not?" Mihra joked.

"Whatever, it made me even more determined to shake an order out of that jerk."

"I think I would have been offended."

"Ah, I've gotten used to it. If my skin is anything, it's thick." Martin suddenly realized how quiet the subway was, even though packed with people. He and Mihra were the only two talking. He lowered his voice. "Like you wanna know why I've been wearing a suit on Fridays, even though it's dress-down day on the trading floor?"

"Yeah, I've noticed. Why is that? I thought maybe you'd lost one of those silly bets you guys are always making."

"No, I'll tell you what happened. Some new guy in the currency pit saw me in my khaki's and a pullover shirt and mistook me for one of the mailroom boys. Starting bitching at me how one of his overnight packages wasn't sent out until the next day."

"You're kidding."

"Not at all. You know, I could have gone to human resources and filed a complaint or something like that. But I just told myself to let it go and always wear a suit so that it doesn't happen again." Mihra didn't say anything.

"You look around that trading floor," Martin continued, "and you can count on one hand the number of people just like me."

"Racism at work once again?" Mihra said.

"I don't know if it's all that." Martin lowered his voice almost to a whisper. "My people have a ways to go. I mean, you wouldn't believe the amount of shit I get from some of my own just for working on Wall Street. They talk like I'm some kinda traitor, well almost. That this is just a white shoes, white man's game. Black people are always talking about power, but as soon as one of us gets some, they accuse him of being a sellout, an Uncle Tom."

"A la Clarence Thomas," Mihra said.

"Yes. Hell, I almost got into a fist fight with my brother over Colin Powell."

"Your brother, Henry? Why, I remember him from that one time he came to visit you at B-School."

"I was surprised he even came that time, all the grief he used to give me for getting an MBA. Can you believe it, of all people, my own brother? He's a walking negative stereotype. Grew up in a nice neighborhood and what does he end up doing? Deals dope. Go figure."

"You never told me that."

"Yeah, well, it's not something I brag about. Just pisses me off when I think what he put our parents through. But in a way, I guess I have to thank him."

"For what?" Mihra asked.

"'Cause seeing him screw his life up made me even more determined to make something out of mine," Martin answered, staring straight ahead.

The train began to slow as it entered the Bleecker Street Station, Mihra's stop. She lifted her shoulder bag, heavy with laptop and research material, kidding herself she would read on the couch that night.

Just before she began working her way toward the door, she said to Martin, "So the main reason you're working at Whorman Skeller is not the money but to prove a point?"

Martin thought for a second. Prove a point, be a role model, a pioneer blazing a trail, be a—dare he say it—a hero? He looked at Mihra and answered, "Yeah, I guess you could say that."

Mihra smiled, gave a little wave goodbye, and made her way into the flow of bodies spilling out the shiny silver doors.

CHAPTER 4

JUST DO IT

"C'MON, DON, YOU CAN GET IT UP," LIBBY COOED, AS she ran her fingers through the curlicue gray chest hairs of Don Languano, her most active client, both sexually and trading-wise. She lay sprawled across his body, her legs intertwined with his and the flannel bed sheets covering the queen-size bed.

"But Lib, baby, you're asking too much. I just can't do it." Don was a man in his late fifties and tried to do what he could to please this sex tigress, twenty-five years his junior.

"Oh, sure you can, Donny," she murmured, her fingers wandering down past the paunch that revealed the years his hair weave and discreet eye surgery tried to conceal. "Sure you can, daddy."

Don's face turned red with exasperation. "And what would you like me to get it up to?" he asked with a trace of annoyance.

Libby demurely put her index finger to her lower lip and pondered a moment. "Hmm...I was thinking...fifty million."

"Fifty million!" Don sat up in the bed. "You think I'm gonna invest fifty million of my portfolio in that piece of shit pie-in-the-sky satellite deal? I love ya, babe, but you're nuts."

Libby knew that she should have gotten the Lodestar order pre-coitus rather than post, a tactical point that even a half-wit streetwalker should know, even more so a Phi Beta Kappa graduate. "You can certainly do better than ten, especially since Lodestar has contracts with the Defense Department covering over a third of the debt service on the bonds.

"Wooly'll blow a gasket when I tell him that my best and closest account is only putting in a pittance."

"Let him blow then."

"He may even assign you to one of the other sales people, and that might make it harder for us to see each other," Libby added, a not-so-subtle threat. Don made the trip to New York from Chicago once a month and he had come to value these trysts with Libby as one of his spicier catnips.

He turned and looked down at her, his salt 'n' pepper mustache twitching. "What do you mean by that? Is that all that I mean to you? Money? You'd end this gig just because I didn't do enough trades with you?"

One of the few things that endeared Don to Libby was his knack for questioning the obvious.

"Of course not, Donny. It's just that you know I'm in a real pickle here. If I don't do well on this Lodestar deal then that prick Dick Moore might fire me. It's times like these when you have to turn to your loved ones for help." She reached out to scratch his back.

"Fifty million is a helluva lot of help, girl. I'll up it to fifteen."

"Quit being a damn cheapskate!" Libby shouted as she hopped out of bed and stomped into the bathroom. She plopped down naked at the gilt—trimmed vanity with the big round white light bulbs, one of the several amenities that the Pierre had specially installed in its honeymoon suites. She looked at her reflection looking back at her, the light bulbs encircling her reflection like cherubs around the Madonna.

"I just can't believe you're letting me down like this," she said in the most pathetic voice she could muster. "And forget about that long weekend ski trip to Vail. I'll probably be looking for a job." The bathroom tile walls hollowed her voice.

"Oh Libby, don't be that way. Fifty is just too much. The investment committee will scrutinize me down to the last letter if I put that much in a deal like Lodestar. What if I gave you an order for twenty? Would that make baby happy?" Don Languano had adopted a silly, saccharine voice that was much unlike the one millions of investors heard when they regularly saw him on CNBC and other financial TV programs touting himself as the world's most savvy junk investor.

There was silence in the bathroom. Then a meek little peep, "Do you think you could make it twenty-five million? Please? For me?"

Don shook his head. "Oh, all right! I'll give you an order for twenty-five million. How's that?"

After a few seconds, Libby leaned her torso around the bathroom corner so that Don could see her bosoms hanging like a garden of earthly delight. A sloppy lascivious smile corrupted her face, half-hidden by disheveled hair. "You're the best," she giggled. "And now you're in for a really special treat," she added, holding up a jar of Vaseline.

Skeets Daniel steered the golf cart around the seventeenth green, the bent bermuda grass as soft and smooth as the baize on a pool table. Sitting next to him was Earl Fuller, one of the largest managers of the State of South Carolina Employees Pension Fund. Skeets had flown down to Myrtle Beach to hook up with his old pal and do some hunting, golf and, yeah, pitch Lodestar.

Skeets waited until the fifteenth hole before mentioning Lodestar to Earl, figuring that four holes would give him plenty of time to close the sale. But coming to the last hole, Skeets had encountered more resistance than anticipated.

"But, damn, Earl, they got those doggone Defense Department contracts. Takes a lot of the risk out of it, you know."

"I know, Skeets, but...

Skeets stopped the cart at the tee box on the eighteenth hole. He and Earl, both big time gamblers, had been betting a hundred bucks a hole, and now Skeets was ready to raise the stakes substantially.

"What do you say we do this, Earl? Make a special bet on this hole."

Earl eyed his buddy warily. "Yeah, like what?"

Skeets cocked his head and considered things for a moment. "If I birdie this hole, then you put in for fifteen million of those Lodestar bonds. If I don't birdie it, then I'll never mention it to you again."

"Hmm," Earl mused as he gazed beneath his golf visor over the eighteenth fairway and estimated the odds of Skeets birdying the hole. It was a par four but a difficult par four. The fairway had a sharp dogleg to the left and blind shot to the green from the other side of the turn. Earl had played enough golf with Skeets to know that he had a natural slice and so would have a tough time with a dogleg left. No way Skeets was going to play this hole in three, Earl finally concluded. No way.

"Okay, you're on, Skeets, my boy." He reached out to shake Skeet's hand. "But remember your end of it. If you lose, not a peep more about Lodestar." Earl considered this a perfect and painless way out of telling Skeets that he wouldn't invest in his crummy deal. And saying no in this way would be a lot more fun, besides.

"Not a peep, Earl. Not a fuckin' peep. You'll be off the hook."

"Shoot, you better put better bait on that hook next time if you wanna catch this catfish."

Skeets chuckled as he strolled up to the tee. He bent down with a groan to set his ball squarely on the red tee. Skeets was a tall, lanky sort, but at fifty-eight his knees had that crunchy sound, like he was churning gravel into cement inside, and his swing wasn't quite what it used to be, either. Addressing the ball, he moved his left foot some six inches behind his right, as he had done earlier that day at the driving range when trying to develop a hook shot. And why would he be trying to develop a hook shot? Because he had been thinking about this hole and thinking about this bet all weekend.

SCCHHWWIIINNKK! Skeets laid into the ball and sure enough it went sailing left and cut the corner on the dogleg.

"Yep, she might not be purdy but she's got big tits," Skeets muttered, characterizing his shot as he bent down to pick up his tee.

"Not bad, Skeets," Earl offered. "But it's a long ways from the turn there to the hole. Too long for three strokes total."

"We'll see. But don't forget, Earl, there's a real downhill slope toward the green. You get a good bounce and you're knockin' at the front door."

Earl stepped between the blue markers to tee off. His coral pink pants and parakeet green shirt bludgeoned the retina. Earl wore a blue suit and white shirt everyday to work. But golf offered Earl and other staid, conservative middle-age men like him the rare chance to get away with being a bit "queer" in the golfing attire.

After Earl's tee shot, which was straight and far, so that he had a direct line to the green, they rode down to the turn to see where Skeet's drive had taken his ball.

"Where is it?" Earl asked as searched the fairway in front of him. "I'll be damned!" he exclaimed as he espied Skeet's ball right on the edge of the green.

"Yeeedoggie!" Skeets hooted when he saw his ball.

"Any chance you let me out of this bet if I take ten million of those puppies?" Earl asked, the wind completely gone from his sails.

"No, siree. But I'll do double or nothin' that I can eagle this hole."

"Shit, no! If you're lucky enough to get a bounce like that, then you're lucky enough to sink that putt! Damn!"

After playing the last hole, they rode to the clubhouse to dispose of their bags. Afterwards, Earl headed to the men's grillroom while Skeets took care of some last minute business with one of the caddies. "See ya up there in a few, Earl. Order me a Whiskey Sour, Maker's Mark. And don't look so damn downcast. You look sadder than a sow at the smokehouse."

Skeets then walked over to Clarence, the head caddie at the club, who was in the process of wiping clean Skeet's club heads. Skeets and Clarence had developed a friendship over the twenty years that Skeets had played at this club, or at least as much a friendship as a white golfer and black caddie could develop at a country club in South Carolina.

"I do good, Mr. Daniel?" Clarence whispered.

"Yeah, you did great, Clarence." Skeets looked over his shoulder and then began counting a hundred dollars from the big roll of cash that he had pulled from his pocket.

"I didn't know how close you wanted me to sets dat ball. I almost gots carried away and put it right on the lip of the cup."

"That would have been a little too obvious. And nobody saw you run out of the woods and pick up my ball and move it to the green?"

"Nope. I sat in those dang woods, jus waitin' for you to come up, likes you tole me to do this mornin'. I must have mistimed it, though, cause I sat there waitin for almost an hour. You old boys play slow, Cap'n."

"Slow and steady, Clarence. All right, here's your bread." Skeets discreetly placed the cash in Clarence's palm as he shook hands with him.

Skeets Daniel sauntered to the grillroom, happy with himself and his place in life. Once again he had finagled and finessed his way to a trade. He had started twenty-eight years ago in Memphis, selling municipal bonds. In those days, he was a conglomerate of permed hair, manicured fingernails, pinky ring and loose hanging wrist bracelet, cuff links in the shape of champagne glasses, bright yellow suspenders arrayed with dollar signs and a funeral parlor cologne that clung to you after shaking hands. He smoked cigarillos, which he lit with a monogrammed Zippo lighter, and the flame turned extra high just for a laugh. He drove a Mark IV Lincoln with a hole in the trunk where a mobile phone had been before it had been repossessed for lack of payments. After his boss was found in the trunk of a car with a bullet in his head, both flies and rumors about unpaid casino debts buzzing around the corpse, he had fled to Little Rock where he discovered the fool's gold called zero coupons. Later, he hauled ass with a junkyard dog lawyer in hot pursuit to Houston where he got in bed with a bevy of beauties named Ginnie Mae, Fannie Mae and Sally Mae.

With such an abundance of talent, it was only a matter of time before Skeets found his way to Wall Street. There he had transformed from a sorghum-mouth good ol' boy with a toothpick hanging from his lip and wearing a fifteen hundred dollar suit designed by an Italian whose name he couldn't pronounce. Once slick, country slick, he was now a managing director at one of the oldest, blue blood, white shoe, patrician firms on the street. The culture at Whorman Skeller "felt" more Waspish than Jewish, Italian or Irish, and that somehow gave a lot of people comfort, even if they were Jewish, Italian or Irish. Suddenly, he was wearing tortoise-shell glasses. If his suit was not tailor-made, then it was at least Paul Stuart's. His briefcase was ensconced in dark leather, cracking with age and signifying an indifference to fads and frenzies. He carried a pocketknife whose handle was inlaid with scrimshaw, which everyone took as a sure sign of gentility. The slow and steady accumulation of capital through sound advice and underwriting exuded from Vernon Barton "Skeets" Daniel.

As he entered the grillroom and saw Earl sitting at the table, drink in hand and still sullen from losing the bet, Skeets couldn't help saying aloud to no one but the devil on his left shoulder, "Yeah, yeah, that was a good one..."

Chapter 5

Account Development

MARTIN STRETCHED LENGTH-WISE ACROSS THE wooden bench and gazed at the robin-egg blue sky. The afternoon was unseasonably warm for early spring, and he had sneaked off the trading floor and gone outside to the small park next to the building. Sporting four benches, some planted shrubs and a half dozen poplars, the park was usually empty, except for the occasional Whorman Skeller employee escaping to have a quick smoke. Martin found the serenity of the place a respite from the commotion of the trading floor and came here once or twice a week for a ten to fifteen minute break from insanity. Paranoid that one of the Whorman Skeller powers-that-be might happen into the park, Martin always brought along a conspicuous research report that he pretended to read. He certainly would never have thought to prone out on one of the benches as he was doing now, not wanting to give anyone the opportunity to cluck their tongues and say to themselves, "Look at that lazy, shiftless black guy." Martin was always on guard against presenting such opportunities.

But at that moment, lying across the bench with one arm over his face, he didn't care what some Whorman Skeller overlord might think or that he might be providing fodder for some bigot's prejudice. He had been pounding his accounts nonstop for three days, trying to entice the buying of Lodestar bonds. Wooly had been ceaselessly pacing the aisle that ran between the high-yield sales desks, barking, scolding, coaxing and pleading. Dick Moore would make a cameo appearance at least once every hour, wouldn't utter a word but just let his glare slowly drift from one salesperson to another, as if he almost hoped that the deal wouldn't get done so that he would have an excuse to line them all up against the wall, then open fire with a .44 magnum.

Just as the drone of traffic on Park Avenue was lulling him into semi-consciousness, he was jarred by a raspy voice saying to him, "Better watch those pigeons up there don't shit all over you." He didn't have to look to know the particular Queens accent belonged to Lyle Shiner. Martin opened an eye and saw Lyle standing over him, a cigarette dangling from his slack mouth. With the sun behind Lyle, his thick, combed-straight back hair looked like a large helmet that his slight frame should have trouble holding up.

"Those rats with feathers up there aren't particular about what they crap on," Lyle said, wagging his thumb toward the three pigeons roosting on a poplar limb above the bench.

Martin gave a heavy sigh and sat up on the bench. "So what. My accounts have been crapping all over me about this Lodestar deal."

"Oh man, it'll be a miracle to get this baby done," Lyle said as he flicked the ashes off his cigarette.

Martin sat there, intellectually worn out; irritated that Lyle had interrupted his moment of forgetfulness and not in the mood to muster up chitchat with him. It wasn't that Martin disliked Lyle. He just didn't respect him. Martin constantly marveled at how Lyle did so well selling bonds, given his total lack of discipline. Discipline, Martin thought, was the key to all success, in any business. Without it, talent was useless and luck wouldn't last. Martin found Lyle's unabashed prurience, distasteful in its own right, another manifestation of his lack of self-control. That Lyle was a product of Bensonhurst didn't help engender any affinity toward him, as Martin knew first hand what the prevailing attitude toward blacks was in that community. Nonetheless, he maintained a cool but cordial working relationship with Lyle.

"Hey, but what are you bitching about," Lyle continued. "You got that big fucking order out of Brosky."

"Yeah, but I had to lie to get it," Martin said, realizing as soon as he had spoken how silly that must have sounded to Lyle.

"So? We're in the business of selling bonds not truth," Lyle said, barely concealing his incredulity at Martin's naiveté.

"Don't ever let truth get in the way of doing a trade, right," Martin answered, the tone of his voice half-heartedly ironic.

"Damned straight, man. Don't let anything get in the way of a trade, dude."

"It's just a good thing you got that monster order out of MLAS, otherwise we'd really be in the hole," Martin said. Lyle had astonished everyone by getting Minnesota Life Assurance Society to pony up a commitment to buy a hundred million dollars worth of Lodestar bonds.

"I'm glad you mentioned that, Marty. How I got that order proves the point I was just making."

Oh no, Martin thought, *another one of Lyle's bond daddy "lessons."* Martin found it both amusing and annoying that Lyle, the bond veteran, was always eager to provide instruction to him, the novice.

"You know Kurt Kirsen, right."

"Sure," Martin answered. Kurt Kirsen ran the high-yield portfolio for MLAS.

"Yeah, well, how do you think somebody like me could get a nerd-geek doofus like Kurt Kirsen to buy a pig like—"

Martin wondered what he had meant by *somebody like me,* but didn't noticeably dwell on it. "Doofus is the right word for the guy, all right," he responded, remembering when Kirsen had visited the trading floor looking like what had he always imagined an insurance executive from St. Paul would look like—tall and trim, close-cropped light brown hair, standard black frame glasses, and blue pin-striped suit purchased on sale at Brooks Brothers. The final impression was that the man had never failed to vote or slow when the light turned yellow.

"Look, all you need to know about Kurt is that he's got the usual middle—age baggage. Married to the same skank for twenty-four years, two daughters he's trying to marry off and a junior who's off in college blowing all his dough on nose-candy and ecstasy. Get the picture?"

Martin nodded.

"So even though the dude might be an active member of the St. Paul Rotary Club and a deacon at the Greater Lutheran Church, when he makes trips to Sodom and Gomorra, who better to call than me for a little razz-ma-tazz? Who better to help him lift all that baggage off his sore little shoulders?"

"I couldn't think of anybody more footloose and fancy free," Martin answered in reservation.

"So he calls me last week and says he just happens to be coming into town. I'm thinking, great, I can pitch Lodestar to him face-to-face. So I plan the usual night on the town. Rent a stretch for the evening. Book an early reservation at Elios. Scalp a couple of Rangers tickets since I figure being from ice country he'd be into that. In other words, the whole smear."

Hockey, white man's last refuge in the world of team sports, Martin mused out loud.

Lyle paused, not accustomed to hearing Martin make racial references. Indeed, Martin did make a determined effort to avoid drawing attention to that which distinguished him from everyone with whom he worked. If he pretended to be colorblind, maybe that would help them pretend as well, he hoped. Mihra was the only person with whom he abandoned such pretense.

"Yeah, whatever," Lyle muttered. "But I'm real worried 'cause I know where Kurt's gonna wanna take it."

"What do you mean by that? Take what, where?"

"Don't worry, I'm coming to that. So anyway, we meet at the Plaza, where Kurt always stays when he comes to town. Have a couple of eight-dollar beers at the Oak Bar, get in the limo, head a few blocks over to Elios, get a little loose on a couple of martinis and a bottle of Brunello di Montalcino. By the time we're finished, we're both cracking up at the crooked toupee on top of a big-wigged real estate developer two tables over. From there, we're off to the Garden for the Rangers game. But we don't stay too long cause I can sense that Kurt is restless, that he was thinking about the rest of the night, about where to take it. It didn't help that a gang of lunkheads from Patchogue wearing Rangers jerseys and mean drunk on draught beer are yelling shit at us like 'Take your suits off, geeks. Die, yuppie scum.' Such shit is surely one of the charms of a Rangers game. When cups of beer start flying our way, I suggest to Kurt that we take it somewhere else. So we head over to Benson's."

"The gentlemen's supper club?"

"Gentlemen's supper club? It's a titty-bar, Marty. They call it a gentlemen's supper club so the corporate types won't feel grimy taking their clients there."

"So that's where you're worried Kurt would 'want to take it,' as you put it?"

"Hell no, that's just the warm-up act. He's gonna take it way beyond that, believe me. But right then I'm not worried about much cause Kurt brings up Lodestar while we're in the limo on the way to Benson's.

"'I got a chance to read the red on the Lodestar deal you sent me,' he says to me out of the blue, in that tightly wound, roof-of-the-mouth voice that drives me fucking crazy. 'Doesn't look bad,' he says, much to my surprise. And he starts going on about the Defense Department involvement and asks if I could get him copies of the contracts. I tell him, hey, that'd be a tough one, classified, TOP SECRET and so on. But I do tell him that I could get him that statement from Defense saying how long the contracts are to run and the generated cash flow, in total. 'Well, that would probably satisfy me,' he says. 'Give me a call next week. I can see us putting in an order for as much as fifty million.' Oh, yeah, baby. I'm smiling like a crocodile offering a frog a free ferry ride across the swamp."

"Fifty million? So how did you manage to get him to double that to a hundred?" Martin asked.

"I'm getting to that. So we head over to Benson's, or Bosoms, as Kurt calls it. A little while later, I'm sitting in one of those plump, cushy chairs and staring at some kinky haired Puerto Rican's tits while she's gyrating her sweet ass in Kurt's face. Man, her ass is so tight you can strike a match on it, and Kurt's studying it like a proctologist. By now, his glasses are lopsided and halfway down his nose and I'm nervous as shit 'cause I know where he's gonna take it. Then she slips her g-string down her thigh and puts it on Kurt's head and he swills another shot of Jagermiester, yuppie crack, and his face comes together on the tip of his nose and he shouts 'Yeeeeeehaaaaaa!'

"'Can Loriana dance for you another?' she asks. Kurt says, 'That's all right, darlin', but me and my partner here wanna sample all the wares here tonight. So you run along now.' Kurt's suddenly talking Texan and that scares the crap out of me. So eight more dancers rotate through, Kurt chasing each dance with another shot of Jagermiester and now I know I got a Jagermiester monster on my hands. He slips each chick a twenty and for that they wring his neck with one of those Hawaii Lei things. He pinches one on the ass and she cuffs his ear and he looks at me with a jack o' lantern smile. 'Hey, I kinda liked that!' His shirttail's out, tie unloosened down to his navel. Then the music stops and the hyperactive jerky DJ comes on and reminds everybody that the midnight buffet is free and features crab imperial and chili con came.

"Then it happens. Just like I knew it would. Kurt stands up with those nine pink Lei around his neck and yells over a Van Halen number, 'Time to walk on the wild side, Lyle. Time to take it to Hellfire and back!' Oh, fuck!"

"Hellfire?" Martin asked. "What kinda joint is that?"

"It ain't no coffee bar, I can tell you that. So we're back in the limo, cruising toward downtown. I look over and see in Kurt's mouth—you're not gonna believe this—a plastic pipe. He's gotta lighter over the bowl."

"You're telling me that Kurt Kirsen was toking off a crack pipe!" Martin shouted in disbelief.

"That's what I'm telling you, bro. My heart gagged a couple of beats. I grabbed the pipe from his mouth and hurled it out the window. He claimed that one of the dancers had slipped it to him for an extra fifty. Better than a triple martini, extra dry, she'd told him.

"So we're down in the meat packing district, driving by all these dark warehouses, looking for a red door that's the entrance to Hellfire and—"

"Oh, Hellfire," Martin said, interrupting. "That's the S&M Club, right? What in the fuck were you going there for?"

Lyle blushed. "I dunno. The first time we'd gone there was sorta on a drunken lark. Some jerk investment banker from Morgan Stanley had told Kurt that it was kinda 'avant garde cabaret.' A spiritual douche, if you will. So Kurt wanted to try it out. We went a second time when he last visited. Gotta tell you it was too weird the first time, and, well, sorta interesting the second time, you know, in a clinical way. But man, the third time, I was scared shitless.

"So we go through the red door. You enter this foyer, I guess you call it, unpainted stonewalls and all. This big fat sissy dude is sitting behind a wire-mesh counter. Got a shaved head, half a dozen nose rings and a 'come-on, dude' smile. And he says to Kurt and me in his fag voice, 'Oh, my dears, I remember you two. Back for more, huh? Really now. Just hand over twenty apiece and read the house rules one more time because I know how naughty you heteros can be.' I swear if the fat fuck didn't wink at me.

"Hellfire's got house rules?" Martin asked.

"Oh, yeah, they go something like this:

> Rule 1.—Do not disrupt scenes unless asked to join in.
>
> Rule 2.—No guns, knives, cattle prods. Bull whips okay but cat o' nine tails with metal tips a no-no.
>
> Rule 3.—Cameras verboten!
>
> Rule 4.—You must clean the floors after any act of defecation. pooper-scoopers available.
>
> Rule 5.—Condom machines are found on the first floor behind the pillory.
>
> Rule 6.—No animals, except gerbils.
>
> Rule 7.—Have fun, if that's what you're into."

"I get the picture, Lyle," Martin said.

"Okay. So as I'm pulling forty bucks out of my clip, I notice this strange guy in a trench coat leaving the foyer and looking over his shoulder at me. A little weird but I don't think anything about it cause everything about this joint is weird. Kurt, meanwhile, has got this look on his face like he's on a mission. He's breathing real loud and horny and walks right past me like I'm invisible, steps right into the next room he does.

"The space was real dank and dark except for the unshaded light bulb hanging from the ceiling. There's a couple of Nancy boys dressed up like Nazis standing there, and a couple of yup couples in formal attire and giggling nonstop, a chick in red leather jump suit unzipped to her navel, and some black guy wearing a fur-trimmed fedora. That kind of scene."

"Just another typical Manhattan cocktail party," Martin said with a chuckle.

"Yeah, get this. In the corner was some guy crouching and wearing nothing but a leather harness, handcuffs, and a red ball gag. I kid you not!

"So the black guy in the fedora raises his flashlight and shines it on him and then the chick in the red jumpsuit pulls a riding crop out of nowhere and lashes the guy two or three times across the back. Whether he's wincing with joy or pain, or both, I couldn't tell you. Everybody in the room glances over at him and goes on with their conversations.

"I look around for Kurt and damn if I don't see him and that strange pervert in the trench coat traipsing out of the room together. Boy, do I panic. Kurt is, after all, my number one account. It takes me about two seconds to calculate in my head that my monthly production would drop by at least 28% if something bad happened to Kurt. If I could sell him fifty million Lodestar bonds, that would mean close to a hundred grand in my pocket. So, needless to say, I haul ass after him.

"Marty, you wouldn't believe some of the weird shit I see running down that dark hallway trying to find Kurt. All kinds of noises are echoing from everywhere, people laughing, moaning, shouts, some dog yelping somewhere. This woman rushes out of a room to the left and bumps into me. I can see her face from candlelight coming from that room and she looks like she's just seen a ghost or something. So I look in there and see this naked female body hanging upside down by a chain attached to the ceiling. I'll never forget her hair, real long and bright red, hanging like upside down fire. Her skin's as white as the candles on the floor and her shadow covers the whole wall. She's singing, 'This diamond ring doesn't shine for me anymore…' The only thing in the room besides the wine bottles holding the candles is one of those metronome things, I think they call it, keeping time to the song."

"Too strange," Martin said, mesmerized. "Was Kurt in the room?"

"Fuck no. I lost him. I hear loud cheers coming from down the hall, so I go that direction. I come to a room filled with at least a dozen people. They've formed a circle and are clapping their hands and shouting and I'm freaking out cause I'm afraid Kurt might be in the middle of that circle, in the middle of a 'scene.'

"I move up to the edge of the crowd and what do I see but two old paunchy codgers with gray chest hair and wearing nothing but boxing gloves. One of the gent's noses has burst like an overripe tomato and most of his lower face and neck is smeared with blood. The other guy is winding up a haymaker that the old dude's too dazed to dodge. I don't stick around to see it land but everybody cheers like it must have landed real sweet, and final.

"I'm freaking out by this point, running from room to room in search of Kurt. I don't even wanna tell you some of the shit I saw. But like in one room are these dwarfs doing nasty stuff to each other that only dwarfs could do. In another room is an old-fashioned 1960s orgy, people all tangled up, squirming and wriggling over, around, through each other like grubs under a rock.

"Finally, I come to what looks like a locker-room shower. You know, shower nozzles on the tile walls and a drain runs along the perimeter of the floor. In the far corner is this porcelain tub. Two bodies are sitting in the tub—two dudes—two naked dudes. One is rubbing the other's back with a sponge, a loofa, I think. The one whose back is getting rubbed is really into it, you know, moaning with his eyes shut. They're facing away from me, but I see that the guy whose back is getting rubbed is wearing a pink Lei. Then I notice the blue pinstriped suit lying on the floor. Then he turns and looks at me, the guy doing the rubbing, that is. God help me! But it's that weirdo who was wearing the trench coat. The fucker looks right at me, and smiles.

"So I'm thinking I should go and shake Kurt by the shoulders, dress him real quick and get the hell outta here. But then I think maybe shaming him like that wouldn't be good, wouldn't be good for my business, that is. Probably the best thing to do, I say to myself, is run away from it. But then I have a stroke of genius, a bright, sinful thought. Maybe I shouldn't leave but maybe let Kurt see me seeing him. Let the word "blackmail" creep into his brain without me having to utter a fuckin' word. Let a certain understanding imply itself: You, Kurt, must perform penance to atone for your wickedness. A cleansing is in order, as my old neighborhood priest used to say. The wages of sin must be paid and who better to pay them to than me? I would gladly settle for a hundred million dollar Lodestar order instead of fifty million. That would be easy enough."

"So you stood there until Kurt finally saw you, huh?" Martin asked, barely concealing his disgust.

"Hey, I got the hundred million dollar order, didn't I? Just call it 'account development,' Marty. That's all it was, baby."

CHAPTER 6

DREAM STREET

BEHIND THE SIGNATURE SILVER DOORS OF THE Georgette Salon on Rodeo Drive, in a room awash in soothing tones of white, sea green and gray, sat Lori Putterman. Even though the leather chair, low-slung in a chrome chassis, offered the utmost comfort and the rain forest spritzer muzak mist was easy on the ear, her patience-meter was running at a fast clip. For over twenty minutes now, she had been watching her client, Gloria Shanks of Shanks Asset Management, have her eyebrows done. Twenty minutes, for chrissakes, and that eyebrow auteur, Mr. Ilya Petrossius, aka the Queen of Wax, hadn't even finished one eyebrow.

At that moment, Ilya, tweezers in hand, was lecturing Ms. Shanks, who sat in the upraised suede leather salon chair underneath an unforgiving array of thirty-watt light bulbs. "Dahlink, neva, neva, pluck the white hair. It won't grow back. You don't want holes on your face now, goodness gracious." Ilya's effort at American idiom came out gudnass greeshus.

Tedium finally forced Lori to take another slurp of the vegetable pulp drink in her hand, which the salon offered their customers as they waited to be remade. Lori found the Beauty Squeeze, a blend of liquefied aloe vera, carrot, cucumber, ginger and apple (she declined the wheatgrass) to be thoroughly yucky. But she sipped on it anyway just to impress upon Gloria that she "got it" and was "with it," even though she couldn't have really explained what "it" was in the first place.

"I tell Demi Moore just last week, I say, 'Demi, don't over pluck. Nyet, nyet!' Okay, so she has mink stoles for eyebrows, but too skinny not good. Yah?"

Quit the name-dropping and pluck away, you fairy Cossack, Lori thought to herself. She also wondered what this job would cost her, what with the armload of GiGi, Lancôme and Shiseido products that Gloria would surely want before they left. At least three hundred bucks, maybe more. And that was in addition to the one hundred fifty dollars for the Eight-step Facial Treatment that had preceded the eyebrow plucking. (Chris O'Donnell had taken the exact same eight steps before this year's Academy Awards, the solicitous beautician, or "beauty enabler," had told them.)

And the salon was just the first stop. Lori knew that Gloria would want to conscientiously work her way up from South Rodeo to North Rodeo, stopping at every boutique, haberdashery, home furnishing store and kiosk to conspicuous consumption on the strip. Gloria and Lori had an unspoken gentlewomen's agreement that Lori would foot the entire bill if Lori wanted Shank Asset Management's business. This arrangement was left unspoken because such an arrangement was blatantly illegal. But Lori was getting a little annoyed that so far this shiksa had dodged her every inquiry about Lodestar, even though she had attended the roadshow presentation at the Beverly Wilshire just the day before. *What was a little feedback going to cost her?* Lori wondered. *How many hundreds, maybe thousands, for a simple yes, no, or maybe?*

Nonetheless, Lori would indulge Gloria's every whim and fancy. Lori was sorry to say that Shanks Asset was her most active account, sorry because it was a really pathetic account. Gloria Shanks had got her start in junk at the infamous LA office of Drexel Burnham Lambert. Her resume claims she was a high-yield trader who sat somewhere on the notorious X-shaped trading desk, the star-crossed center of the universe which was occupied by the 1980s demigod, the father of junk, the ruler of perdition, Michael Milken. The truth, however, was that Gloria was one of numerous babes who were hired more for scenery than skills, a hiring practice which all investment banks engaged in during the pre-politically correct, Neanderthal, good ole days. Every trading floor was a talent show, a bimbo expo. Gloria's actual title was "Trading Assistant," a job requiring she get the coffees, take messages and look good while doing it.

She launched Shanks Asset with the fifty million she squeezed through a divorce settlement from Bernie Shanks, one of Milken's star goodfellas. Like the Melanie Griffin character in the movie *Working Girl,* she had a lot of street smarts for a secretary and was able to hold her own in the rough and tumble world of high-yield bonds. But the Wall Street crowd regarded Shanks as a "flipper," an account that bought into a new issue with the intent to immediately sell the bonds back to the underwriter after the bonds had run up in price. Flippers were not held in high esteem or endearment by trading desks. Lori often had a hard time getting Dick Moore to allocate new issue bonds to Shanks, unless the deal was a tough one and the desk was looking to unload bonds to any and all comers. "Scummer" was the pejorative that Moore used to characterize firms like Shanks. But Lori figured that Lodestar would be one of those desperate deals and so she was willing to do what it took to weasel an order out of Gloria, including funding a shopping spree on Rodeo Drive. The word "kickback" might have peeped way down in the murky depths of Lori's conscience, but the words "You're fired!" blared loud and clear, like a siren drowning out all peeping scruples.

Ilya finally finished with his latest masterpiece, the eyebrows of Gloria Shanks. Before releasing her from the salon chair to the world at-large, he graced her with a few pearls of wisdom: Always brush brows up, trim overgrown hairs at an angle and wax every two weeks. After Gloria loaded up on facial and hair care products, Lori paid the five hundred and ninety-five dollar gouge-bill. Everything that Lori purchased for Gloria on this excursion would be with money from her own pocket since Whorman Skeller would only reimburse for meals. The two large bags of products were to be delivered free of charge to Gloria's apartment on Santa Monica Boulevard, as Gloria wouldn't have been so gauche as to haul the loot around like some mule or tourist. Besides, she expected plenty more stuff and stash would be carted away to her apartment before the day was done.

Looking Gloria over as they exited Georgette's, Lori felt gypped. This was all she got for all that money, all that cosmetic pampering? Puh-leese. Lori vindicated her own worth by imagining that something was off kilter, askew, even freaky about Gloria's appearance. Wasn't there something sad and pitiful about so many of these women sauntering down the Drive? So many of these once-forty women desperately trying to look like their daughters. Lori would have bet that at any one moment there was enough silicon on Rodeo Drive to supply a semiconductor plant for three months! But the collagen lips! They reminded her of the goofy wax candy clown lips she once bought at the Brighton Beach Five and Dime when a kid. She smirked thinking how Gloria must have devoted most of her waking, non-working hours to retaining a few tantalizing hints of the trading assistant head-turner she had been only fifteen years before. "Well honey," Lori wanted to say, "I'm here to tell ya that all that effort backfires 'cause it's just a little too obvious."

Not that she would have put herself up against Gloria in the looks department. After all, Lori realized she couldn't compete, five-three in heels—tops, Gloria, five-eight in flats and with legs up to here. Lori couldn't do a thing with her short, kinky, dishwater brown hair while Gloria tossed around a shoulder length, henna-tinted mane. The mop, though, was a little thin and ragged in spots and Lori wouldn't have been caught dead with those high school bangs Gloria wore to cover her forehead wrinkles. Lori was acutely aware that she was shaped like a cinderblock with a round hump where her shoulders and neck joined. No one had to tell her that she wasn't a "looker" but she had quit pitying herself about that ages ago. After two husbands and two divorces, who cares? She consoled herself that she had nice eyes, with chestnut brown irises, long lashes, sort of exotic really. Gloria, on the other hand, had managed through liposuction, tummy tucks and a boob lift to keep an hourglass figure; a pear-shaped hourglass maybe, but still more appealing than a cinderblock with a hump. The bottom line was that Gloria looked, well, silly, wearing a leather miniskirt three inches above the knee, the balloon lips, sawed-off nose. And this was a woman a few hormone imbalances away from menopause, for crying out loud. Like her uncle Harvey used to say, "Nobody ever won an argument with age."

Lori and her top client exited Georgette's and ambled along the dreamy drive lined with glistening, cream-colored buildings, marble storefronts, curved glass and gilt, and street lamps belted with geranium pots. A seventy-two degrees breeze stirred the leaves on the fichus and fig trees. Striding briskly, Gloria turned toward Lori, smiled and said, "Thanks a bunch for the make-over, sweetie. I feel like a million bucks."

Lori saw her opening. "Speaking of millions, why don't you spend a few on some Lodestar bonds," Lori said with a soft-sell smile.

Gloria squinted behind her Channel sunglasses, and stretched her plump lips in due consideration, "Whadya say we talk about it over lunch." Lori only now had to figure out how to maneuver through the hole just opened by Gloria's comment.

Lori dutifully stepped along to Wolfgang Puck's latest enterprise, ObaChine ("Oba" after the minty Japanese leaf and "Chine" for China in French.) They entered the copper-bar area and were directed to a sweeping staircase carpeted in Pacific Rim colors like dusty peach, eggplant, and celadon. The stairway led to the dining room. The room was dimly lit in jade and amber but that didn't prevent onlookers from gazing about the room, hoping to catch a glimpse of somebody famous. Was that Tori Spelling over there by the Thai temple stone carving? Wouldn't that be a laugh if we were all three together, Lori mused—Lori, Tori, and Gloria.

Since lunch was going to be on the company tab, Lori intended to make it sumptuous. First they ordered cocktails, a couple of Polynesian concoctions but thankfully sans little paper umbrellas. Halfway through the drinks, and after putting their order with the waiter, who was thought to be a dead ringer for Ben Affleck, Lori felt it was time to work her account with the nice eyebrows. "Okay, quit tormenting me and tell me what you think about Lodestar. We've been schlepping all morning and you haven't even mentioned it, darling."

Gloria shrugged. "Well, you know, the presentation yesterday went okay, I would think. That Kinkaid fellow is kind of a strange bird, isn't he?"

"Nebbish," Lori uttered in agreement as she drained her drink. Gloria blushed with slight embarrassment when Lori very conspicuously circled her finger in the air to inform Ben Affleck they wanted another round.

"It has some risk to it, surely," Gloria continued.

"Got those Defense contracts, though," chimed Lori with the standard line. "Government contracts mean secure bucks, anyway you looked at it."

"Yeah," said Gloria, again shrugging her shoulders. "Look, I'm leaning toward doing something. I just wanna mull it over a bit. Walking around like this really helps me to do that. Really it does." Gloria reached out and lightly touched Lori's hand.

Yeah, I bet it does, Lori thought to herself. *Me blowing my bank account on your lipo-sucked rump really helps, I'm sure.*

"I promise I'll give you an answer by the end of the day," Gloria said with a sympathetic smile. With several more hours to go before the end of the day, Lori figured some more mulling was going to cost her a lot of dough.

The second round of cocktails seemed a little more rummy, but that didn't stop the two ladies from deeming them delightful or from ordering a one hundred and eighty-five dollar bottle of Hermitage to go with the meal. Famished from all that shopping, Lori attacked the tea-smoked Peking duck laced with kumquat, orange and plum sauce while Gloria worked on the grilled lemon and ginger Malaysian Pad Thai chicken. Normally not a big imbiber, Lori surprised herself by ordering another bottle of wine. *I'm not such a paskudnika as to think I can get a Lodestar order from Gloria just by getting her drunk, am I?* Lori mused, almost giggling out loud with devilish delight.

Lori credited the second bottle of wine for the flagrant come-ons that Gloria hurled at their hunky waiter, even going so far as to slip him a card when he brought the check.

"Hey, Gloria, you think Ben Affleck there's got a wad he can give you to manage," Lori teased.

"I'll let him put his wad in my little ol' purse any time he pleases."

The two gals stepped out the low-lit restaurant and into the sun-lacquered late afternoon and felt like conquering the world. Gloria stood outside on the sidewalk, raised her hands toward the sky of unearthly blue and pronounced, "God, what a wonderful day!" She slipped her arm inside Lori's and thanked her for the splendid lunch.

"Look there's Frette," she then said, pointing at the gleaming glass storefront across the street. "Let's check it out."

"Sure, check it out," Lori replied, giddy enough for anything. "Why not—"

"Let's do like the celebs do and go in through the back," Gloria said in a low, conspiratorial tone. "Celebs always enter from the alley to avoid paparazzi."

They skipped across the street like two schoolgirls cutting class. They startled the Asian kid doing inventory in the stockroom when they nudged open the heavy backdoor. "Whad-da-fuck," he uttered. Then, after a little teasing on Gloria's part, directed them to the showroom where a snooty clerk suspiciously examined them as they emerged from the stockroom. Gloria decided to show the clerk that they were for real by wasting no time in buying two sets of Egyptian-cotton jacquard sheets. Lori grimaced when the clerk rang up one thousand three hundred and fifty-three dollars on the register. Oink! She could already feel the hangover coming on.

Back on the street, Gloria again put her arm though Lori's and whispered. "Guess what? I made up my mind and I want some of those Lodestar bonds."

Lori's mood suddenly mirrored the sunny afternoon. "Terrific! How many do you think you'll want?"

"I don't know. Let me think about it. Let's wander through Tiffany's first."

After the diamond tennis bracelet at Tiffany's, the green leather handbag at Louis Vitton, the clear crystal puffed-heart paperweight at Baccarat, the shotgun (for Gloria's boyfriend) at Holland and Holland, the horse-bit stilettos at Ferragamo and a tailored, hot ticket suit at Gianfranco Ferre, Gloria was ready to cease fire. (A quick visit to Fred Hayman did cross her mind, but hey, enough's enough and she didn't want to totally abuse Lori's generosity.)

"I'm caput," Gloria moaned while stirring her decafe cappuccino at Cafe Rodeo. They sat outside to get a better view of the sunset.

"Yeah, so am I," said Lori. "My credit card, too," she let slip.

Gloria smiled. "Now I gotta make it up to you, hold up my end of the bargain. You're a good shop mate. Thanks."

"As in *'finally* give me an order' for some Lodestar bonds?" She put heavy emphasis on "finally." She was tired of being ginger and demur with Gloria. She was foot sore, rum groggy and broke.

"Put me in for five million."

"Five million, huh?" Lori did her best to hide an obvious disappointment.

"Yep."

"You're done, baby." Lori raised her cappuccino glass and touched it against Gloria's. No, five million wasn't the biggest order in the world, but she at least had more than a goose egg to show Dick Moore. A confidence booster to say the least—she would happily take it.

The redeye back to New York was relaxing, and there was something about a little wine at 32,000 feet that made things just right. Lori took out her calculator, tallied up her receipts from Gloria's shopping extravaganza, which totaled a little over $10,000. She then figured her take from the five million dollar order—two and half points on five million, divided by two, since half the proceeds went to the banking side, times the sales payout of fifteen percent, equaled nine thousand three hundred seventy-five dollars to her. Then it hit her—hard. She had spent over ten grand just so she could put $9,375 in her pocket. How could she have been such an schnook! After the sting, her heart sunk and insides shrunk. After all that profligate groveling, she was out $625! She looked out the window at the crazy quilted patchwork world below and tried her hardest not to cry.

CHAPTER 7

POPS

THE TAXI PULLED TO THE CURB IN FRONT OF A yellow brick house, one of those middle class black neighborhoods you never hear about. Actually, it was about the only halfway black neighborhood in Massapequa, as far as Martin knew.

Martin paid the fare, got out and walked up the driveway past the Buick Electra that his father had owned the past nine years. The front yard was perfectly edged and trimmed—as always. The front door was locked, so Martin pressed the doorbell and a few seconds later the door swung wide open and there stood his father, Henry Stallworth, smiling big and proud.

"You finally made it," he said to Martin. "I was worried you hit some traffic." The elder Stallworth wore a red crew neck, virgin wool sweater, which Martin had bought for him last Christmas, over a pair of beat-up overalls. Martin smiled and slightly shook his head, thinking how his father had left the farm in Georgia over thirty years ago but still couldn't give up overalls, or that smile.

"What you grinnin' like a possum at?" Henry asked, ushering Martin in.

"Oh, nothing, Pops, just happy to see you, as always."

They walked down the hallway to the den. "This place hasn't had Annie Belle's touch in over five years, so don't mind if it's a tad dusty, son."

Following behind his dad, Martin remembered the last time he had seen Annie Belle, his mother, the day he had gone back to Duke University to finish his last semester. He remembered how she had tapped on his bedroom door at the ungodly hour of 7:00 a.m., ungodly at least to a twenty-one-year-old college kid.

"Martin, before you head back to school, could you drive out to Chester's barn and fill me up four bags of manure. Go back there behind the barn where the horses roll around in the dirt near that maple tree. Usually a lot of manure back there. Make it five bags while you're at it. It'll help my azaleas look bright when they bloom this spring."

And so on a cold January morning he had driven out to a riding school in Suffolk County where Chester worked, an old friend of his parents. *What great preparation,* he had wryly thought as he shoveled manure into a burlap sack, *for receiving a degree in English Literature.* Later that cold day, as he backed his Honda Civic down the driveway to return to North Carolina, he had waved bye to his parents standing at the back door with their arms around each other. His mother, who always wore a wig to church, had her gray brillo-hair pulled back in a bun, her eyeglasses, which Martin guessed were at least twelve years old, catching the bright winter sun and, for an instant, looked on fire.

Martin had noticed Pops limping in the hallway and asked about the problem. "Oh, I got the gout, believe it or not. Doctor said I got to quit spicy food. No more Mex."

Martin flopped down on the sofa, its fabric cushions protected by plastic slip covers, while his father turned into the kitchen opening into the den. Pops had added this room onto the house after Annie Belle's death, to distract him from grief. He had decorated the den in a slapdash but comfortable way. A purple shag rug on the parquet floor, a Laz-e-boy recliner, metal bar stools along the counter that divided the den from the kitchen, one of those standalone, self-contained fireplaces that people in the '70s called futuristic. In front of the sofa was a glass top resting on four wood blocks, offering several issues of "Ring Magazine," a made for coffee tables *Photo Essay: Africa!* and a one-piece porcelain set of dogs—a German shepherd, boxer, beagle, English terrier—all dressed in bachelor garb and playing high stakes poker.

But Pop's signature upon this room was the gallery set up against the varnished plywood wall. Gold and silver trophies were massed together like the towers of some space-age city. A brigade of tin and copper boxers, caught in perfect jabs and right crosses, kept watch from their spires and pedestals over the city. The superb gleam showed they were polished regularly. Besides having taught in the public school system for over twenty-seven years, Pops had also run the boxing gym at the local "Y" and had coached many golden gloves champions. "Pop's Gym" was well known in amateur boxing circles across the country. He had been a champion himself and had once even fought in the Olympic Trials. Behind the trophies were the thirty or more photos of all the young men who had won trophies and otherwise had made their marks. From the first photo on the top row to the last on the bottom, Martin could follow the change in hair styles from the greasy kids' stuff to crew cuts to long hair over the eyes, back to short hair, and finally a pony tail in the last frame. For the black boys, the transition went from Afros to Jeri—curl to "Fades."

Pops emerged from the kitchen, carrying in his hands a birthday cake with twenty-eight lit candles crowded on top. His baritone voice, a mainstay at the Mount Zion Baptist Church, broke into birthday baroque, "...Happy birth-d-a-y, dear Mar-tin, hap-py birth-d-a-y to you—"

He set the cake on the coffee table. Martin inhaled and with some effort blew out the candles. "There you go!" Pops said. He then walked over to the bookcase and retrieved a small gift-wrapped item. "Here," he said, handing the present to Martin. "Happy birthday, boy," he added as he bent down to lightly hug his son.

Martin removed the wrapping paper to discover a leather-bound edition of Langston Hughes collected poetry.

"I know you're a fan of his, as is your mother."

Pops hadn't yet given up speaking of Annie Belle in the present tense.

"Thanks, Pops." Martin couldn't remember the last time he had read Langston Hughes, and felt a pang of remorse. There was a time, in college, when he had even fancied himself a poet. His mother had encouraged him in that endeavor. It occurred to him at that moment that he had stopped writing right after she died.

Pops then leaned over the cake with a knife in his hand. "I know Doc Walters told me not to be eatin' stuff like this, but to hell with it. My boy's birthday only comes around once a year."

Martin lay back on the sofa and his father kicked back the Laz-e-boy, the two of them eating birthday cake and reviewing who had recently been born, gotten married, had children, or died.

"You datin' any gals?" Pops wondered.

Mihra's face flashed through Martin's mind. "Nah, not anybody particular. Playing the field, Pops."

"Nothin' wrong with that...Why you scratchin' at yourself like a some hound dog with fleas, Martin?"

Martin had mindlessly been raking across his arm. "I don't know what it is. Some rash has been eating at me." He roiled up the sleeve of his flannel shirt.

His father put on the eyeglasses that were always on the stand next to the Laz-e-boy and peered at the rash on Martin's arm. "Shoot, you know what that looks like? Looks to hell like shingles. I used to get those myself back in the service. Nerves cause that, sure enough."

"Nerves?"

"Yeah, I was nervous about gettin' my ass shot off by some Korean. What do you have to be so nervous about?"

Martin exhaled, put his plate on the coffee table and sat silent for a few moments. "I guess work, I dunno. We got this deal we're trying to do. Big, important thing."

"Deal?"

Martin didn't feel like explaining once again to his father the intricacies of Wall Street and how "the deal" was the light bulb all the moths hovered around. His dad did once ask him to explain Wall Street in a way he could understand. The best analogy that Martin could offer was the Wizard of Oz: You see a huge, all-knowing, all-powerful head surrounded by smoke and fire and speaking with a voice as loud as a tornado. But if you looked behind the curtain in the corner, you would discover a short, bald-headed old man frantically pulling on a clutch of levers.

"Yeah, you know, that's how we make money. They're telling us that if we don't get this deal done, then they're going to can us all like a pack of sardines."

Pops raised himself up on his elbows. "They're not pickin' on you 'cause you're black, are they?"

"No, no, Pops," Martin answered with a tone of exasperation. His father was from the old school, always thinking that white people were out to get "the colored folk," always suspecting that the Boogey White Man was behind every problem every black person encountered. Too many African-Americans, Martin believed, used that suspicion as a reason not to try, as an excuse for failure, a built-in "it ain't my fault." *You'd think that after working with white people in the school system for all those years, Pops would know better,* newly twenty-eight year old Martin thought.

"We're all in the boat together," he continued. "Of course, I am the least experienced and have the least seniority of the group, so I'd probably be first to go." He scratched his arm once again.

"Well, I guess I have to give them some benefit of the doubt," Mr. Stallworth said. "They did hire you in the first place, so they must believe in 'some affirmative action.'"

"Damn it, Pops, I didn't get hired because of affirmative action!" Martin said with a raised voice.

"Okay," his father said as he pulled the wooden lever on the side of the Laz-e-boy and kicked the leg-rest back under. "Let me ask you then, Martin. How many blacks did Whorman...what's it's name...have before you got there?"

"I don't know about the overall firm. My group didn't have any."

"There you go. I bet there wasn't many anywhere else at that doggone place, either."

"Probably not," Martin grudgingly admitted.

"So then you're tellin' me that they hired you only cause ya was so god awful brilliant compared to any other blacks they'd ever talked to? And that was why you was the first? You was just so far superior to any brothers or sisters that they'd done seen before you happened along—"

Martin noted with some displeasure how Pop's grammar and diction deteriorated when he got his dander up. But he really had no answer to his questions. "I tell you what, son. I'm glad you have self-confidence. In a white man's world, that's what it takes. But there's a world of difference between self-confidence and misplaced pride. One raises you up and the other brings you down." He then kicked the Laz-e-boy back into a reclining position with considerable authority.

Agitated, Martin got up from the sofa and walked toward the kitchen. He sat at one of the bar stools at the counter so that he wouldn't have to suffer Pop's glare.

"I hate to see you so distressed about your job, Martin," Pops said, softening his tone. "I just wonder if it's good for you workin' in a place like that."

"What would you have me do, Pops? Quit and then do what? I'm not a quitter."

"I know you're not. But you're young enough to start anew if you want. You used to talk about being a teacher, before you ran off to business school."

Martin almost laughed out loud. What a little naif, a cute little moonbeam he had once been. Be a teacher and make the world a better place! Save the children! Save the planet! Fortunately or not, somewhere on the road to Damascus, Martin had become enlightened real fast to the fact that money was all that mattered. Maybe it was when he saw how life changed for that scrawny, geeky Willis kid in high school after he started trading commodities. All of a sudden, he was a hometown hero to everyone, the kid they used to hang in lockers and stuff in trashcans. Money can transfigure a dumb ass into a genius, a jerk into the greatest guy around, a sinner into a saint, a black man into someone to be reckoned with. Black folks like Martin's father were always spouting off about freedom and power, and Martin hoped that one day he'd realize that money, capital, is the root of freedom and power. Money doesn't just talk and it does more than scream. It opens all doors. No, you can't take it with you when you die, but you can leave it to charity and people will be praising you for decades after you're dead, no matter how big an asshole you were. Be a teacher? Yeah, right. Pull in what, 15K a year? Put up with all those monsters, brats and bureaucratic nonsense? Hell, Pops had been teaching for twenty-seven years and the most he ever made was 50K. Martin expected to make five times that this year—if he kept his job.

"I decided teaching wasn't my bag, Pops. I know it was for you. But I wanna do something a little more, uh, different, a little more real."

"Real? You wanna make money, or 'serious' money, like you yuppies say. Is that what you mean?"

Martin insouciantly shrugged his shoulders.

"There are plenty of rich people out there who are miserable, Martin. Assholes besides."

"Well, Pops, they'd probably be even more miserable if they were poor and assholes."

"Maybe one day, you're gonna realize that all those bags of money you're scratching your arms off about only weigh you down, boy."

Martin had enough of Pop's platitudes. Especially when he started calling him "boy." He didn't come here to argue, but there was a limit to anything. So he remained silent, hoping the subject would just go away by itself.

He glanced at the family photos his father had arranged on the kitchen counter. There was one of his mother taken about six years before, just before that lump appeared under her arm. Even though she believed in Jesus, she had always sworn that in another life she had been an Egyptian queen. In that photo, she certainly looked regal.

Hovering behind her in another color photo was Pops. Martin studied his father's face, eyes, the same eyes as his, big and shaped like teardrops turned sideways, tucked under perfect, jet-black eyebrows. The irises were more than brown, almost orange, burnt orange, like the color of both his and Pops' skin. Pops liked to tell people he had some Seminole Indian in him and adduced skin color and a broad nose and angular face as evidence.

In another photo was the entire Stallworth family, taken when Martin was twelve years old. Pops and Annie Belle stood behind Martin and Henry junior, Martin's older brother. Henry—Martin's first reaction was to avert his eyes, but instead they lingered over the photo, over Henry's face. While Martin favored his father in looks, Henry looked more like his mother. He had a smallish face, slender nose and high cheekbones and looked like a little Ethiopian prince. "Henry—" Martin absent-mindedly murmured.

"Yeah, he came by here around a month or so ago," Pops uttered, startling Martin.

"Who? Henry?" Martin said.

"You just mentioned him, didn't you?"

"What did he want?"

"Nothin' in particular. Wanted to give me something."

"What?"

"He laid a thousand dollars on that coffee table there. Told me to use it for a down payment on a car or something."

"Did you take it?"

Pops hissed through his teeth and shifted in his chair. "I tell you what I did. I went back and got a box of kitchen matches, picked those hundred dollar bills up, struck a big ole match and sent the pile to Hades. A thousand dollars, up in smoke."

"Man, I would like to have seen Henry's face when you did that. Did he throw a conniption fit?"

"Nah. Just looked at me. Sorta smiled in a sick kinda way. Got off the sofa, said, 'so long, Pops,' and shuffled out the door." Pops stared down the hallway at the front door, his eyes vacant, a little sad suddenly. He then asked Martin when was the last time he had talked to Henry.

"Oh, mama's funeral, I guess."

"Yeah, I remember that," Pops said, arching his voice, not wanting to recount the details of that incident. On the day of the funeral, Martin had confronted Henry about what everyone had known for a long time, namely that Henry was dealing drugs. The discussion devolved into a shouting match that degenerated into a fistfight in the lobby of the funeral home. Pastor Hooks, who had performed the service, got his nose bloodied trying to pry apart the two brothers.

Pops turned his head toward Martin behind him and asked, "What happened to Henry, Martin? Did your mama and me love him any less than we did you? Why have you gone down one road and Henry down another? Why?"

"Don't know, Pops," Martin answered, his voice full of resignation. "I guess when we were living in Bed-Stuy, there was just a lot more bad stuff going around there than here. You know, Henry was just getting into those teenage years, times when you're easily influenced. I was too young for all that. But that was a rough crowd he was running around with, rough for anyone."

"He still kept runnin' around with them even after we moved all the way out here," Pops added angrily. "All the opportunities and good things for him out here and he had to sneak off to Crooklyn all the time."

"You and Mama did your best, Pops. It wasn't your fault."

"Yeah..." he grumbled.

Martin and his father spent the rest of that Saturday afternoon watching "March Madness" college basketball games, having discussed enough heavy matters to last awhile.

Finally, Martin had to leave.

Pops struggled out of the Laz-e-boy and gimped with his son to the door. Martin couldn't help noticing how at sixty-four his father's frame was becoming more squat and settled. He was thirty pounds heavier than the light heavyweight whose ring name had been "Blood King" and who had fought in the same Olympic trials as a skinny kid from Louisville named Cassius Clay. The frame creaked and sagged and his head had weathered gray. But he still moved gracefully with a slight shuffle in his step. His hands handled everything gingerly because they weren't so sure anymore. The orange fire in his eyes had weakened to cool ochre and his complexion had blotches of plain ol' brown. Martin had no doubt, though, that the old panther still had a bite, dentures or not.

Pops stopped at the doorway and turned to Martin. "You know, there's something else I wanna give you for your birthday?"

"What's that?"

"This," he said as he twisted a finger on his right hand. "This ring they gave me when I fought in the Olympic Trials." He then handed Martin a solid gold ring with a miniature gold boxing glove soldered to it. On the back of the ring was the inscription, "Olympic Trials 1960. Henry Stallworth. Light Heavyweight Class."

Martin wouldn't take it. "No way, Pops. You've worn that ring ever since I've been alive. I couldn't imagine you without it."

"No take it, son," he said, still holding the ring out to him. "I know it ain't the prettiest ring you'll see, and you might have to wrap some scotch tape around it to make it fit. And yeah, I know I tried to get you interested in boxing when you was a tyke but you wanted to read your books instead. But I want you to have it, whether you wear it or not. Now take it."

Martin shushed and tossed his head. "All right, if you say so. I don't know what to say, Pops. I'm, uh, honored."

"Whenever you find yourself in a jam or some kinda fix, just look at that ring and remember that all Stallworths are fighters. That ring'll bring you some strength and, who knows, maybe a little luck."

Martin took the ring and studied it under the hallway light. He was reminded of the cartoon "Hercules" he watched as a kid and how Hercules would gather strength from the special ring he wore.

"Okay, Pops," he said as he slid the ring on his finger. "I guess a little luck never hurt anyone," he said as he gave his arm another scratch.

CHAPTER 8

WHEN THE WHIP COMES DOWN

WOOLY FINNEGAN PLACED BOTH HANDS ON THE conference table and leaned slightly forward toward the sales force—including Arnie Markum—assembled before him.

"We've got a problem, people," he announced. "We've been pounding the pavement for a week now on this deal and we have a total of one hundred and seventy million in orders. One hundred and seventy million! That sucks! This is a five hundred million dollar deal and we have the rest of this week to sell it. We're up that proverbial shit creek without a paddle and the boat has sprung a leak and filling fast with shitwater and right around the corner is Niagara Falls. Get my drift, folks?"

"Hey, guys, I'm running a special on life preservers this week. Anyone interested?" Arnie wisecracked.

"Shut up, Arnie," snapped Wooly. "You think this is vaudeville or something? I'm as serious as cancer. And don't think because you're a research geek that you're not as vulnerable as the rest of us. This was your deal. Fielding any calls from accounts, have you?"

"A few," Arnie said with a shrug of his shoulders. "They all wanna know about the Defense Department involvement, and of course, there's hardly anything I can tell them about that. That's the real hitch to this deal."

"Yeah, I know. Damn it!" Wooly ran his hand through his thicket of hair. "What about you, Lyle? You got more in the pot than anybody, I think. You got anywhere else to go?"

Lyle bobbed his head slightly, a habit of his that somehow made him seem even more cocky, if possible, but degenerate nonetheless. He slouched in the chair, and turned sideways to the table, elbow resting on the table. "What can I tell you, baby? I've turned up every rock out there. You know, I got Kirsen to step up to a hundred on this thing. He started out at fifty. Took a lot of convincing, a lot of hand holding, you know what I mean?"

"Yeah, I got you," replied Wooly. "Thank god for that order, otherwise we'd be dead meat on hooks. Good job, Lyle."

"Wad'n nothin' to it, boss," Lyle said with a wink.

"Skeets, what about you, brother? Any prospects?"

"I got that old coot, Earl Fuller, to come up with fifteen million. Goddamn stick-in-the-mud, that guy. Cried like a baby about it, but, you know, we go way back, and it's on deals like this you gotta call in the markers. It's on shit deals like this that your account has to be more than an account. It has to be a pal." Skeets always liked to emphasize how old and close his account relationships were, that being the only advantage his age offered in this young man's game. "But I got a few more pockets I can still pick. Give me a couple more days and I think I can come up with at least another fifty."

"Lord, I hope so," Wooly muttered. "Libby?"

"Don Languano jammed me for twenty-five. I think he shot his wad on that, no more there. Two or three of my other guys I'm still stroking. Then there's—" Libby stopped, finally noticing that everyone at the table was tittering with their hands over their mouths at her unintentional double entendres. "You guys are so puerile," she sniffed.

"Hubba hubba," Lyle exclaimed, titillated.

"Wow, I was getting a little moist there, honey," Lori said, intentionally trying to blow out the boys, all of whom moaned "Ugh!" in unison.

"You keep jamming and stroking, Lib. Keep your guys coming. What about you, my little Jewish princess? What you got working?"

Lori hit her head with the butt of a hand and then raised both hands level with her ears, palms open. "Nada. They shoot bond bitches, don't they? Go ahead, I'm worthless. Maybe selling real estate wouldn't be so bad after all. All I got is five million out of that junk hag, Gloria Shanks."

"Oh man, we're really scraping bottom now, aren't we?" That was all Wooly could say.

"On a brighter note, our rookie sensation, Marty, got a twenty-five million dollar order out of the meanest SOB in the biz, Owen Brosky. Way to go, Marty!"

Everyone at the table congratulated Marty with a round of applause.

"And I didn't even have to stroke or jam him!" Martin said, causing even Libby to smile. "But, even so, I had to put a few thousand in his kid's college fund," he joked. "That's okay, isn't it, Wooly?"

"Hey, whatever it takes, Marty. Kickbacks, blowjobs, snuffing out mother-in-laws. Whatever works, anything goes."

If anyone had been observing Lori, he would have noticed that her smile evaporated and she shifted in her chair at the mention of kickback.

"Last and certainly least, Hap. Hey, man, you don't have one fucking order on the books. What gives?"

Hap leaned back, sighed heavily and yanked at the hair at the base of his skull. He knitted his eyebrows, thick and almost joined.

"Jesus, Wooly, I don't know what to do," Hap bellowed. "I just can't sell this fucking deal!" He slammed his fists down on the wooden table, causing everybody to lean back in their chairs.

"Well, then eat some more of those Flutie Flakes," Wooly said, hoping to defuse the lit powder keg that he knew Hap was always on the verge of becoming.

Hap was in a slump and that made everyone nervous. Hap Boggs was a top-notch producer, a "big hitter," always had been. But his production was erratic and his prolonged slumps were notorious of late. Wooly and everyone else on the high-yield desk knew that when Hap went into a slump, it was time to hide the steak knives, lock up the guns, warn the neighborhood children and dress the dog in kick cushions.

All bond salespeople dread the awful slump. The post-trauma stress syndrome, the pre-menstrual syndrome, writer's block, Jekyll and Hyde syndrome, none compare to the Bond Slump Blues Syndrome (BSBS). Maybe it's wrong to say that bond selling is like sex or religion. Maybe a drug is more what it's like, an addiction. The first sale, no matter whether big or small, hooks you quicker than the purest Afghan heroin. Still, one day without a trade is headache time. Another day without a trade and then another and you begin to worry a little. A few more empty days and you begin to worry more than a little.

No one would ever forget the terrible slump Hap had gone through two months before. The long, torturous days during which Hap had printed no tickets had become long, torturous weeks. "I feel like I'm crawling across the desert and no palm tree anywhere in sight," he had told Martin, Wooly bearing down on him like the withering desert sun, day after day.

"Hey, can't you give me a break?" he had said to Wooly. "Aren't we buddies?"

"Yeah, well, what have you done for me lately, kid?" Wooly had responded.

Selling bonds had once seemed a cinch, recess stuff, a slam-dunk, like peeing a hole in the snow. Now it had become mission impossible. The most important thing that Hap had, the only thing he had, namely his self-confidence, had started to seep away during the last slump. He had begun to think he had lost that ineffable thing called "touch." "How in the hell did I ever convince anybody to do such a crazy thing as buy a bond from me in the first place?" he had begun to wonder. He had tried not to panic but had grown increasingly certain he would never ever sell another bond the rest of his life. *Then what,* he had asked himself. *Sell stamps at the post office?* After all, what technical skills did he have that could be transferred to another profession? Good phone voice?

He had begun to act strange, increasingly intolerant of other people. He could barely muster a "good morning" to his colleagues. To top it off, he had threatened to kill Lyle because he had got his lunch order wrong: "Didn't I tell you rye and not whole wheat, you fuckin' shit-head!" Too, his appearance had grown increasingly disheveled, his hair uncombed, the same stinky shirt worn several days in a row, pants fly constantly open. And he had taken to pacing in the back of the trading room, all the while mumbling incoherently. Going into the fifth week of dearth, he had begun bringing a bible to work and quoting scripture aloud, developing a special appreciation for the Book of Revelation. "Come, I will show you the Judgment of the great Harlot who is seated upon many waters, with whom the kings of the earth have committed fornication, and with the wine of whose fornication the dwellers of the earth have become drunk."

One day he had asked Martin if it was better when drowning to keep your mouth shut until the oxygen had left your brain or to open your mouth and let the water rush in. But it was the glassy-eyed giggling that had really spooked everyone. They kept a safe distance from Hap, and with good reason. Of course, he suspected, no he indeed knew that they were all talking about him behind his back. He had overheard Skeets making a joke about the Soldiers of Fortune magazines he had begun buying at the newsstand downstairs.

Hap's BSBS had been aggravated by the fact that Lyle, who had sat next to him, had been on a roll that month, a hot streak. He had been having a jolly ol' time selling bonds, sailing along while Hap barely had one nostril above water. When Lyle had asked to borrow a trade ticket from Hap since he had exhausted his supply, Hap had growled at him, "I guess even a stinking, shit-covered, blind pig finds an acorn every once in awhile, huh?"

Lyle had chuckled. "Don't worry, buster, you'll do a trade again one of these years. Hee-hee-hee—"

"You know what I feel like doing?" Hap had all too calmly continued. "I feel like getting a really sharp knife, slicing open your chest, ripping out your heart and holding it in your fucking face a full two seconds before you die."

Lyle had demanded that Wooly find him another seat immediately after that spiraling episode.

So everyone shuddered with trepidation at the thought that Hap was sinking into BSBS once again. But Wooly didn't have time to worry about that.

"So what am I supposed to do, gang," he said as he raised his hands hopelessly into the air. "Let me ask you this, what can I do to help you? Should I send Arnie out to visit accounts? Should I go and pay some calls to accounts myself. Hell, I've covered just about everyone out there at some point in my career. Look, I know you guys are good. I know that this is one of the best high-yield sales teams on the street, anywhere in this town. I'd put you up against any other house in the business, any of those motherfuckers. So I know it's not lack of ability. I also don't think that it's lack of motivation, since I've made it crystal clear that all our jobs are in jeopardy if we don't get this deal done. So I think that the most important thing we can do is—"

Wooly stopped in mid—sentence as Dick Moore barged into the room. Wooly rolled his eyes and inched up his brow. Why, he wondered, couldn't Big Dick just quietly enter a room during one of their meetings instead of rudely busting in like the conference room was his kitchen or portable toilet?

"Okay, chowder heads, I gotta catch a flight on the Concorde on my way to Geneva shortly so I'm gonna make this quick."

So that's why he's wearing his best get-up, Martin thought. The Serge Armani suit, the Thomas Pink custom made shirt with the blue striped body, starched white collar and French cuffs. The Ermenegildo Zegna mauve tie that seemed too Euro-trash for a WASP poseur like Moore. On his feet, Martin noted with disdain, were the Bruno Magli slippers. Of course, he cradled in his hand as always that cute little Star Tac cell phone, even though he worked in a place chock full of phones. Martin knew that Moore dressed his best not for the benefit of the officials of the Swiss bank in Geneva that owned Whorman Skeller and whose asses Moore was expert at sticking his nose up, but for the other grandees and "eminence grise" he would be hobnobbing with on the Concorde. "Dickhead," Martin muttered under his breath.

"I just got a look at the book of orders on Lodestar. You guys are joking with me, right? Funning me? You really got a whole stack of orders that you'll dump on me at the very end, right? That book was a joke, a real laugh."

"Look, Dick, we've been busting our butts on this," Wooly interjected. "We still have a good number of prospects who—"

Moore raised his hand in Wooly's face to silence him. "Save that for your therapist. So I see you retards didn't take me seriously when I told you somebody'd have to pay if this deal didn't go well. You chumps are the most overpaid salesmen on the street. I bring in one slam-dunk deal after another, deals so easy that a monkey could sell them.

"You know, we have a saying in this business—you eat what you kill. You know what the Dick Moore corollary is to that? If you don't kill, then you get killed. I don't have the time or patience for losers. So I'm going to have to make an example out of somebody. I'm going to have to do the dirty job of publicly executing somebody."

Not a sound could be heard in the conference room, just eight hearts rapidly beating at a panic pace. The sales force's attention was as focused as a herd of wildebeest sensing that the jackal was about to make a charge.

Moore then turned to Wooly, who was standing less than five feet from him. "Wooly, you're outta here."

Wooly shot a puzzled, disgusted look toward Moore. "Outta here? What the fuck you mean by that, Dick?"

"You're fired. You been playing the game long enough to know where the buck stops. Like my pappy used to tell me, the fish rots from the head down. So pack up your desk and have your shit out of here by five o'clock today."

"I've been working at this joint for over five years and you've been here less than a year and you think you can whack me that easy?"

"I already cleared it with the higher-ups. Go see Human Resources and you'll see I got you a sweet severance package, really more than you deserve."

Wooly's face reddened with fury. "You, who doesn't know dick-squat about this business, who doesn't have the support or loyalty of one person in high-yield except your little bitch, Barker—You, who gets by totally on kissing any ass above your head and shitting on the face of anyone below you—You, a bogus fraud, are firing me, the person who everyone knows runs this show?"

Moore smiled maliciously at Wooly. "You got it, champ. Now quit being a damn crybaby and get out of here! You're embarrassing yourself."

Wooly then smirked and nodded his head, slowly and with purpose. "Really, okay..." He walked toward the door, but as he passed Moore he faced him square and said, "But let me kiss you goodbye first." Out of nowhere he threw a left hook that caught Moore dead center on his protruding chin. A big guy at six-four and two-fifteen, Moore reeled against the wall and slumped down a bit. Everyone was flabbergasted.

Moore shook off the punch enough to say to Wooly, "Are you fucking out of your mind."

"What can I say, just a love tap, Dickey boy." Still smiling, Wooly calmly took a step closer to Moore, still slumped against the wall, and let loose with an upper cut to the rib cage. Libby emitted a loud gasp as she heard a bone break.

Moore's face burst crimson and his eyes looked like they were about to pop through his spectacles. "Ugh!" he gasped and crumpled over, clutching his side. Wooly then reached to the back of Moore's head and slung him onto the floor.

He then turned toward those in the room; all of them shocked silent, and said, "Behold the Great Pretender." Moore was now on all fours, crawling toward the door, hoarsely uttering, as loud as he could, "Security! Security!"

Hap began clapping. Then Martin joined in. In a few seconds, everyone at the conference table was standing and applauding, yelling, "Wooly! Wooly!"

Wooly turned toward his audience and shouted, "I'm not done yet. I think our boy Dick has gotten himself dirty crawling all over the floor like that. Whadya say we give him a shower?"

Wooly unzipped his fly, straddled over him and proceeded to hose him down, thoroughly soaking his four thousand dollar suit and giving his hair a rinse job that he would never forget.

Moore stayed on all fours, crawling half blind like a mole because his glasses had fallen off. Pale yellow rivulets of urine streamed around his ear and off the straight and long "Mayflower" nose of which he was so proud. "You'll pay for this, Finnegan!" he shrieked, his voice high-pitched and loud with hysteria, people on the trading floor outside the room turning their heads in disbelief.

CHAPTER 9

DOUBT AND REDOUBT

"MAN, IT WAS THE WILDEST THING I'VE EVER SEEN, bar none," Martin said to Mihra, sitting in the saloon at the Oyster Bar in the bowels of Grand Central Station, recounting the pissing match, literally, between Wooly and Moore earlier that day. The Oyster Bar Saloon, with its checkered tablecloths, the paintings and to-scale models of famous sailing ships on the walls, the bowls of oyster crackers on the cherry wood L-shaped bar, was his favorite watering hole.

"So Skeets and I finally got up and helped the son-of-a-bitch off the floor. Got Wooly's piss all over my hands, which wasn't so nice. Libby found his eyeglasses and Moore put them on. I gotta give the jerk credit—he raked his hand through his hair a couple of times, wiped the urine off with his silk hanky, straightened his tie, tugged on the bottom of his suit coat, and strolled onto the trading floor like Prince Charles stepping from his carriage." Martin finished by slurping straight from the shell one of the raw blue oysters on the tray before him.

"Didn't he say anything to you guys?" Mihra asked, raising her voice above the hubbub of the bar packed with train commuters.

Martin shook his head. "Not a word. We were all a little nervous wondering whether he heard us applauding, I mean, whether he knew which ones did the applauding. He was kinda dazed, so you never know. Anyway, we're probably dead ducks, so who gives a fuck."

"Nice rhyme," Mihra said, nudging Martin with her elbow. "You really are a poet." The crowd had been pushing them closer and closer together so when she had turned to smile at him, he could see close-up everything that had always charmed him about her smile—the perfect teeth which only the Pakistani plutocracy could afford, the shy dimples, the lips not overly fat but lithe and curvy. Martin sucked down another oyster chased by a gulp of draught beer to distract him from her distracting mouth.

Boy, she is indeed looking fine today, he noted to himself. She was more dressed up than usual. The pearl gray silk blouse that jiggled every time her bosoms did, the tight gray wool skirt and matching jacket, the high heels—the whole package. Her hair, which she usually kept up, was hanging down past her shoulders. She was wearing makeup for a change so that her eyes looked even more striking than usual.

"Hey, you know you're looking hot today, Mihra," he said, taking great pleasure in breaching the politically correct etiquette that one should never comment on a co-worker's appearance in any way that could be construed as sexual.

"Beg your pardon," she said, straining to hear above the din and bringing her ear almost to his lips.

"You look good today."

"Oh, thanks. We had a presentation to a healthcare client on a new deal we're trying to bring. Since I'm the healthcare analyst, I had to be there. But don't ask me about it or I'll have to break about half a dozen SEC regs to tell you anything."

"Don't worry. After this Lodestar fiasco, I don't wanna hear about another new deal for quite awhile."

Martin speared an oyster with his little prong and held it up to Mihra's mouth. She drew it in with her tongue and sucked it into her mouth with a grin which Martin deemed extremely lustful. "Way to go," he said in that tone that guys use to encourage girls to behave like guys even though what they really want is for them to behave like girls, bad girls that is.

Mihra leaned closer still to Martin. "You know, Martin, even though that scene between Wooly and Moore was comic in a way, I detected a little sadness in you when you related the story." She gave him an inquisitive look.

"Yeah, I am sad, I mean, I love Wooly. You know, I hate to see him blown out like that. I don't know how we're gonna make do without him."

Mihra took a sip from her beer. "Ah, I thought that maybe, umm…"

"Maybe what?" Marty asked.

"You sounded really disillusioned. I thought that maybe you were having real doubts about working at Whorman Skeller. That maybe you were having doubts about being in this business, period." She glanced at Martin to see how that went over. "Don't be such a tight oyster, open up some," she added with a laugh.

Martin chuckled. "You mean after that little manifesto I delivered on the subway train just a week ago, you think I'm ready to quit? Hell no. I'm more convinced than ever that selling bonds is a black man's game. Before, I was worried that I was too black for Wall Street; now, I'm worried that I'm too white. Like what is it that we do? We grovel and kowtow before our accounts to get a trade. We shower them with gifts and Giants tickets and meals at five star restaurants. Well, sheeit!" (Martin suddenly shifted to what Mihra would have called "ghetto talk.") "Us black folk been doin' dat for three hundred and fifty years, shuckin' and jivin', steppin' and fetchin' just to survive. We be experts at bendin' da knee and smilin' big and sayin', 'Yassuh, Massa Client!' What else do a bond salesman do? Bullshit and hustle his master, the client? Now what homey ain't good at that? We da bomb at pullin' one over on ol' whitey. Rippin' off some honkey while he ain't payin' attention, what so new 'bout dat? So when it comes to whuppin' somebody upside da head like Wooly done to Big Dick, hey, just show me where I gots to go. Wall Street be just like the NFL, just a matter of time fore wees takes over."

Mihra failed to smile at Martin's minstrel show. Martin hunched over the bar, sulking over his beer. His eyes, usually narrow with intensity of purpose, were now only smoldering.

"So you answered my question in your own rather Persian-bizarre way that you are disillusioned with this business," she said."

Martin leaned back and let his breath out. "Beating people over the head and licking their butts for a solid week to buy some shitty deal and knowing all along that you're probably gonna get fired anyway, then watching one managing director of the firm urinate all over another one, yeah, all that might be enough to send one into a spell of weary disgust.

"I think back to when I was wondering what to do after I got out of Columbia. I was seriously thinking about going into the publishing business, believe it or not."

"Yeah, I remember," Mihra said.

"But then the investment banks came to recruit. Lehman Brothers even sent a black guy to interview black prospects, blackly speaking, of course."

"Hey, I remember," Mihra said. "A nice guy, really. The only black guy I ever remember representing an investment bank. He was one of the few traders, too.

Most of the firms sent the bankers, not anyone from sales and trading. Always some dressed-to-the-nines, moussed-down, urbane, oh-so-civilized banker."

"Pompous prigs," Martin added.

"Yeah, they wanted to give the impression that this business is genteel, elitist, even respectable. Ha!"

"That's all just a front, Mihra. Out there on the trading floor, that's what Wall Street's all about. A dogfight everyday and the devil take the hindmost. Eat what you kill, and if you don't kill, then you get killed. Who really gives a damn what the client wants or needs. We're just more honest about it than the bankers. But they're salesmen just like Lyle Shiner's a salesman. They're trying to pull one over on some CEO who's thinking about taking his company public or merging it with another company or bringing a bond deal. We salesmen are trying to pull one over on the accounts guys who buy whatever product is generated by that action. Sure, the banker's a little slicker about it than Lyle, but it's basically a sales job, a con job, a hand job just the same. What a great racket, huh?"

"But this guy from Lehman convinced you otherwise?"

"The dude gave it to me straight up. He said, 'Listen, man, nobody at Lehman gives a shit what you look like. You might be a redheaded Cyclops, but if you produce, if you make money for the firm, you'll look like Prince Charming to everyone. Just all a matter of numbers, man,' he said. 'That's simple to understand.'

"And that really appealed to me, the idea of a colorblind meritocracy. Really struck a chord with me. Except for the military, I couldn't think of anything else that pure. So I thought, hey, why not give it a try.

Mihra nodded in resignation. "Yeah..." She knew she wasn't in any position to muster a rousing defense. Lately, she had been wondering how she had ended up here. Many nights when she was still in the office at 9:30 p.m. working on a research report, she had asked herself, *How did I ever get it in my head to work on Wall Street?* Of course, she partly and conveniently blamed it on her father, an industrialist who had always pushed her to go into business. She was his eldest child and he had no sons, thus she was his heir apparent. The plan, his plan, had always been that she get her MBA and some valuable investment banking experience before coming home to join the family conglomerate. Even though journalism had been her major and first love, she had enrolled in business school. She had got it into her head that New York, Wall Street, was the only place to be. *If I can make it there, I can make it anywhere,* she told herself over and again. So here she was.

"See this ring?" Martin said, showing off Pops' ring.

"Yes, I noticed it earlier. No offense, quite ugly, really," Mihra said, slipping into the faint British accent that she had gradually been losing since she had moved to the States.

Gazing at the ring, Martin said, "My father gave it to me. He was a champion boxer. Every time I look at this ring, I realize I can't quit, not ever, on anything. Let the game play out however it might, good or bad, but I can't quit."

Mihra wanted to say, "I understand you have something to prove. But please, Martin, follow your heart, not your will." But that would have sounded a little too Hallmarkish. So instead she reached out and took hold of his ring hand. Martin turned and looked at her. "What do you say we go somewhere for dinner?" he asked finally, fully aware that taking her out to dinner could be construed as a "date," the first real one they ever had together.

"Sure, I'd love to."

Hap Boggs lay sprawled on his couch, wearing nothing but his underwear and scratching his nuts as he watched the evening news. The apartment he rented on Central Park West came furnished and the decorator certainly didn't have the likes of Hap in mind when she had installed the wool satin drapes, the stiff-backed Victorian sofa and chaise lounge (chosen for their discipline of line) the bow-front English Regency dresser in which the table linens were stored, and the chenille fabric rug on which Hap had tossed two empty thirty-two ounce cans of Foster beer. He did, however, consider the white baby grand piano in the corner to be a real hoot and intended one day to learn how to play the damn thing. He had even gone so far as to buy a Billy Joel songbook, notwithstanding that he couldn't read sheet music. He had placed on the piano a silver framed photo of Doug Flutie and him arm-in-arm just after beating Miami on that historic day in November 1984, maybe the happiest moment in Hap's life.

Look at that fop Peter Jennings, Hap thought to himself as he popped open his third Foster. *What decent, self-respecting guy has plastic surgery done to his eyes! The prissy, fuckin' Canook! Can't take Brokaw though, talks funny and Rather is a fuckin' nut! Wooly, god almighty, man, what are we going to do without Wooly? Where's that blonde chick correspondent with the nice rack? Wooly, man, what a bummer! He looked out for me. Moore hates my guts and would jump at a chance to whack me. Oh, shit! Better get my resume together.*

Wow, look at those Palestinian kids hurl those rocks. Might be a budding Doug Flutie amongst that rabble yet. That one there has a nice arm. It's awesome ol' Dougie is doing well in the NFL, finally. Too short my ass. Outta give him a call sometime.

Speaking of Flutie Flakes, what am I gonna eat tonight? Oh, yeah, nice fart, Hapmeister. Geez, get a whiff of the Moo Goo Gai Pan from last night! Yowzah!

Wooly, the guy knows how to go out in style. Moore stank like Penn Station on a hot summer night. Look at Clinton! Bogus Bill. Gotta give him credit for that cigar dildo idea, a stroke of genius that was. Even smoked the damn thing afterwards. Soaked in pussy juice! Almost made me like the guy. Hillary otta give him a box of exploding cigars for Christmas in case he wants to try it again.

Lodestar, shit! Not one order. I'm a dead salesman walking-dinner—Chinese, Italian, Mexican, the three great cuisines of the world. Lodestar. Zilch. Guillotine. Need to call Belinda for Saturday night. Time to drain the ol' dragon again. Wonder if she's still pissed about me blowing my wad in her mouth. Hell, the way she carried on, you would have thought it was monkey snot. Ah, fuck her anyway. She could stand to drop twenty pounds, anyway, the fat pig.

Hey, hold it, what's that, a satellite? Turn up the volume, moron. Fuck, where's the damn remote! Chinese satellite strayed from its orbit and lost communication, important part of telecommunications system the Chinese government is developing, major setback. The Chinese are decades behind the U. S. in satellite technology, but gaining. Hmm…Lodestar…Chinese…Those chinks have a lot of dough, don't they? Billions, right? Gave Bogus Bill a few million for his election, didn't they? Like it was pocket change. Throw money around like water!

Maybe, they would…Holy fucking mackerel! Maybe they would put some money in Lodestar! Maybe they would wanna get involved in the company for the technology! They could probably buy the company if they wanted. Gave Clinton money. For sure they could at least buy some bonds just to get an inside peek.

My god! They could take down the whole goddamned five hundred million if they wanted. The Chinese! Lodestar…Who ever said Hap Boggs was a dimwit? Coach Coughlin called me a puddin' head that time. Well, fuck you, coach! I just saved the day!

Hap decided he now had no choice but to order Chinese take-out for the second night in a row, picked up the telephone and ordered a "Happy Bird Nest Mandarin."

CHAPTER 10

GUNG HAY FAT CHOY

HAP BOGGS OPENED HIS EYES AND GLANCED AT the clock radio, 6:14 a.m. A brilliant idea had aroused him from slumber, exactly one minute before the alarm had been set to go off. Hap had thought that a person could not think while sleeping, but this idea had arisen as sublimely as the hard-on that usually greeted him every sunrise. The idea was this: Why fly to D. C. and go through all the trouble to find the Chinese embassy and then hassle trying to get into the joint, when there was probably one of those consulting—or consulate—offices right in Manhattan. Sure there would be some chink there high enough up the pay scale who would understand the Lodestar deal and what a tremendous potential opportunity it offered the Chinese government, someone there with a bat big enough to be worthy of Hap's best pitch. (Chinks do play baseball, don't they? Or was it those geeky Japs who were the baseball freaks? He couldn't remember. They all looked the same to him.) Better avoid baseball metaphors when spinning the spiel, he concluded. Table tennis, aka Ping-pong, that's what the Chinese love, he remembered. *Try to think of some Ping-pong analogies later on,* he thought. In any case, it was another stroke of brilliance in what was becoming a scintillating streak of good ideas.

Hap pondered whether he should eat Chinese food every night from now on, seeing how the junk was real brain food.

Hap called information to find the address of the Consulate for the People's Republic of China and a short while later found himself at the corner of 40th street and 12th Avenue. *What a friggin' place to have a consulate,* Hap thought as he stood in the drizzling rain of a gray March morning, so struck by the fact that the aircraft carrier Intrepid was permanently docked on the Hudson River directly across the Westside Highway from the consulate that he almost achieved a rare conceit of irony.

Hap found the building housing the consulate to be as non-descript as communist Chinese fashion. The bottom half of the building had a veneer of slate-colored faux brick. Above that were large gray panels of concrete and compressed gravel that had no openings other than a row of large air vents. Rising upward was a dingy apartment tower sheathed in the same faux brick material but aquamarine in color. The building appeared to have once been a hotel, but the windows on the ground floor had been boarded up and the metal porche-cochere in front was rusting and in need of a fresh coat of paint. The only improvement the present occupants had apparently made to the building involved security cameras strategically located along the facade.

Hap walked to the metal front door, tugged on it and discovered it was locked. He peered inside the glass peephole, for some reason thinking he would be able to look inside. It was early morning, not quite eight o'clock, so why wasn't the place open? He searched the entrance corridor but found no sign stating when the consulate opened for business. The only evidence that the building was in fact the consulate was the seal of the People's Republic of China—four small red stars arrayed around a large star in front of something that looked like a pagoda—hanging precariously over the entrance.

Hap jumped at the sudden, clamorous opening of a large metal door several yards from the front entrance. He froze to attention. "Uh, oh," he uttered, half expecting a contingent of Red guards to march out and seize him. Instead, a silver Lexus sedan mysteriously emerged from what must have been the garage. Relieved, Hap hurried towards it. "When does this place open?" he shouted at the driver, a young Chinese woman who Hap thought way too pretty to be a communist. Unwilling to lower the driver side window, she pointed toward 40th street and mouthed the words, "Around the corner."

Hap made his way around the corner and found another metal door. This door was not as big as the front entrance but it was unlocked. A plaque at the side of the door read VISA AND PASSPORT OFFICE, but Hap didn't let that stop him from entering.

Hap entered a large room that was partitioned by a glass wall, fully drab as the building's exterior. Naked fluorescent lights lined the ceiling and the dull linoleum floors contained random islands of brown blotches, cinderblock walls painted light yellow. In front of the glass partition were four scuffed and scratched wooden desks, each of which was occupied by a Chinese official of some genus or another. Behind each desk on the glass partition was a sign in Chinese ideograms, English and Spanish that demanded the presentation of a birth certificate and another acceptable form of identification. The only sounds in the room were mumbled exchanges in Chinese and the regular staccato of a stamp pounding a document. A line of two or three supplicants, all of whom appeared to be Chinese, stood in front of three of the desks. The military-attired floor guard directed Hap to the fourth desk after taking down his name and examining the contents of his briefcase.

Hap approached the desk. Sitting behind it was a middle age, overweight Chinese woman who had her gray hair severely pulled back and who wore a neck high, black satin blouse underneath a gray woolen cardigan. Her lit cigarette smoldered in the ashtray and provided the only odor in a room forever deprived of fresh air. Hap, a former chain smoker, savored the aroma now prohibited in every public place except consulates. She peered at Hap over the reading specs perched on the end of her short, broad nose. "Visa or Passport?" she asked.

"Uh, neither," Hap answered quickly. He then flopped down into the metal foldout chair at the side of the desk, slightly unsettling the interrogator.

"I'm not here for any of that stuff," he continued, as he placed his elbow on the desktop. "I need to talk to somebody, one of the head honchos in charge here."

"Hable usted Espanol?" the official asked uncertainly, evidently taking the word "honcho" as a sign that this big, ugly qualan might be of "Latino heritage," as phrased in her training manual.

"No, no, of course I don't speak Spanish. Do I look like a Puerto Rican to you?" Hap's agitated gesturing caused the lady official to make eye contact with the guard standing in the corner behind Hap.

"Okay. Visa or passport then."

"Look lady, you're re not getting me." Hap had turned the chair so that he was now facing the official square. He hunched over with his arms on his knees and his hands chopping the air with each word he spoke. "I don't wanna talk to nobody about a visa or passport. I need to see somebody here about something really important, something way beyond visas and passports. You follow? Believe me, you get me through to the right person and I'll tell them how sweet and nice and oh so helpful you are. This could be big, lady, and it'll be a real feather in your cap that you had something to do with it."

"I do not understand you. I do not wear cap with feathers. Only visa or passport here."

"Damn," Hap said as he slapped his hands down on her desk, drawing the attention of all four guards in the room. "Look, let me show you something." He then opened his briefcase, at which point one of the guards put his hand on the large handgun holstered at his side. Hap then pulled out a Lodestar prospectus. Waving it in the air, he said, "See this here. Your boss would die to get his hands on this. Let me show something." He then hurriedly opened the red to the first page and pointed at a word.

"You read English?" he asked loudly. "You see that word there, right there." He jabbed his finger at the page.

The official, becoming increasingly alarmed, turned her eyes askance to the page.

"You see that word there," he shouted. "You know what that word says? It says 'satellite.' You follow me? Sa…tel…lite. That's what I wanna talk to somebody about. Satellites. I got something that'll blow their socks off."

Upon hearing the word "satellite" bellowed from Hap's mouth, every person in the room stopped what they were doing and turned. The four guards in front of the glass partition, the three officials who sat at the other three desks and the line of supplicants who stood before them, the guards behind the glass partition who were running metal detectors over each supplicant who was allowed entry to yet another layer of officials sitting behind wooden desks, they all simultaneously turned their heads and focused their attention upon this crazy American, this stranger in a strange land who had uttered a word that had recently attained an almost magical aura about it within the People's Republic, obsessed as it was with American high technology.

The official then pushed a button under her desk that sounded a loud buzzer. She stood up and waved toward a guard behind the glass partition and began motioning for him to come to the front. She spoke loud and rapid Cantonese to the other guards on that side of the partition. Just moments after uttering the word, "satellite," Hap found himself surrounded by the guards, two of whom gripped him by his arms.

"Hey, what's going on—I'm an American citizen," he hollered.

"They take you to head honcho," the lady bureaucrat answered, smiling in a way that could have been either mocking or solicitous.

Hap was bum-rushed through the glass partition and past the gaping supplicants. "What the hell is going on here," he shouted. Hap's ushers marched him down a dark hallway and into a conference room. "Stay right here. Someone come to help you," one of the guards said in as reassuring a tone as he could manage.

Hap, disconcerted, sat down at a conference table and inhaled/exhaled several times in order to collect himself. As roughshod as the galoot guards may have been, Hap felt that he was at last getting somewhere and that helped him regain his equilibrium. He looked about the conference room and found that, like the overall environs, there wasn't much to it. He rose and walked to a mirror hanging on the wall only because it was the only object in the room other than the conference table, chairs and a plastic fichus tree in the corner.

He studied his reflected mug. He admired how large and square his head was with its cantilevered brow. Hap was too ugly and too base to be vain, but he did consider once again whether he should do something about the pits above his jaw line that a vicious bout of teenage acme had ordered. Maybe sandpaper it or a peel, whatever. He then fancied what he might look like if he were Chinese. To get an idea, he put his index fingers to the corners of his eyes and pulled slightly. Besides takeout food, watching Charlie Chan movies was about as close to anything Chinese as Hap had ever got, so it wasn't long before he lapsed into the Charlie Chan impersonation that used to crack everybody up in the high school locker room.

"Ah yes, my most favowite son and I go to Shanghai to find the lost heirwoom that is key to solving the murda. Confucius say, 'Tea leaves like the tongues of men. Some tell truth, some don't'. Ching kung toa ping pong wonton egg fu young."

On the other side of the two-way mirror, two colonels in the People's Liberation Army sat observing Hap Boggs and his take on Chinese culture. They turned and looked at one another, both lost for words.

Hap's attention was quickly drawn away from the mirror, as two men entered the room. The shorter man, hurried over to Hap, his hand extended and smiling anxiously so that his large teeth were revealed in all their yellowish splendor.

"Hello, Mr. Boggs. My name is Sam Wong. I am Deputy Consul." Hap failed to wonder how this gentleman knew his name, so distracted was he by the gentleman's enormous head, made even larger by the helmet of longish gray hair. The man wasn't dressed like a communist apparatchik but more like a NYU professor of ancient Chinese history, wearing a cloth tie and tweed jacket, gray polyester slacks, Rockport's on his feet. Like his name, everything about the man seemed Americanized. His eyeglasses had silver square frames, standard People's Republic issue. Hair was growing from his ears.

Hap shook Mr. Wong's small, damp hand, Mr. Wong bowing as he did so.

"This is Mr. Zhu Lai," Mr. Wong said as he turned to his cohort behind him. Mr. Wong did not bother to state Mr. Zhu's title or position. Hap was surprised by Mr. Zhu Lai's stature, having been under the assumption that all Chinese were short in height. But Mr. Zhu was at least six-four and heavy-set. He was wearing the traditional Mao Tse Young gray jacket, with a buttoned neck collar. He combed his hair straight back and also wore square framed eyeglasses, but his were black instead of silver. He did not offer his hand to Hap or even bow.

"Okay. Let us talk," Mr. Wong said as he directed Hap to the conference table.

Hap sat at the conference table and quickly reconnoitered his audience so as to determine the best tact, right angle, and the most effective tone. In truth, Hap didn't have much to work with, but it would have to do. Mr. Wong was smiling a little too much, to the point of making Hap uncomfortable. The other gent was smiling too, but in a funny, sly way, like Mona Lisa, like the Cheshire cat that swallowed the canary. He sat very erect in his chair while Mr. Wong slouched back with one leg resting on the other's knee.

"You have something to tell us about satellites?" Mr. Wong asked in a halting English.

"You bet I do," Hap said, shifting into gear. "I got something here that you'll lick your chops over, something that'll let you get a glimpse into the twentieth-first century, something that'll—"

"Something about satellites, right," impatient Mr. Wong interjected.

"Oooh, yeah. Now I know you Chinese were once good at inventing things, like gunpowder and firecrackers way back when. But you've lagged a bit lately in things technological. Am I right?" Hap stopped, waiting for his audience to respond.

Mr. Wong looked at Big Cat Zhu, who nodded back. Both Mr. Zhu's smile and patience were growing shorter. "Right," Mr. Wong answered.

"Okay. So we all admit we have a problem here. Recognition of a problem is the first step towards solving it. Now I have here something that could very well be at, the very least part, of the solution and, at the very most, an answer to your national prayers." With the fluid hand skills of a magician, Hap then popped open his briefcase and retrieved the Lodestar prospectus and dramatically flourished it in the air. Mr. Wong's hands twitched in his lap as he repressed the urge to snatch from Hap's hands the document, containing, he was certain, TOP SECRET satellite technology.

"What I have here is not only the end product of a major technological breakthrough, not only a window into a revolutionary advance in satellite telecommunications—" Hap paused to let that last bullet point sink in and then with a parenthetic smile added, "And, if I'm not mistaken, you guys have staged a revolution or two, am I right?" Again, Hap waited for the audience response.

"Right," Mr. Wong grumbled.

"Well, this window into a revolutionary advance is now open and you, Mr. Wong and you, Mr. uh..." (Hap stalled, not remembering Big Cat's name until the mental image of a zoo came back to him), "Mr Zhu can leap right through that window, take another great leap forward, and the price of admission is only five hundred million dollars!"

Mr. Wong winced while Mr. Zhu, barely understanding a word Hap said, continued to smile. Mr. Wong wondered if he was hearing right. This gorilla in a thousand dollar suit wanted half a billion dollars in exchange for information? The most he had ever paid for espionage was low seven figures. What was in that document he was waving about that could be worth that? Blueprints for a state-of-the-art satellite? Outlines for a space-based missile defense system? Still, what could be worth five hundred million dollars?

"We must know more about what you have before we say what we pay you," Mr. Wong diplomatically proffered.

"I haven't even mentioned the best part," Hap said, leaning forward. "This deal'll probably come with at least a twelve per cent yield."

A puzzled look muddled Mr. Wong's face. "Twelve percent?"

"Hey, I said at least. Don't start chiseling me before you've even seen the deal. A twelve percent coupon is not bad in this market."

A light bulb as blinding as a lighthouse beacon went off in Mr. Wong's head, bleaching away all prior assumptions about this man's intentions. "So you wish that we invest in some...some...what you call...deal?"

"Well, duh," Hap said good-naturedly.

"And this investment is for what?" Wong said, his voice stilted with shock and disappointment.

"Faxing! Lodestar is putting up a satellite system so people can carry fax machines around with them. They need the proceeds from this bond issue to build the system and get it going."

Mr. Wong fell back into his chair. "A bond salesman..." he uttered in Chinese to Zhu. Mr. Zhu's transcendent smile turned into a menacing scowl.

Mr. Wong then turned to Hap. "Mr. Boggs, we have no interest in your fax machines. Time to go." He and Mr. Zhu then abruptly rose from the table.

"Hold it there, for a second, will ya," Hap pleaded. "I haven't even mentioned how the U. S. Department of Defense is involved in this thing."

Mr. Wong paused. He murmured to Mr. Zhu. The two gentlemen quickly sat back down.

"Department of Defense?"

"Yeah, that's the beauty of this deal, Sammy. The Defense Department has entered into long-term contracts to use the Lodestar system. What they pay out under those contracts covers a good chunk of the debt service. It's almost like buying U. S. treasuries."

"What does your government need fax machines for, Mr. Boggs?"

"Hey, I can guarantee you that their interest in Lodestar has nothing to do with faxes. That stuff is classified so there's not much I can tell you. But my hunch is that it has something to do with Star Wars defense or something along those lines. You follow me?"

Mr. Wong was following Hap so well that he squirmed in his seat. "Do you understand Chinese?" he asked Hap.

"My Chinese doesn't go much past 'chop suey,'" Hap said with a chuckle.

Mr. Wong then launched into an animated conversation with Mr. Zhu. Hap sat nodding his head, even though he couldn't understand a word of what they were saying, as if his nodding might emit positive vibes toward his two pigeons.

Mr. Wong finally turned to Hap and said, "I'm sorry to say to you, Mr. Boggs, but my government cannot invest in such a project. Would not be...how you say...kosher."

Crestfallen, Hap sighed as long and loud as a balloon deflating.

"But," Mr. Wong continued, "I know investor who could give you money. He runs a, what you call it, hedge fund. His name is Jo Hu."

"Jo Hu? Runs the Dragon Funds, right? Sure I've heard of him." Hap like everyone else in the global financial community had heard of Jo Hu; and like everyone else he knew next to nothing about him.

"Yes. I will courier this document to him. Someone from his office call you to set up meeting. That okay?"

"Of course it's okay. Let's do it, baby!" Hap's sudden outburst of exuberance startled Mr. Zhu.

"Give me five on that, Sammy," Hap said as he held his palm in Mr. Wong's face.

Mr. Wong, blushing sheepishly, slapped Hap's hand, causing Big Cat Zhu's bulk to shiver with giggles.

Chapter 11

Oh Happy Day

HAP RECEIVED THE CALL FROM A WOMAN WITH A lovely British accent requesting that he come to the offices of Dragon Funds to discuss Lodestar with Jo Hu. After getting the call, Hap bolted from the trading floor and tried to hail a taxi outside but all the cabbies were off duty as this was the time of day (4:00 to 5:00 p.m.) when they changed shifts. So Hap sprinted from Whorman Skeller's offices on 54th and Park to Dragon Fund's on 48th and Third, covering the distance in a remarkable eight minutes. If it hadn't been for that old biddy he had plowed over on Park Avenue, he would have probably made it in six minutes flat.

Hap paced the Dragon Fund's 23rd Floor reception area. He was too anxious, too sweaty, too out of breath to even flirt with the cute Asian receptionist, an indulgence that Hap rarely passed upon. Finally another cute woman entered and asked Hap in her silky British accent (the same one that he had heard on the phone earlier) to follow her.

They entered Dragon Fund's trading room from the reception area. The trading room was not overly large, approximately 10,000 square feet. The trading desks were lined in three rows running the length of the room. Everyone, it appeared, had a phone to his or her ear. Hap was surprised to see that they were all dressed casually, not a suit or tie in sight.

One shorter row of desks stood separate from the three lines. This row was elevated against the floor-to-ceiling windows overlooking Third Avenue. Pacing back and forth was an Asian gentleman talking into a phone headset. Although his pacing was hurried, his demeanor was cool and collected. He wore a black silk tee shirt and black pleated, light wool pants. The Reeboks, however, were white. Hap guessed that this person was Jo Hu, judging by the way all the other people on the floor paid him their utmost attention.

The secretary led Hap across the trading floor and to a corner office. "Mr. Hu will be joining you in a moment," she informed Hap with a flight attendant smile.

The office did not stand out from all the other executive offices honeycombing the buildings lining Third Avenue. Large windows dominated the far corner of the office. In front of the windows was a sitting arrangement of antique, chintz-covered settee, two Duncan Fife chairs and a cherry wood coffee table. On the other side of the room, nearest the door, was Mr. Hu's desk, a large, flat semi-circular slab of polished mahogany suspended by steel cables running from the ceiling. Behind the desk was a high-backed, black leather swivel chair, and behind the chair was a bank of sixteen trading screens. Little red and blue and yellow lights blinked across the flat green surfaces, signaling market changes, like synapses popping off within the Great Market Mind. With the window blinds drawn, the only light in the room was that of computer screens and the track lighting over the desk, giving the office a deeply private, insular ambience. A large silk banner with black ideograms against a red background hung against the wall across from the desk. The banner bore a quote from Tse's, *Art of War*. "One can only know one's enemy by knowing oneself." On the credenza underneath the banner were the framed degrees from Harvard College and Stanford Graduate School of Business and three photos of Hu shaking hands with various Chinese officials, one of whom Hap recognized as Zhu Lai. Hap, however, did not recognize the porcelain bowl in the temperature-controlled case as a priceless artifact from the Ming Dynasty.

A few minutes later, the man in black strode into the office. He introduced himself to Hap and shook hands without breaking his stride and while simultaneously squinting at the trading screens behind his desk. "Have a seat," he said to Hap as he pointed at the chair in front of his desk.

Hap, a borderline homophobe was not one to consciously notice another's man's looks, but even he found Jo Hu's features striking. His face was broad, with cheekbones high. His nose was flat, leonine. His jet black hair, short on the sides and long in the front, swept across his forehead. His skin was the brown that Caucasian sunbathers shoot for in suntan lotion commercials. His dark, narrow eyes, limned with lashes as stark and pronounced as mascara, endowed his face with certain fierceness, even when laughing.

Hap was struck not only by Hu's looks but also his youth. Hap guessed that he couldn't have been any older than the early thirties.

Sitting at his desk and turning to peruse the trading screens, Jo Hu said to Hap over his shoulder, "I got the red on Lodestar. Looks interesting." His accent was as Californian as Palo Alto.

Hap nodded, struggling to overcome his awe. This, after all, was Jo Hu, the notorious rogue trader who had almost single-handedly precipitated a global financial crisis by taking on the central bank of Thailand. Hu had thought that Thailand's currency, the baht, was overvalued, vis-à-vis the dollar, the yen, the mark. The Thai central bank had thought otherwise. Jo Hu proceeded to sell billions of bahts, which the central bank proceeded to buy. Mano-e-mano, Hu sold and sold and the central bank bought and bought. Spending its reserves of U. S. dollars, Japanese Yen and German Marks to buy bahts from Hu, the central bank vowed to devalue its currency only when hell froze over. Detecting a strong chill arising from that nether region, other speculators joined in the fun and also began shorting bahts along with Hu. Before long, the central bank reserves had dwindled to almost nothing and the devil was ready to strap on his ice skates. The Thai government finally had no choice but to devalue its currency. Other nations within the Pacific Rim, namely Indonesia, Malaysia, Korea, were forced to devalue their currencies as well in order to keep the price of their goods competitive with Thailand's exports. So a vicious whirlwind was set in motion, as the Pacific Rim countries, the so-called Asian Tigers, spiraled into economic depression. Since the rest of the world marketed much of their goods to these economies, the "Asian Contagion," as the press dubbed it, spread rapidly. Russian defaulted on its bonds, South American financial markets crashed, the Dow Jones Industrial Average plummeted almost two thousand points. Standing in the middle of the vortex, within the eye of the storm, was thirty—three year old Jo Hu, who had pocketed over one billion dollars in trading gains from the turmoil. Suddenly, everyone wanted to know who Jo Hu was; Hu was not eager to oblige the curiosity.

This is just another pitch, just another pitch; Hap kept telling himself to maintain his verve. "It's more than interesting," he said to Hu. "Is it okay if I call you Jo? It's a great opportunity to get into a deal that has the backing—"

Hu raised his hand, cutting Hap off. "I don't need a snow job." He again swiveled in his chair to check the screens behind him. "I've studied the red thoroughly. What I need from you is information about how the deal is going." He then turned and transfixed Hap with eyes whose irises were the same color as the mahogany desk but more opaque.

Hap shifted in his seat and wondered how far he should go in lying to Hu. "It's going okay, you know. We've had a good order flow."

"Bullshit," Hu said matter-of-factly. "Is that why you were loitering around the consulate, trying to get money out of the Chinese government, because the order flow has been so good?"

Hap blushed, chagrined.

"I'll give you credit, Mr. Boggs, you got some nerve." The fact that Hu had called him by name and even smiled at him, okay, maybe it was more of a sneer, helped set Hap at ease.

"Now don't jerk me off. How much in orders you got on the books. Firm orders, not indications of interest?"

Hap emitted a low groan of resignation. "Around two hundred million, tops."

"A five hundred million dollar deal and you got two hundred million in orders, huh? Yeah, the deal's going well, all right—"

Hap shrugged his shoulders once again.

"What's the price talk?"

"Uh, like eleven and three quarters to twelve percent."

Hu turned to his screens and, after a few moments, turned back to Hap. "I want to get into this deal. But I don't want to get in and then discover that Whorman Skeller is still sitting on a boatload of bonds after the deal breaks. You guys have a nasty reputation for dumping bonds, not supporting your deals. So, all of a sudden, my investment turns to shit because you start throwing paper out the window, start selling at whatever price it takes to clear the overhang."

"I wouldn't say our reputation's nasty," Hap feebly countered. But once again Hu interrupted him by raising his hand.

"I'll cut to the chase. I'll take the balance of the deal that's not spoken for."

Hu's phone, with its twenty-three lines, then rang, or rather trilled. "Goldman London," he mumbled as he looked at the phone bank. He picked up the phone and said to the person in Goldman Sachs' London office, "Stay right there." He then said to Hap, "I got to take this call. You clear on my order?"

Hap put his hand to his head. "You say you want the balance. But I told you the balance is three hundred million."

"That's right. I'll take the three hundred million or whatever the balance is, give or take fifty million, at the price talk. Got it?" Hap, stunned, couldn't utter a word but only nod his head. "Get back to me with regular updates and any change in the price talk," Hu said before returning to the Goldman Sachs call.

Shocked numb, Hap rose from his seat, his head as light as a helium balloon and his body as insubstantial as a string attached to it. He exited the office and shuffled across the trading room, his mouth slightly agape, his face pale, his gait so mechanical that at least one trader in the room was reminded of the zombies in Night of the Living Dead.

By the time Hap had returned to the Whorman Skeller trading floor, his zombie shuffle had improved. He strode to the high-yield pit as jaunty and imperious as McArthur stepping into the surf at Corregidor. But the scene he came upon did not befit the grandeur of the announcement he had to make, which was that he had saved the day once again. A small crowd had gathered around Lori Putterman's desk. They were laughing and shouting, "You go, girl. C'mon Lori, you can do it. Somebody move the trash can next to her in case she pukes." Hap got close enough to see Lori Putterman sitting at her desk, cramming a hotdog into her mouth. Lying on her desk in a neat row were four more hot dogs, Coney Islands with sauerkraut and mustard, which the commissary was serving for lunch that day.

"Okay, that's two down and four to go," shouted Skeets, who was standing behind Hap. "You've only got eight minutes left."

Lori took a big gulp, her face turning a ghastly pale. She reached for another Coney Island, belched, and slowly began inserting it length-wise into her mouth.

"Better step on it, Lori," Lyle said. "I got a hundred bucks riding on you."

"What the hell's going on?" Hap asked Martin.

"Oh, we got a little bet going. Skeets bet Lori she couldn't eat six hotdogs in fifteen minutes and keep 'em down for at least half an hour. She bet Skeets five hundred dollars she could. I got a side bet with Lyle that she couldn't."

"Ah, shit, look at the poor girl," Lyle moaned. "Her eyes are starting to cross. She ain't gonna make it. It's a shame she'll end up losing both her lunch and five hundy."

Hap, suddenly turned haughty, shook his head. What a bunch of juveniles, he could afford to say to himself, even though normally he would have been right in the thick of the shenanigans. "Can you hand me one of those order tickets there behind you?" he asked Skeets.

"Sure. Five more minutes, Mrs. Putterman." He handed Hap a ticket and offhandedly asked what his order was, just as Hap was hoping he would.

"Got an order on Lodestar. Where's Moore. I got to give him this order so he can give it to syndicate."

"You can bet he ain't here, otherwise we wouldn't be sittin' around watchin' Lori shovelin' doggies into her mouth. How many Lodestars?"

Hap didn't answer but handed the order ticket to Skeets.

"Hey, thirty million. We could use it. Way to go, boy."

"No, read it again, Skeets," Hap commanded as he tilted his head back.

Skeets moved the piece of paper closer to his face and squinted at it. His face slid two inches down his skull. "Three hundred million? You're pulling my leg. You got an order for three hundred million?!"

"You got it," Hap said, snatching the order from Skeet's fingers.

"Lyle, you hear that? Hap got a three hundred million dollar order on Lodestar!" Skeets shouted.

Upon hearing that, Lori began gagging on the Coney Island dangling halfway out of her mouth. But no one around her noticed as they had turned their attention to Hap.

Hap sauntered over to the trading desk. "Where's Big Dick," he asked Terry Barker, who had glumly been observing the festivities in the sales pit.

"In a meeting. What the fuck you want with him?"

Meanwhile, Lori had fallen to the floor, her face turning crimson while everyone else was grossly involved in discussing the commission that Hap would earn off this trade.

"I have something for him." Hap replied.

Martin finally noticed that Lori was writhing on the floor, clawing at her throat, her legs frantically thrashing. "Holy shit!" He reached down and picked her up, hugged his arms around her chest and began to administer the Heimlich maneuver. Three times Martin squeezed until finally a stream of mashed and partially digested sauerkraut and beef by-product spewed forth from Lori's mouth four feet through the air and all over Lyle's back. The pink and yellow splatter upon his tailor-made green checked shirt achieved an effect worthy of Kandinsky. Lyle shrieked like a hysterical old lady who had just witnessed her cat being run over.

The first words immediately following the bits of chewed up hotdog from Lori's mouth were, "THREE HUNDRED MILLION DOLLAR ORDER!"

"You're in luck, Happy," Terry said. "Here comes Dick now."

"Hap has been asking where you were, Dick," Terry said, cuddling his tongue inside his cheek, anticipating Moore's reaction to Hap's presumptive inquiry as to his whereabouts.

"You remember Hap, don't you, Dick? He's that guy who used to do a trade every once in awhile."

"He better sell some fucking Lodestar bonds or else he'll be a distant memory," Moore said as he slid into his seat.

Hap nonchalantly tossed the trade ticket up into the air. It fluttered into Moore's lap. "What are you doing, you big ape?" Moore asked, unaccustomed to such insolence.

"Ah, yes, Lodestar," Hap responded. "Consider it done, Big Dick, put to bed, tamed, slayed!"

Moore glanced at the ticket. He glared at Hap. "You back to those five martini lunches again. Didn't I tell you to never show up here sauced?"

"I'm as sober as Judge Judy."

"So you're telling me that you sold three hundred million in Lodestar bonds?"

"That's what it say, don't it, boss man."

"You better not be shitting me, Hap."

Hap held his hands up and began moving them from side to side as he wiggled his hippo hips and sang three notes off-key, "Happy days are here again, the sun is shining here again—"

"Damn," Terry Barker exclaimed as he held the ticket in his hand. "Dragon Funds? I didn't know they were a junk investor."

"This better be legit, Hap," Moore snarled.

"That's right, Dragon Funds. Boy, are you fellas out of 'the know.' Jo fucking Hu, the man himself, gave me the order personally."

"Jo Hu is buying three hundred million Lodestars?" Moore and Terry asked simultaneously in disbelief.

"Yep! We're in the money! We're in the money!"

Moore turned to Alex, the clerk who oversaw trade clearing and credit checks for the high-yield desk. "Check out Dragon Funds, Alex. We've never done a trade with them so make sure they're cleared and eligible to buy Lodestar."

"I already have, Dick. Hap called from his cell phone thirty minutes ago, all in a panic, telling me to run a check. They're fine. They're registered in the Netherlands Antilles, an offshore fund. This Jo Hu guy is a Chinese national, lists his main residence as Hong Kong. But that's no problem since it's Dragon Funds and not him buying the bonds. Their credit's good here. Dragon Funds does a shit load of trading with Whorman Skeller's currency and government desks."

Moore nodded his head and then looked at Hap. "I guess I have to hand it to you. Good work, man." Moore held out his hand to shake Hap's.

"Yeah, you make sure you hand it to me when bonus time comes, boss."

"Good work, Hap," Terry chimed in.

"Oh, go fuck yourself, Barker," Hap retorted. Moore then turned toward the sales pit and shouted, "Okay, all you mullets. Lodestar is done! We'll price this mother two days from now at the high end of the price talk, twelve percent. Get around to all your accounts and let them know."

A burst of cheers and applause arose from the high-yield area and resounded throughout the cavernous, acoustically refined trading floor.

Overcome with joy and elation, Hap broke into a dance, a cross between the Watusi and the Bugaloo. He shimmied and sashayed his way back to his desk, like King David entering Jerusalem. Even Moore had to smile. His belly sloshed sideways, his arms flailed the air, his backbone slipped, his facial expression turned manic and goofy as he ran a gauntlet of high fives and pats on the back.

Chapter 12

Fortune's Fool

HAP BOGG'S LIFE HAD CHANGED. WHEN HE walked onto the trading floor the next day he felt eyes following his every movement. Eyes in the foreign exchange trading area or the government bond pit or on the equity-trading desk. He had achieved an aura, a magnetic aura attracting eyes to him, admiring eyes everywhere because by now everyone on the floor had heard about Hap Boggs, the guy who had saved the day. "There he is!" he imagined them saying, as he strolled across the floor, "The guy who saved the day!"

Hap was already taking a mental inventory of the young and pretty trading assistants and secretaries whom he would now have a shot at, anyone of whom he was sure would be honored to escort him for a romantic evening of wild, kinky sex. The cock-of-the-walk he was, indeed, the stud of the stables. Of course, his own colleagues, who had once mocked and derided him, now bestowed the respect due the mighty one who had saved their jobs. They remained silent when he spoke and did not snicker and make rude raspberry sounds as once was their wont. Terry Barker, who had always scowled at his presence, now approached him eagerly at regular intervals, smiling and asking what Dragon Funds was up to, asking whether they might have interest in whatever bonds Whorman Skeller owned. Hap had no doubt that whenever Lori Putterman's eyes lighted on him, she would think, "What a macher!" Dick Moore might even occasionally deign to say hello or good morning to him—would wonders never cease! Whereas, before he might be standing at the next urinal in the men's room and still not even so much as acknowledge Hap pissing beside him.

The topper was when he was walking down the hallway and who should be walking toward him from the other direction but Hans de Saint Phallas, CEO of Whorman Skeller, surely followed by a cavalcade of soldiers uniformed in blue suits and red ties. They stopped when Hans pulled up in front of Hap.

"If I am not mistaken, you are Mr. Boggs," Hans intoned in his sonorous voice with its continental inflection.

Hap, surprised that Hans should know who he was, answered yes.

"That was a brilliant job you performed yesterday in obtaining that Lodestar order." The members of the cortege all nodded their heads in approval.

"Mr. Hu is a valued customer of this firm and I am pleased to see that he is now being served by our high-yield group."

"Nothing to it, sir."

Hans examined Hap through the eyeglasses that were a throwback to pince-nez. "Keep up the good work." Hans de Saint Phallas and his convoy then sailed away, leaving the good servant Hap in their wake.

This recognition of his abilities was long over due, Hap believed, and he rested assured knowing that his new found stature would be confirmed in the most material of ways after the Lodestar deal closed and he would have $1,350,000 in commissions credited to him.

Then the phone call came.

The silky British voice once again summoned him to the offices of Dragon Funds for a meeting with Jo Hu. A short while later, Hap again found himself seated before the flat circular desk while Jo Hu, wearing again a black tee shirt and black wool pants, studied the trading screens behind the desk.

After several moments of silence, Hu finally turned from the screens to Hap. "Ever been to Hong Kong, Hap?" he abruptly asked.

Hap, who had never been outside the country except for a college spring break trip to Cancun, answered no.

Hu sat back in his chair and pressed his fingers against each other. "You know the biggest thrill Hong Kong has to offer is landing at the airport. The old airport, that is. What's so wild about that airport is it's right smack in the middle of downtown Hong Kong. So the planes coming in for a landing have to swoop down and veer between the skyscrapers like an obstacle course. I mean, imagine looking out the window of a jet and seeing right into the windows of an office building fifty feet away, seeing somebody at a copier or reading a newspaper at his desk. It's a real rush, man." Hu spoke wistfully of Hong Kong. No matter how Americanized his speech and manner, Hong Kong would always be home sweet home.

"Flying in like that can also scare the crap out of you. You have to remind yourself that the pilot has flown in there probably dozens of times before. And the flight plan and flight path have been calibrated to the nth degree. There are no variables, unknowns, nothing left to chance."

Hap nodded, wondering where the hell Hu was going with this.

Hu then looked directly at Hap. "I'm canceling the Lodestar order."

Hap blinked his eyes. "Come again?" He didn't believe he had heard him right.

"I can't go through with the Lodestar transaction," Hu reiterated. Hap's gulp was deep enough to be clearly audible. Actually, it was more a gag than a gulp.

"You can't do that," he gasped in desperation.

"Sure I can. Look, here's the problem. This deal has way too many unknowns. I mean, you keep harping about these Department of Defense contracts, how critical they are to Lodestar being a success or not."

"That's right," Hap said as he shifted to the edge of his seat. "They cover a third of the—" Once again Hu's raised hand cut Hap short. "Yeah, yeah, I know. But then, what do I really know about those contracts? What do you know? Nothing really. Neither one of us has seen the contracts. You have no idea what the U. S. government's involvement is in this project, do you?"

"That's because all that stuff is TOP SECRET," Hap replied.

"That's a problem for me. I live on info. For me to know next to nothing about what your government is doing in this investment that you want me to stick three hundred million into, well, that's like asking the pilot to land at the Hong Kong airport blindfolded. The more I thought about this deal, the crazier it seemed."

"But…but," Hap sputtered.

"I don't know what else to tell you."

Hap's mind scrambled for some way to salvage the situation. If he lost this order, the $1,350,000 would vanish like a mirage. Moore would fire his ass right on the spot. "Do something," he screamed to himself.

"Okay, what if I could get you more info on what the Defense Department is doing?" he desperately offered.

"Like what?" Hu asked, his eyes narrowing.

"I dunno. What exactly do you need?" Hap answered weakly.

"I need the contracts." Hu now leaned over his desk and stared hard at Hap. A flush of intensity shattered his impassive mask. "There's got to be some way for you to get your hands on them. Somebody in the high-yield group has access to them. There's got to be a way."

Hap's face squinted with pressure. He put his hand to his forehead. "I don't know. I just don't know."

"Quit saying you don't know," Hu, barked. "You look like you're about ready to cry. Think!"

"I guess one of the bankers has the contracts, or should have. Probably Arnie Markum does, he's the analyst covering the credit. At least, he talks like he's got them. But he's always talking big."

"Find out. Figure out a way to get him to hand them over to you. Share some of your commission with him, for example."

"You mean, bribe him?" Hap asked, not with outrage or incredulity but as if the idea might be worth considering.

"If that's what it takes. All I'm telling you is that I'm pulling the order. You get back to me within the next twenty-four hours with what I need and I'll re-think it. Now I got some trading to do."

Hap rose from his seat and shuffled across the trading room, his face pale, mouth slightly agape. "Hey, you ever see that movie, Night of the Living Dead? one trader asked another in broken English as he watched Hap amble by.

Arnie Markum winded his way through the matrix of desks constituting Whorman Skeller's trading floor. His short legs pumped a quick pace as he whistled Barry Manilow's "I Write The Songs." Arnie had promptly arrived at the usual time, six-fifteen a.m. He carried his briefcase stuffed with research material and the usual coffee—large regular, skim milk, no sugar, and an onion bagel with a smear of cream cheese and olives. Arnie usually purchased his breakfast at the kosher deli next door since the trading floor commissaries didn't open until 6:30 a.m. Living in a Murray Hill co-op not far from the Whorman Skeller building, he was usually one of the first to arrive on the trading floor.

Arnie, very much a creature of habit, found nothing unusual that morning until he approached his desk and saw the figure of Hap Boggs conspicuously taking up space. Seeing Hap in his seat gave Arnie pause; indeed, he halted in mid-stride. Hap was not one of Arnie's favorite people. He displayed no capacity for research, didn't know how to use it properly to generate trades the way Libby did, for example, and evinced no desire to learn. Hap, in fact, went out of his way to denigrate the work of Arnie and the other analysts, characterizing it as "geek droppings" or "brain dumps." He derisively referred to the area where the analysts were assembled as Whorman Skeller's "nerd center." Arnie would have bet that in high school Hap was one of those bullies who lifted guys like him up by their underwear, a practice known as a "wedgie," or pushed their heads into a toilet and flushed it, a "whirlie."

Notwithstanding his disdain and vague fear of Hap, Arnie proceeded to his desk as if it were business as usual. He greeted Hap with a smile and a chipper good morning.

"Don't tell me you spent the night under my desk, Hap-meister," he joked.

Upon seeing Arnie, Hap leapt from his seat and returned his cheerful good morning. *Hmm, now's that a bit unusual,* Arnie thought. *Hap's being friendly. Wonder what he wants?*

"Oh, no, I just got here myself," Hap replied. In truth, Hap had stationed himself at Arnie's desk over a hour before, knowing that Arnie got to work early but not sure how early. "I need your help on something."

"Okay," Arnie said as he casually placed his briefcase, coffee and bagel on his desk and thought to himself, "You need my help all right, bub."

"You know Dragon Funds put in that huge order for Lodestar."

"Sure, that was the trade of the year. Way to go."

"Yeah, well they still have a few follow-up questions that I figured you could answer."

"Probably something to do with the Defense Department, right?"

Hap started in surprise, his lips parting and his eyes opening wide. In the next instant he worried that his reaction had been too obvious. *How in hell did Arnie know that was what he was after,* he wondered. Hap hadn't slept a wink the night before, thinking about his meeting with Jo Hu earlier that day, thinking how he could get his hands on the information that Hu demanded.

"What makes you say that, Arnie?" he chuckled nervously.

"Because that's what everybody wants to know."

"You have the agreements and what-nots between Lodestar and the U. S. government, right?"

"What-nots? I'd say it's a hellava lot more than what-nots." Arnie pushed his eyeglasses, whose lenses were oversized as to suggest intelligence, up the bridge of his nose, an action which usually preceded an illustration of how important he was.

"You wouldn't believe all the bullshit I had to go through before they let me have all that classified stuff. The friggin' FBI interviewed me three times...even fingerprinted me. They told me that less than a dozen people had access to that info, and I was one of them."

Hap nodded, for once keenly interested in what Arnie was saying. "And let me tell you, there's some shit in there that would make your eyeballs pop out, if you knew about it. I can't tell you anything, but believe me, it ain't got nothing to do with faxes. Think missile defense is all I got to say about that. And I'm one of a dozen people in the world who has it. Got it filed right here on the ole PC."

"Wow, that's cool," Hap said to stroke Arnie's ego and stoke his babbling.

"Yeah, I imagine there are some people who would pay a pretty penny for what I know about the U. S. government's plans for Lodestar. Plans so big it's almost dangerous to know about them." Arnie's eyes grew large and his squeaky voice affected an ominous tone.

"What I need is no big deal like that, Arnie. Dragon Funds just needs your most recently revised pro-forma."

"You haven't sent that to them? I put it out last week."

"Yeah, I faxed it, but you know how things get misplaced."

"No problem. It'll just take a second for me to pull it up."

Arnie then reached down to boot his desktop computer. A click and a whirring sound and then the log-on prompt appeared on the monitor. Hap moved close behind Arnie and the eyes of a hawk watched, as the latter's hands hovered over the keyboard. All neural passages throughout Hap's brain were completely cleared for receipt of Arnie's login ID and password. His vision was riveted to Arnie's fingers over the keyboard. He was poised, tense. It all would happen in an instant, the fingers typing the ID and password. If he missed even one stroke on the keyboard, he would miss everything. If Arnie had been listening closely, he would not have heard Hap's breath, bated as it was, but his teeth grinding.

Hap had once read in the newspaper how a scientist had discovered a buzz behind everything, a faint echo of the Big Bang that had started it all. At that moment, Hap believed it because he could hear the buzz roaring in his ears as Arnie's fingers stayed suspended over the keyboard. Then they moved, filling the spaces in the user ID slot. A-R-N-I-E the fingers typed. Okay, that was easy enough, Hap thought.

Now for the five numeral password. The fingers pressed the keys, 1-2-3-4-5. That was it. Easy enough. "What's so funny?" Arnie asked

Hap stood behind him laughing with relief, laughing because it had been that easy.

At approximately 8:30 p.m. that evening, Hap entered the Whorman Skeller building, flashed his ID to the guard at the security desk and rode the elevator to the trading room on the sixth floor.

"Well look what the cat dragged in," Lenny, the security guard stationed at the entrance to the trading floor, said when he saw Hap step from the elevator. "What brings you here at this indecent hour?"

Hap and Lenny were buddies, mainly because Lenny was a fanatic about football, the only subject of which Hap could claim a broad and deep knowledge. Hap would occasionally leave the trading floor during dead hours on slow days to talk sports with Lenny, whose shift usually started in the afternoon.

"Ah, damnit, I left some research I promised myself I would read before tomorrow."

"Hey, big game for the Bills this weekend. Playing the Jets. You think your pal, Flutie's ready?"

"Dougie was born ready, Lenny."

Lenny allowed Hap to enter the trading floor, no questions asked. Hap walked to the high-yield section, casing the joint as he did so. A few cleaning personnel were still at work, but otherwise there appeared to be nobody around. He reached Arnie's desk. He looked around one more time just to be safe; the high-yield analysts were notorious for hanging around until midnight or later, churning out reports. Again, he spotted no one.

Hap sat in Arnie's seat in front of his keyboard. He booted the PC. He then typed A-R-N-I-E when the user ID slot appeared and 1-2-3-4-5 in the password slot underneath that. A programming menu materialized on the screen and Hap placed the cursor on a task bar heading, FILE and double clicked. When prompted, Hap typed in Lodestar as the file name. A few seconds of downloading and there it was, everything Arnie had about Lodestar. Hap brought up a sub-file labeled DEFENSE. A large letter warning emerged on the screen: THE FOLLOWING CONTAINS HIGHLY CLASSIFIED INFORMATION THAT IS THE PROPERTY OF THE UNITED STATES DEPARTMENT OF DEFENSE. UNAUTHORIZED USE OR DISTRIBUTION OF THIS INFORMATION IS ILLEGAL AND MAY CONSTITUTE A FELONY VIOLATION OF SECTION 2, PARAGRAPH III OF THE U. S. SEDITION CODE, THE VIOLATION OF WHICH MAY BE PUNISHABLE BY A MAXIMUM OF TWENTY-FIVE YEARS IN THE U. S. FEDERAL PENITENTIARY SYSTEM.

"Yes! Fuckin' A! Rock and roll!" he said to himself as he scrolled through pages of legalese and technical jargon, no more deterred by the warning than he was by the FBI warning at the beginning of a movie video rental. Hap didn't take time to read it. He was both too elated and anxious to read. He simply printed off the entire sub-file.

Hap had spoken to Hu earlier that day, telling him that he thought he would have the information in hand later that evening. Hu had told him to call as soon as he got it, no matter the hour.

Hap didn't disappoint.

"I got what you want," Hap said when Hu picked up the phone.

"Where are you?"

"Whorman Skeller building."

"Go to your apartment. I'll meet you there."

"Cool."

CHAPTER 13

DEFENESTRATION

HAP LEFT THE WHORMAN SKELLER BUILDIING TO return to his apartment. Since he didn't think Hu would be at his apartment for at least another thirty minutes, he took the time to stop at Pogo's, one of his favorite haunts, to have a celebratory beer. He figured the pressure that had been squeezing him the past day or so might even justify two beers. Careful to keep the envelope containing the two-inch stack of material relating to the Defense Department and Lodestar securely in the inside pocket of his overcoat, he sat at the bar, eating salted peanuts and sipping a draft ale beer in an ice-cold mug. *Ahhh!* He was in such an ebullient mood that he bought a round for the three barflies slumped next to him.

Just about the time Hap started on his second beer, Dick Moore entered the lobby of Hap's apartment and was greeted by Karl, the doorman. "Gut evening, Mr. Moore," he said in an accent that still retained a Teutonic harshness even though he had lived in the United States for twenty-eight years. Karl knew Moore because he occasionally came to Hap's apartment and also that Moore was Hap's boss and therefore treated him accordingly.

"What's groovin', Karl," Moore said with his studied nonchalance. "Our boy, Hap, in?"

"No, he has not yet arrived home, Mr. Moore."

"Probably out getting plastered like he does most nights of the week," Moore casually responded. Karl didn't say anything.

"Look, Karl, he has something for me to pick up at his apartment. I've got a dinner engagement to be at in fifteen minutes, so would you give me the keys to his apartment so I can get what I need and get outta here?"

Karl tilted his head for barely two seconds, considering. "Sure, Mr. Moore. Let me get the keys." There really wasn't anything for Karl to consider, since Moore was, after all, Hap's boss and this wouldn't be the first time Karl had let him into Hap's apartment when Hap wasn't there.

Moore entered the apartment and flipped on the light. He had some serious business to attend to so he hurried over to the white, baby grand piano in the corner and lifted up the top. *Okay, now where is that cassette?* he mumbled to himself as he rifled through a couple dozen videocassettes, causing piano wires to twing and twang as he did so.

Hap used the piano as a place to store his library of porno tapes because he didn't want to take the chance that a friend, relative, or even worse, a date might happen upon them if he stored them in a more conventional spot. Therefore he figured that inside the piano was the last place anybody would look for anything—unless they were a piano tuner.

Moore was the only other person who knew about the hiding place, and to retrieve some delicious porn from the innards of the baby grand was really the only reason he had ever visited Hap in the past. Of course, Hap was always willing to oblige his boss and enjoyed having a dirty little secret to share with him.

Tonight, Moore was particularly anxious to find what he needed because he had a hot date with Selena, who worked on Whorman Skeller's emerging markets desk. Moore idly wondered, *Is the chick a mulatto or possibly Puerto Rican? It doesn't matter...she has such pert little tits ripening on that twenty-one year old body and those long legs... Wow! She's always showing them off by wearing skirts almost all the way up to her fuzzy peach.*

Moore had wolfishly eyed this little mocha-colored lamb whenever she sauntered around the trading floor. And now the husband of twenty years who had always bragged to everyone how his marriage was "the most wonderful fulfillment of a fundamentally insane concept," this father of three children, of whom Charlotte, his eldest, was only one year younger than the sweet young thing with whom he was about to gorge himself, was frantically searching for a hardcore video tape. Lately he found he needed the extraneous stimulations the videos provided in order to become thoroughly aroused and to ardently perform.

"Damn it," Moore grumbled, "Where is that 'Cock-a-Doodle Do Me!' tape?" He tossed the cassettes about on the piano wires, inadvertently composing something that could have been mistaken for a John Cage rendition.

His search was interrupted when the intercom buzzed. Moore walked over and barked, "What!" into the speaker.

Karl's voice crackled, sounding rather thin, "Dinner is here for Mr. Boggs. They say he ordered take-out from his office and I have sent them up. Please let them in."

"Yeah, yeah, all right," Moore hurriedly answered. He then wheeled from the intercom, struck by a sudden hunch. He hurried over to the VCR in the walnut cabinet, turned it on and punched the eject button. Sure enough, the "Cock-a-doodle Do Me!" tape popped out.

Should have known that sleazebag Hap had been watching it, Moore thought to himself. *Probably jerks off to it every night while he's having dinner.*

Just then the doorbell buzzed and Moore opened the door and admitted two Chinese delivery boys into the apartment. "Damn, is Hap having a party or something?" Moore said aloud as he eyed the armloads of take-out the two carried. "Just set that stuff over there on the dining room table. Shit, I guess I'm gonna have to pay for all this too," he muttered as he reached for his wallet.

"Whada dogumens?" one of the delivery boys asked after putting his sack of food down on the table. Moore was taken aback by the demanding tone in his voice.

"What did you say," Moore answered indignantly. He really didn't understand what the delivery boy had said through his thick accent. *Whada dogumens? Does Hap have a dog?* Moore wondered.

"Whada dogumens?" the boy shouted this time.

"I don't know what the fuck you're talking about, but why don't you get the fuck outta here!" Moore shouted back in the intimidating voice he utilized so often on the trading floor. He wasn't too worried about the one who was doing all the shouting; he was skinny, with a large adams apple and hair that stuck out in every direction. But he did keep a wary eye on the partner with the short, squat build of a wrestler and the shaved, bowling-ball head that looked as if it had been mashed down onto his massive bulk thus obviating the need for a neck. Moor thought he could have been a stand-in for "Odd Job" in the James Bond movie, Goldfinger.

"Satellite! Satellite!" "The Skinny One" shrieked with a deranged look on his face and took a couple of steps closer. Moore now could see his tiny, sharp teeth jammed into the front of his small mouth, reminding Moore of the stuffed piranha his son had mounted in his bedroom.

"Satellite, is that what you said?" Moore responded, his face scrunched up with disdain and bewilderment. "Look, I'm telling you for the last time to leave or else I'm calling the cops. And they'll have your dog-eating gook ass on the first boat back to Shanghai!" Moore stood on the balls of his feet so as to be more threatening and moved a step closer to The Skinny One.

But The Skinny One did not wilt before the infamous and intimidating Dick Moore snarl. Instead, he spoke something in Chinese to his partner; something that could have been translated as "sic him," for the latter sprang off his feet, reached up and in one quick motion managed to get Moore into a headlock.

"Goddamnit, I can't breathe!" Moore cried. "You're gonna break my neck!"

The Skinny One now bent low to speak directly into Moore's face, which was turned down toward the floor. "Where satellite document?"

"I don't know what you're talking about. Hap will be home soon and he can tell you." Moore's voice had lost its commanding tone and now had a whimpering quality to it.

Not understanding Moore, The Skinny One grabbed the latter's hair in frustration and pulled.

"Ahhheeee. Let go of my hair!"

"You tell where papers are for Mr. Hu. You tell or else."

Moore then tried to break free of the headlock and flung himself and Odd Job onto the dining room table. Szechwan chicken and General Ho's shrimp spilled over the two. Moore reached for a steaming container of hot and sour soup and hurled it at Odd Job's face. The big guy screamed bloody murder and put his hands to his face as he released Moore. Moore stumbled toward the door and The Skinny One grabbed hold of Moore's leg. As Moore continued desperately toward the door, he dragged The Skinny One along with him. In the meantime, Odd Job recovered, ran up behind Moore and got him into a Full Nelson.

The Skinny One angrily issued an order to Odd Job and the two of them grunted and groaned as they slowly maneuvered Moore toward the tall windows overlooking Central Park West. "Don't you know who I am?" Moore cried weakly. "I'm Dick Moore and I'm gonna make you pay for this."

While Odd Job held Moore, The Skinny One pushed the double-hung window up as much as it would go. "Okay," he shouted to Odd Job as he reached down and took hold of Moore's ankles. Odd Job released Moore, who was quickly tiring from the struggle, and grabbed him by his thighs. The next thing Moore knew, he was hanging upside down out the twelfth-story window, getting a bat's-eye-view of the traffic streaming down Central Park West.

Then The Skinny One stuck his head out the window and yelled toward Moore, "Where satellite documents for Mr. Hu?"

Moore scared out of his wits couldn't utter a word or even cry for help to the passersby below, none of whom noticed him swaying in the wind even as his glasses, keys and pocket change pelted the sidewalk below like anomalous hail.

Now quite panicked, Moore violently kicked his feet and thrashed his legs. One leg wriggled free as Odd Job struggled to hold onto the other one. As The Skinny One dived halfway out the window to grab Moore's other leg, Odd Job, worried that his comrade was about to fly out the window, reached for him. One second after doing so, he uttered, "Oops."

The Skinny One quickly pulled himself back from the window and looked at Odd Job, his face wracked with shock and horror. Then he snapped to and slapped and punched Odd Job, who meekly held his hands up in defense against the blows that really couldn't hurt him. The Skinny One yelled in Chinese what could be loosely translated as, "You fucking idiot! Now, look at what you've done. Let's blow this joint and fast."

Hap traipsed up Central Park West, a wee bit tipsy after he had decided he deserved five beers instead of two, plus a shot of Wild Turkey to boot. But he stopped and quickly sobered up when he saw the body dangling out the twelfth-story window. "Oh my god!" he said when he figured out that the window was to his apartment. Just then, the body plummeted down as swiftly and soundlessly as a hot-air balloon ascending toward heaven.

Hap ran to the crumpled heap on the pavement along with a half-dozen other bystanders. When he leaned over to peer at the body, he didn't recognize Dick Moore's face, devoid as it was of its scowling arrogance. Instead, the face was forever locked in an expression mixed with wide-eyed horror and abject amazement.

Unable to comprehend, Hap instinctively ran for his life.

Chapter 14

This Importunate World

UNTIL THE BLUE LINES BEGAN TO FUZZ AND SHIFT, Martin stared at the blank page. Just before the page blurred toward total whiteout, he blinked his eyes, jiggled his head, set his pen down and slumped back in his chair. *Meditation is as difficult as tying a rope to a monkey and forcing it to run perfect circles*—an African proverb Martin remembered from college. And he thought how trying to write a poem is like that too, except that the monkey is a ghost, the rope silly putty; and rather than running in circles, the ghost must march through an intricate and very precise dance.

He went back to square one: *Conjure up an image, something concrete, engaging, perhaps even surprising, startling.* He straightened his body, retied the belt of his terry cloth robe, bit down on a pinky fingernail and shut his eyes—the pen poised over the page. *Image...imagine...person...object.* Patches of light bloomed in the blackness, but no image. After two or three minutes, Martin opened his eyes and stared down at the page until the lines once again began to fuzz and shift and whiteout completely.

Then Martin rose from his position, padded on slippered feet into the kitchen, opened the refrigerator door and gulped down several swigs of orange juice right out of the carton. After that he walked to the window, looked at nothing, really, then padded back into his bedroom. Again he sat down at his writing desk and repositioned his head within the small circle of light cast by the reading lamp. He rubbed the back of his hand against his jaw and again leaned over the page and awaited that blank plane of silence.

The night before, he had watched the documentary about Martin Luther King, "From Selma to Montgomery," and the film had inspired him to write something about the man after whom he had been named. Martin thought he had known what he wanted to write about but his "image-engine" needed a jump-start.

He arose from his seat and went into the living room. There he lay supine upon the floor, propped his feet onto the couch, clasped his hands together and placed them on his forehead and tried to create a spark out of nothingness...foment a big bang.

For almost an hour, Martin had lain there on the floor, as he strained his imagination—but all he developed was a terrific headache. Headaches had harassed Martin regularly over the past few weeks and hurt like a nest of termites in the middle of his cranium. Martin wouldn't admit that these migraines, like the rash running up his arm, resulted from the pressures of work. If he admitted to that, it would be an admition of weakness.

Also lately, he hadn't been sleeping so soundly—habitually waking up three or four times every night. Many times he saw people in his room—rather, imagined he saw people in his room. Reaching out to touch them, he found he was only touching a coat draped over a chair or maybe a lamp on a table. What had been breaking Martin's sleep cycle was a profound restlessness—a subliminal uneasiness. The wheel of his night dreams was missing spokes, its rim bending out of shape.

Martin had hoped to dispel his agitation and tonight had forced himself to sit down and compose a poem. In college writing had been his favorite recreational activity. Every semester he had enrolled in some type of creative writing course. He had even vaguely daydreamed he might one day become a professional writer. *The happy man is one who makes his avocation his vocation.*

He rolled over onto his stomach, propped himself on his elbows and tapped his clinched fists lightly and mechanically against his lips, pursed with concentration and the pain of a migraine. He was completely without repose. His inner gyroscope was spinning wildly, unloosened from its axis...oh, how he longed for genuine peace.

There was a time when he had found it in words—as in writing a good poem. At one time it had provided him with the most unadulterated satisfaction he knew. Even those poems that had a dark tone could, if well crafted, infuse him with joy. Harmony clarified the pessimism within and after such an act of creation, Martin would rise from his desk and subsist for days upon that joy, that taste of truth, that feeling of insight and self-mastery.

Now, however, Martin was seized with nothing but a headache and an angry rash on his arm. He lay his face down upon the carpet, he became more restless as each silent minute passed. The pressure to write something, anything, intensified.

Biting off one last snippet of fingernail, he rose from the floor and walking, again to the window, found himself looking out at nothing but a couple of pigeons roosting on his terrace. Writing a poem had never been easy, but usually after a certain amount of ruminating, an image or two began his conceiving process and words would begin burbling up and flowing steadily. But now his well was only issuing echoes of emptiness.

Martin felt claustrophobic, a feeling he hated above all others. It seemed that since he had moved to New York, everything had been pressing too close around and upon him. Crushing mobs rushing everywhere, people pushing against other people like ants, dodgem cabs daring one another on the cramped avenues, babelesque-type buildings cramming the sky like steel fingers pricking the sky. Everything pressing against everything.

When he rolled once again onto his back, he gazed at the ceiling and noticed a tiny spider bouncing up and down upon an invisible thread attached to the ceiling's light fixture.

Boing, boing, boing—*it looks like fun. How neat spider webs are...those deadly little poems.*

He remembered how he had always avoided those old abandoned spider webs stretched across leafy branches or peeling gables. His grandmother had told him they were really witches' hair and he had better not linger too long around there or he would turn into a toad. He had said phooey to that, but actually he'd been a little spooked by spider webs ever since.

As Martin watched the spider go up and down, up and down, the tension within him eased. Up and down, up and down...his arteries expanded a bit, passages throughout his body dilated and his mind emptied itself of everything but that spider and its perfect rhythm. And he thought about weight and gravity. *Up and down. Tum-de-dum. Gravity. Everything falls. Down and up.*

Soon this led him to remember something he had seen on the news the night before—a woman's face, seemingly hovering bodiless among angles of an auto's crumpled metal, the ripped edges sharper than shark teeth. That news report about a crane falling from the sky onto that automobile had for some reason haunted Martin's mind all day long. Numbers had given a certain gravity to the event...a fifty-two year old widow, a sixty-nine ton crane. For over six hours she had lain beneath its burden.

At last Martin had an image—a face swimming in the harsh halo hurled by TV camera lights. The image coalesced, becoming almost shiny and seemingly potent. He was with her; he felt the pressure, oh, the pressure—then his femur pulverized, just as hers had. Either Martin couldn't let go of this image, or the image wouldn't let go of him and it threatened to become a large metaphor—the lines formed on the tip of his tongue...

> The lore of her pulverized femur
> And her sweating awareness of it

Yes, yes, he thought. *And what else happened, what else about the scene was there? What about that fireman?*

> The fireman holding her hand
> For six hours, whispering in her ear
> "We are with you, you are good.
> We love you. You will make it,"

Here feelings fluttered inside Martin.

> Caused some to pause on streets
> And ponder for a moment the sky
> Pricked by fingers of steel.

Martin's pulse quickened. Quickly he got up from the floor, ran to his desk and wrote down those words. Maybe they were the beginnings of a poem, a good poem. He read the lines again and again, as he rubbed his hands together.

He knew how badly the woman wanted to be extricated, knew what it was like to be trapped. She wanted so much to be freed, to get out from under the pressure. The pressure was on him, too—pressure of another kind, impalpable but still weighty, self-inflicted yet still constrictive. For him it was the immediate pressure to sell Lodestar and the over-arching pressure to succeed, to make money—the only measure of success in the bond business.

Also there was the pressure that was, paradoxically, the most intense but also unacknowledged, the pressure to fit in, to be the way most black folks aren't. But even though he had his pedigree of academic degrees, even though his diction and syntax were strictly by the rules, even though he dressed according to the Wall Street assembly-line uniform, he did not feel he was "in," but a little "out." Everybody was just a tad too nice, oh so sensitive that he was black and pleasant to the point of being patronizing. Like when Skeets awkwardly used the phrase, "African-American." Martin almost wished Skeets would go ahead and say "colored folks," say the word he had grown up with; the word he probably used in his own kitchen.

He knew he would still like Skeets in spite of it but at least he would have the comfort of knowing he would never fit in. Also the pressure would then ease because everybody would know where everybody stood and they would accept him as he was—take him or leave him—and not be so damn nice about it.

But at that precise moment, Martin was not actually thinking about himself. He leaned over his desk, his eyes wide as he mined the scene that he had witnessed on TV—her face surrounded by shark teeth. A wave of exhilaration rose within him, as, for those few moments, he was somebody other than himself.

The intercom buzzed but Martin didn't really hear it until it buzzed a second time. "Shit," he muttered as he rose to answer it.

Before doing so, he stood and scanned his latest poetic endeavor. The trance had been broken. His eye turned piercing as he read the few lines. They seemed rough-hewn, off the mark, almost silly. *What had he gotten so excited about? So a crane falls on a woman? Big deal. Just further evidence of our craving for miracles and myths, that was all this media sensationalism amounted to*, he concluded. He picked up his pen and casually scribbled while still standing:

> She is a woman with a lazy eye,
> a fondness for silk undies
> and peppermint schnapps.

The intercom obnoxiously beckoned once again. "All right already," he shouted back at it.

"Who is it?" he asked as he pushed the talk button.

"Marty, it's me, Hap. Let me in. It's an emergency!"

Martin looked at his watch, it was past nine-thirty and he didn't even want to guess what problem Hap might have gotten himself into this time. He did know for sure, however, that he didn't want to be part of his solution, particularly at nine-thirty on a Tuesday night. Nevertheless, Martin pushed the door release button.

Less than a minute later, Hap was pounding on Martin's door, yelling, "Open up, Marty."

Martin opened the door, ready to scold Hap for shouting in the hallway and disturbing his neighbors. But he swallowed the words when he saw Hap's face. Fear and panic had cast a sallow pall over it.

Hap stormed into the room and frantically paced back and forth. "He's dead, Marty! He's dead!" and stopped to press his fist to his mouth and emitted an eerie, anguished whine.

"Who's dead, Hap? Get a grip on yourself, man."

Hap turned and looked at Martin. His face still retained an expression of incredulity as he explained, "Dick Moore is dead!"

"What!" Martin shouted.

"He's dead," Hap said as he flung his hand in the air for no reason except perhaps to indicate how easy it was to die. His face contorted in agony as he explained, "I saw it all! I was standing there and saw it all!"

"Saw what?"

"I saw him drop from my window. Saw him hit the pavement. Saw the dead cat bounce. The son-of-a-bitch was hanging from my window." Hap gesticulated like a madman as he spoke.

Martin's mouth dropped open as his mind tried to quickly absorb this bit of information. "You saw him *hanging* from your window?"

"Yes!"

"What was he doing in your apartment?"

"Fuck if I know." Hap knew but he didn't want to admit to an extensive library of pornographic videotapes.

Martin fell back onto the sofa, completely discombobulated. "Damn, do you think he committed suicide?"

"The way that guy was in love with himself? No way." Hap was still pacing. "You got anything to drink?"

"There's beer in the refrigerator and hard stuff in the cabinet there." Hap went for the hard stuff.

"Wow, Dick Moore dead. So then, it was either an accident or somebody..." Martin continued thinking but couldn't utter the possibility that someone might have killed Moore.

"Accident?" Hap responded with a quizzical look after knocking back two fingers of scotch. "What kinda accident leads to a man to hang by his fingers from a twelfth-story window?"

"So you think somebody threw him out then?" Martin asked in disbelief.

"The guy pissed a lot of people off, so who knows who might have gotten pissed off just enough to snuff him."

"But if somebody intentionally threw him out the window, they had to have been in your apartment. Who could have been in your apartment when you weren't there?"

"Fuck if I know." Hap thought a moment before deciding to reveal more to Martin. "Jo Hu was supposed to meet me at my apartment," he said as matter-of-factly as he could.

"Jo Hu? You're kidding? Why would somebody like Jo Hu want to meet you at your apartment?"

"Because I had something to give him, something that he wanted real bad."

"What?"

"This," Hap said as reached into the inside pocket of his overcoat which he had never bothered to take off. He pulled out the envelope and handed it to Martin.

Martin quickly perused the material. "This stuff has 'Highly Classified' stamped on every page. This stuff is about Lodestar and what the US government is doing with it, right?"

Hap forlornly nodded his head.

"How in the hell did you get this?

"There's no need for me to get into all that. What I can tell you is that Jo Hu said he was gonna pull his Lodestar order if I didn't get it to him. And I don't need to tell you that if he pulled his order, then the whole ship would go down, not to mention I'd be out over a million bucks. So I got it and he was gonna come by my apartment to pick it up. Maybe the doorman let him up. He's the only person I can think of who might have been there while Moore was there."

Hap fell onto the sofa while Martin rose and resumed the pacing that Hap had left off. He ran his hand over his head. "Man, I can't believe this. This is too much. Don't you see what the implication of all this is, Hap?"

Hap didn't answer but only took another swig of scotch.

"The implication is that Jo Hu somehow, and for some unknown reason, threw Moore out that window."

"Are you fucking out of your mind, Marty? You know who Jo Hu is? Why in the hell would he do in Moore like that?"

"I don't know, goddamnit, I'm just trying to piece things together from what you've told me. I do know this, though, you have to go back to your apartment and call the police—tell them everything you saw and know."

Hap's head fell into his hands. "Oh, man," he groaned.

"Shit, what about this, though?" Martin said as he looked at the envelope in his hand. "Forget about calling the cops, Hap. You better call a lawyer first. Do you realize how this looks?"

"How what looks?" Hap asked in a daze.

"You having classified DOD information you were about to give to a Chinese national. It's called espionage, you dumb fuck!"

"Oh get off it, Marty. I'm not a spy or traitor, I was just trying to close the trade, get the deal done. That's all."

"I'm just telling you how it looks, Hap. You need to call a lawyer, immediately."

Hap rose from the sofa with a weary sigh. "Okay, that's what I'll do." Then he said as he held his hand out toward Martin, "Give me that stuff back."

"No, way. I'm safekeeping this."

Hap stepped forward and forcefully said, "Give it to me, Marty." By now the exhausted look had left his face and he was suddenly very intent, very serious.

"No, Hap," Martin answered firmly, gripping the envelope with both hands. "I'll give it to your lawyer but I don't trust you with it."

Hap stared hard at the envelope then at Martin. Martin returned the stare. Eye to eye, they stood there for several seconds, a Mexican standoff.

"Hap, let me keep this for you. It's for your own good. You don't want to go back to your apartment and find the police are there and they find this top-secret shit in your possession. You don't want that, I can promise you," Martin said as he adopted a more solicitous and reassuring tone.

Hap breathed in deeply. He could see that the only way he was going to get the file from Martin was to physically wrest if from him, and he was certainly not up to that at that moment. "Okay, Marty. I'll go back to my apartment and call my lawyer.

As Hap slowly walked toward the door, Martin asked, "Do you want me to come with you?"

Hap answered, "No." He stood in the hallway waiting for the elevator, a forlorn figure in his dark blue overcoat, his face barely illumined by the dim sconce lights. Then he said in his husky voice to Martin, who was standing in the apartment doorway, "Just say a prayer for Moore, Marty, cause if his soul's going anywhere, it's straight to hell."

The elevator door opened, he smiled weakly, saluted and then descended in the general direction of Dick Moore's flaming, tortured soul.

Chapter 15

Hapless

JO HU SAT IN THE STUDY OF HIS PENTHOUSE APART-ment, a computer monitor, as usual, in front of him blinking market information. Usually at this time of the evening, Hu would be fiercely trading the Pacific Rim markets, i.e., Asian currencies and stocks, the Japanese government bond, JGB, and trading until well past midnight. Instead, he was examining the vase sitting on the mantelpiece. A blue vase with gold and silver floral designs that dated from the reign of Emperor Quianlong and its provenance was the town of Jingdezhen, famous for its porcelain.

Recently, Hu had become a collector of such Chinoiserie and had figured that collecting art was the quickest, easiest way for a fabulously rich, but socially non-respected and culturally unsophisticated young man to put a polished veneer of respectability and sophistication on his newly minted riches.

Never having studied art, Hu's tastes naturally gravitated toward where he had originated. Therefore, Sung Dynasty stoneware was scattered throughout the apartment. He'd even had the fabric seat of the Queen Ann-style chair he was sitting in painted with a scene of a rich Manchurian walking through the countryside. The centerpiece on his large dining room table was a four hundred year old Famille Verte Jar, for which he had outbid the Shanghai Museum. (Some dinner guests thought the notion of placing a funeral urn on a dining table very cheeky, while a few others considered it just plain bad taste.) Even the pillows on his bed reflected this Sino flair. Attached to the pillows were jade squares that Chinese superstition held would prevent brain tumors and increase the sleeper's IQ. Hu, like all traders, was deeply superstitious.

But he was not really examining the vase, even though his gaze was directed toward it; his mind was elsewhere. He was thinking about Hap Boggs, whom, he had just been informed, was dead. When his two bungling minions, The Skinny One and Odd Job had haltingly told Hu how they had inadvertently dropped Hap out the window, Hu had become so furious that he punched Odd Job in the nose. But Odd Job, who could have neatly broken Hu into a small stack of fire kindling, only mewed like a kitten as the blood streamed from his nose.

Such a display of emotion by Hu was rare. But now he was in a serious bind as he had just received orders from General Zhu Lai, himself, to use *any* means necessary to obtain the classified Lodestar documents. Hu had no idea what those documents contained but knew there was something there that Zhu desperately wanted. And now he would have to tell Zhu that not only did he *not* have the documents, but also the person who had them was permanently "indisposed."

Hu rose from his seat and looked out his window toward the sparkling Manhattan skyline. That view was the reason he had bought this Sutton Place penthouse. (And buying it had been no easy task, as the snooty co-op board had been leery of allowing into their realm a "chinaman," as one old, crusty knickerbocker had called Hu.) Across the way, Hu could see the Citicorp Building, projecting Egyptian mystical energy. And there were the old-timers, the Chrysler and Empire State Buildings, as durable and splendid as two old spinster aunts who weren't about to be ignored. And if he looked directly west, he could see clear across Fifty-first Street to the Rockefeller Center, its buildings lifting heavenward with a dramatic, spiritual rush.

Looking at the skyline, Hu remembered how he had felt when he first walked these streets seven years before. These buildings had beckoned to him with their grand hauteur and their glittering greatness had promised him everything. Then, he had felt as if anything were possible here; that these buildings, this whole island, could at any moment have wrenched free from the earth and flown away into space.

But here he was, in the here and now, about to disappoint one of the most feared men in China, General Zhu. *How did I get here, now? How did this happen?* he asked himself. *Was it a mistake to have ever let the Chinese Government invest five hundred million dollars into my hedge fund? I knew that trading company putting the money in was a sham, just a cover for the Chinese military. Those pigs are always trying to get their cut.*

But how could I have turned down such a huge amount of money? Without that investment, I would never have gotten into the big leagues; wouldn't have had the wherewithal to be a serious player on a global scale. C'mon, what was the downside to getting into bed with the government? Man, I was flattered that these modern-day Mandarins had such confidence in me. And the importance and status gained from it only pulled me in even more.

Like, think about whenever I went to Hong Kong or the Mainland; think about how I was treated like a prince. I was treated like that because people, or at least the people who mattered, knew the crowd I ran with. And having people like Zhu as partners was almost an insurance policy against failure wasn't it? I knew they would always be there with their big fat coffers for when things might get a little rocky or rough...or so I always assumed.

Still looking out at the magnificent view from his penthouse apartment, Hu continued to meditate on the past—especially about when they had begun asking him to do "favors" for them and reminding him of their "placing their confidence in him."

At first, the favors asked were relatively benign—like information regarding currency flows and other such public data. But gradually...the favors became more demanding, with more overtones of a "cloak and dagger" nature.

Initially Hu had expressed reluctance in carrying out certain missions that smacked of spying. But it wasn't long before he realized that Zhu and his pals literally owned him—lock, stock and barrel and that he really had no choice but to do their bidding. He clearly understood that if he didn't cooperate, then much more than the half a billion-dollar investment was at stake. The stories Hu had heard about how Zhu and his gang handled those who had been foolish enough to cross them were enough to keep him in line. He realized the Mafia didn't have anything over these guys when it came to "teaching a lesson."

Just then, his thoughts were interrupted when he heard a commotion at the front of his apartment. His housekeeper shouted and a husky voice shouted back. Hu, in his pajamas, put on his robe and hurried to the foyer of the apartment. There he saw his housekeeper with her back against the door, pressing it against the hand that was stuck between it and the doorjamb. The features of her small, round face were set in a determined grimace as she grunted and firmly planted her gum-soled shoes.

"Who is there?" Hu asked his housekeeper in Chinese.

"He wouldn't say," she answered as she leaned all her weight against the door, her face flushed with strain.

Hu told her to move away and let the door open just the length of the safety lock. When he peered through the gap to see who the intruder was, he blinked, not believing his own eyes. It was Hap Boggs and for a moment Hu thought he was seeing a ghost. His head suddenly felt light, and he had to lean his hand on the wall to steady himself.

"Let me in, Jo!" Hap hollered, his snarling face pressed so close to the gap that his saliva showered the chain lock. "We gotta talk, Hu!"

Hu released the chain lock and opened the door. Just then, the doorman from the lobby burst from the elevator into the penthouse's private hallway. "Mr. Hu…I am…so sorry…I tried…to…stop…this loony…but he…busted… right…past me," the doorman said breathlessly as he jogged up to the doorway. "Should I call the cops?"

"No, that's all right, everything's under control," he answered as he scrutinized Hap, who was maintaining his composure at least long enough for Hu to drop any thought of calling the police. "Thank you for your concern.

"If you need anything, let me know," the livery-attired doorman said as he indignantly looked Hap up and down one last time. "And you better watch it, buster," he warned before walking away.

Hu closed the door behind his un-invited guest, dismissed the housekeeper and then faced this dead-man-walking, not knowing exactly what to say.

"Why did you throw Dick Moore out my window?" Hap blurted out, knowing exactly what he wanted to say and not wasting any time saying it.

Hu looked at Hap in wonderment. "Wo bu dong," Hu reflexively said in his native tongue. "Let's go back to my study and talk."

Hap followed close behind Hu to his study and Hu indicated for Hap to sit in the leather upholstered brass-studded chair; but Hap, as agitated as he was, refused to sit. Nevertheless, Hu calmly sat down, his forearm resting on one knee and his hand on the other, his arm akimbo. "Now what did you just ask me?" His voice contained both disbelief and indignation.

"Dick Moore." Hap bit down on his lower lip, challenging Hu with his glare.

"Who is Dick Moore?"

Hap looked into Hu's face a moment before answering. He observed that Hu certainly didn't have the demeanor of someone who had just killed someone. *Take it easy,* Hap warned himself, *and remember that this person still has the power to give or take away $1.35 million. No point in insulting him just because Marty had a wild-ass idea Hu, for some reason, did in Moore.*

"He is, or was, the head of Whorman Skeller high-yield. And he somehow found himself falling out my apartment window just about the time you were supposed to meet me at my apartment. That's the only reason I asked you...I wasn't accusing you, I didn't mean anything by it," answered Hap.

Hu now understood this had all been a case of mistaken identity and wanted to curse his two flunkies under his breath. Not only did they blow the job, but they didn't even have a clue as to how *bad* they had blown it. "You 'didn't mean anything by it,' you say? Yet you accused me of killing him, didn't you? And you didn't mean anything by that?" As sarcasm accentuated each word Hu spoke, he intended to keep Hap on the defensive.

Flustered, Hap raised both hands in the air. "Hey man, I couldn't begin to tell you what kinda night I've had. Okay? It's been like the Twilight Zone. I'm waiting for Rod Serling to step from the wings and tell me what the moral of all this bullshit is. It's been wilder than fuck and I think I'm about ready to have a nervous breakdown. So pardon me if I am a little bit off base." Hap changed his mind and plopped down into the comfy cradle of the stuffed, leather chair.

"For your information, Hap, I did go to your apartment. But when I got there, all hell had broken loose about that body lying splattered on the sidewalk. I couldn't get into your building because the police wouldn't let anyone in except residents who had urgent business. So I came back here."

Hap nodded his head in the affirmative as though that explained everything.

"How about a drink, Hap? You look like you could use one."

"Sure, why not," Hap responded.

"I'm having a Glennfidich, you want one?" Hu asked as he walked to the wet bar in the corner.

"Sure, that's fine."

Hu walked over to Hap with the drinks. "And where's the Lodestar info you picked up?" he casually asked as he handed Hap his drink.

Hap took a sip. "You're not gonna believe this, but one of my buddies has it."

"Oh really, who's your buddy?" Hu calmly asked, doing his best to conceal the sudden and dramatic increase in the rate of his heartbeat.

"A guy named Marty Stallworth. Lives over on 63rd and third. A black guy." Hap always added the last item of description about Martin because he never could get over the fact that he was actually working with a black person and he thought others might think him an open-minded, charitable guy for that reason.

"Ugh...and why did you give it to him?"

Hap snickered. "Well, he got this silly notion that you might be a spy and that I could be accused of espionage or something stupid like that."

Hu's entire body did a small jerk and then tensed. "So you told him about me?"

"Yeah, you know, I had to. I told about seeing Moore plummeting from my window and we started going through people who might have been in my apartment. Naturally I mentioned your name."

"All right, that's understandable. And you told him you were bringing these Lodestar papers to me, right?"

"Sure. I told him you had to have them to finalize your order. I also told him that's all there was to it but then he starts talking all this spy shit, like he's seen too many James Bond movies. But when I asked him to hand the info over, he balks, like he's going to protect the Free World from some sinister Chinese spy…no offense intended. I would have had to kick his ass to get them from him, which normally would have been a piece of cake, but I was so beat by that point that I thought I'd just deal with it later."

"I see…" Hu said as he rubbed his chin and stared straight ahead. "Here, let me freshen your drink for you." Hu took Hap's glass and walked to the wet bar.

"But I'll get them tomorrow, don't worry," Hap quickly added, sensing that Hu was suddenly uneasy. "Even if I have to get tough with him."

Hu handed Hap his drink, which he proceeded to guzzle. "Yeah, okay, well, I guess that's what you'll have to do if you want my order. And when's the Lodestar deal supposed to price?"

Hap yawned and answered, "Tomorrow, but they'll have to put if off if your order hasn't been confirmed." He yawned again.

"And so what are you going to do once you leave here?" Hu wanted to know.

"Huh?" When Hap looked up he was so tired his eyes were almost cross-eyed.

"Where you going from here?"

"To see my…see my…lawyer," he slurred. "But it's kinda late and…" Hap's head suddenly slumped, his mouth fell open and his chin hit his chest. The glass in his hand tumbled to the floor.

Hu remained seated and watched Hap just to make sure he really was out as the "Mickey" had worked much faster than he had expected. Then he picked up the telephone and called to the back quarters of the apartment where The Skinny One and Odd Job were hanging out, playing Mah Jong.

When they came hustling into the study a few seconds later, Hu pointed to Hap, spoke a few clipped sentences in Chinese, and then slid his finger across his throat. The two picked Hap up from the chair and lugged him out of the room.

Hu picked up his drink and walked to his desk. He ruminated on the fact that Hap was the first person he had had deliberately murdered. (He wasn't counting Moore since that was an accident of sorts.) Then he glanced at his computer monitor and noticed that he was up two million dollars on a JGB position that he had put in just a couple hours before. "Nice," he said back to his best friend, the computer monitor.

Hu saw nothing right or wrong about having Hap killed. He only saw it as a necessity. If Hap had blabbed the way he had to his friend, Stallworth, then it wouldn't be long before his cover was blown and the FBI would be all over his case. For Hu, good or bad only had meaning as they related to his own, personal well-being. He wasn't bothered one wit by pangs of conscience as he was not a religious person.

His parents had left Mainland China, during the Cultural Revolution, for Hong Kong where they had become successful pearl merchants, but had never relinquished the communist dogma that religion was the opiate of the masses. Lady Luck was the only divinity Hu believed in and his hunch that chance could somehow be manipulated by non-scientific methods was as spiritual as his world-view got.

For some reason he had come to the conclusion that Hap Boggs was bad—a bad trade. Therefore, ordering his execution was no more pleasant than canceling a bad trade or taking a hit. There was no point in feeling guilty about a bad trade; one had to shake it off and go on. But in truth, a thrill had run through Hu when he had run his finger across his throat, a type of thrill he had never experienced when trading.

Now that the bad trade, Hap Boggs, had been closed, Hu had another problem with which to deal. That problem was named, Marty Stallworth. From what Hap had told him, this friend knew too much, and even worse, suspected more. Sooner or later, he would go to the authorities with what he knew and suspected. Thus, he was just as big a problem as Hap. But Hu did not want to have him canceled, at least not until he got those Lodestar documents in his hands and delivered to Zhu. But how could he keep Stallworth from running to the cops?

Hu suddenly had an idea. He rose from his desk and quickly dressed, after which he went outside his apartment and hailed a taxi. Several blocks from his apartment, he had the cab stop at a public payphone where he dialed information and got the NYPD's hotline number for crime tips.

"I got information about the death of Dick Moore," he said to the operator, altering his voice as much as he could.

"Yes," said the operator, "Go ahead."

"Moore didn't fall out of the window on his own. Two individuals who worked with Moore killed him—Hap Boggs and Marty Stallworth. It was something about work is all I can tell you. Boggs got nervous and has already left the

Country; so don't bother looking for him. Stallworth is still around but won't be for long, believe me."

"And who is this calling?"

With that, Hu put down the receiver and got back into the waiting taxi.

The taxi then drove another several blocks and again stopped in front of a payphone. Hu again called information, this time asking for the Channel 24 newsroom.

"Yeah," the voice answered on the other end. Hu could hear in the background the hustle and bustle of the newsroom as the nightly eleven o' clock program would be airing in less than fifteen minutes.

"I got a tip for you guys," Hu said. "A real scoop."

"Yeah, well who's this?"

"That doesn't matter. What matters is that I know who murdered Dick Moore earlier."

"So you say he was murdered, huh?"

"He didn't fall out of that window trying to pet a pigeon."

"Who murdered him then?"

"Two of his co-workers, two subordinates—Hap Boggs and Marty Stallworth."

"Why would they murder him?"

"It was about work is all I can tell you."

"Hey, I got that. A few times I thought about killing my boss, too. What else can you tell me?"

"Boggs has already flown the coop. Gone to parts unknown."

"Okay, that's good info. C'mon, just between us, who are you?"

"I'm in-the-know, that's who I am." Then Hu hung up the phone and got back into the taxi. *That ought to fix Stallworth's wagon,* he mused to himself. Hu's strategy was to set the police running after Stallworth before he could run to them. Then his hope was that Stallworth would run right into his arms. The trick would be to catch him before the police did. Hu deemed it an extra bit of luck that Stallworth was black, a complexion that would naturally arouse suspicion with the police. The trader had just sold Martin Stallworth short.

Meanwhile, back in his apartment, in the master bathroom, Odd Job stood over the body of Hap Boggs. He had placed the body within the large shower stall so that the head was positioned well within it and the stream of water from the shower soaked Hap's head as blood flowed from the large gash along his throat and into the drain. Hap stared wide-eyed, like a gutted mackerel on newspaper, the jagged gash like a gill.

Shortly, The Skinny One entered the bathroom, carrying a chain saw and a carton of trash bags. "You ready to go to work?" he asked in Chinese as he lifted the chain saw up slightly.

Odd Job shook his head no. "Let some more blood drain first. That way there won't be as big a mess when we start cutting."

"Okay, I guess it doesn't matter if it's late and we start this chain saw up. It's not like anybody's gonna hear us inside this mausoleum." The Skinny One looked around the enormous bathroom and marveled at how the entire room had been covered in tile imported from Japan, making it completely soundproof.

"I know one thing," Odd Job said. "The fishes in the East River are gonna have a feast tonight.

CHAPTER 16

HIGHTAILIN'

WEARIED BY THE TROUBLES HE HAD SEEN THAT evening, Martin lay on his couch and glanced at the stack of papers that Hap had absconded from Arnie's computer files. He was beginning to think it was a mistake to have taken them from Hap. His arm itched and he scratched it where the rash had now spread to his shoulder. All he was trying to do was protect Hap, not to mention act as a responsible, patriotic citizen should. But now that he had them, what was he supposed to do? If he gave them back to Arnie, then he would expose Hap. There was no way to get around it, Hap had engaged in an act of espionage, whether he knew it or not. Maybe he should trash the papers—burn or shred them. But if he did that, then he would be putting himself in legal jeopardy—aiding and abetting and destroying evidence. Boy, he sure hoped Hap contacted a lawyer, a good lawyer who could advise him as to what he should do with the lifted documents.

Hap was in trouble, no doubt about it. Not only did he have the US government to think about, but also the people to whom he had intended to deliver the classified information. Martin was convinced that Hu or people associated with him had something to do with Moore's death. He couldn't connect all the dots but he was pretty sure that the most crucial dot was those papers stacked on his coffee table. If they were willing to dump Moore out a window for who knows what, what would Jo Hu, or whoever was behind Hu, do to Hap when he failed to come through? Martin had never considered Hap to be a close friend, even though Hap seemed to think they were buddies. But, he was basically a big-hearted, decent oaf, Falstaff without the wit, and Martin didn't wish to see any harm come to him.

But then an uneasy thought crossed his mind: *What if Hap told Hu that I have the Lodestar documents? No...surely Hap wouldn't be that stupid,* he thought with less than one hundred percent confidence. *Better put that Lodestar crap away somewhere safe,* Martin thought. He rose from the couch and looked around the room as he considered where he should hide the papers. *It has to be someplace where no one would think to look.* He placed the documents in a plastic bag and deposited them in his refrigerator freezer.

Martin glanced at his watch and saw that it was time for the eleven o' clock news. He lay on the couch, picked up the remote and flipped to Channel 24. Channel 24 news was his choice to watch; not only because its news reader was a real babe, a former Miss Duchess County who always stuck her chest out as if she were about to receive a medal, but also because among the tabloid local news programs, it was the most over-the-top. Murder and mayhem were its stock in trade—nothing was too tragic or sensational, and its reporters' schmarmy sad faces could never quite conceal their glee when reporting a deadly house fire, a plane crash with just enough survivors to get a first hand account, or a juicy lover's quarrel turned suicide/murder. Another Channel 24 specialty was the scare stories, like cancer-causing diapers, cancer-causing car antennas, and cancer-causing bricks. Given all the possibilities that Moore's plunge offered, he knew they would lead with that story and give it more coverage than the other stations.

Ah yes, Amanda's looking fine tonight, Martin said to himself as a puff-permed blond, fake eyelash-wearing chickhead appeared on the screen.

"Tony Central Park West was the scene of a gruesome sight earlier this evening. The body of a man identified as Richard C. Moore, an investment banking executive at Whorman Skeller & Company, was found dead on the sidewalk." Martin sat up and leaned closer to the TV set. "Eyewitnesses told police that Moore had plunged to his death from a twelfth story window at a building located at 145 Central Park West. Investigators at first were not sure whether the death was a suicide, an accident, or involved criminal intentions. Channel 24 has breaking information regarding this death. We now go to Warren Lush at the scene of the incident. Warren..."

The scene switched from the studio to Central Park West, where Warren Lush stood, wearing the obligatory trench coat and holding a microphone in his hand. "Yes, Amanda, Channel 24 has received exclusive information that the New York

Police Department now believes that the death of well-known Wall Street executive, Richard C. Moore, was in fact a case of foul play. We have received further, exclusive information that the police now have two suspects who they believe were involved in the killing. Although the police have not, at this point, released the names of the suspects, Channel 24 has learned that they are a Mr. James "Hap" Boggs and a Mr. Martin Stallworth."

Martin leapt from the couch when he heard his name and saw his Whorman Skeller security ID photo flash across the screen. "WHAT!" he yelled.

"The two individuals were co-workers with Mr. Moore at Whorman Skeller. Police have yet to take either suspect into custody. Channel 24 has been told by reliable sources that Mr. Boggs has fled the country."

"Warren, have the police told you a motive for the murder?" Amanda asked her colleague.

"My sources tell me that the motive was work-related, and that's all I know at the moment. I'll report further details as I receive them. Warren Lush here, bringing you another Channel 24 exclusive."

"Thanks, Warren. We look forward to learning more about that horrible tragedy. And now for our feature story: Dangerous levels of toxic bacteria found in calzones served by Hoboken pizzerias..."

Martin paced his apartment, both hands pressed against his forehead. *Am I dreaming?* His gut squirted adrenaline like a lemon being squeezed and sweat dribbled down his back. *What in God's name am I going to do?* Panic took hold. His first thought was to run. His second thought was to run. His third thought was to run. Martin grabbed his coat and ran.

Hu expected Martin to run and he didn't disappoint him. If Hu knew anything about anything, it was human nature and this knowledge had enabled him to become one of the world's foremost traders. He had an uncanny knack for anticipating where the human herd, otherwise known as the market, would move next. Also, he had an innate, extraordinary sense as to when one of the two antipodes, fear and greed, was tipping the market scales one-way or anther.

Knowing Channel 24 could not resist running the story was the reason he had given it to them. They would run it even if the only corroboration they got was some detective telling his ole buddy, Mr. Lush that, yeah, they had received a tip that two of Moore's co-workers, to remain nameless, may have had something to do with his death. But that was all that Warren Lush would need. It was a war out there in local TV news land and victory went to the fleetest—Greed. And Hu further anticipated that after seeing his face on the TV screen, the last thing Martin could do was stay still—Fear.

Martin scampered down the four flights of steps and burst out the front door to his walk-up apartment building. He had no idea to where he would run. Outside his apartment building, by the trashcans were The Skinny One and Odd Job, positioned exactly where Hu had ordered them to be. As Martin ran by, they jumped from the shadows and grabbed hold of him.

"Hey, what's going on here," he shouted as the two men tightly grabbed and held each of Martin's arms.

"You no make noise or else you never make noise again," The Skinny One whispered to Martin. Martin could see that he had a small handgun pressed against his side.

"What do you want with me?"

"Dogumens!"

"Dog what? I don't have a dog."

"Dogumens. Wodestar."

"I don't know what you're talking about," Martin said.

At that precise moment, detectives Fusco and Ayala were walking up the street and quickly sized up the situation and stopped several yards from Martin and his "escorts."

"Hold it," Fusco said to his partner as he pulled a small photo from his pocket. "Ain't that Stallworth right there in front of the apartment building we're going to?"

Ayala peered at Martin. "Yeah, that's him. Who are those two gooks with him?"

"I don't know and I don't care," Fusco answered. "All I know is that's our man. Let's go get him."

The two detectives jogged toward Martin and company. "Police! Stay right there."

The Skinny One and Odd Job looked at each other, wide-eyed. "Run for it," The Skinny One said and they quickly released Martin and fled into the night. Martin took one look at the two NYPD detectives hustling toward him and he too hightailed it.

"Hey! Stallworth, stop! We just wanna ask some questions!" Fusco shouted as he and Ayala chased after him.

First down 63rd street scurried the two Chinese thugs; then Martin followed by the two, overweight, huffing and puffing detectives. Odd Job couldn't believe his eyes when he looked over his shoulder and saw Martin running right behind him, as if he were now chasing *him*.

At Lexington Avenue, Odd Job and The Skinny One split in different directions while Martin headed toward the subway station four blocks away. The two detectives followed Martin in hot, sweaty pursuit.

Martin ran into the 59th street station, clambered down the escalator, and hurdled the turnstile. A train was at the station, filling up fast and the chime sounded and signaled the doors would soon close. Martin almost knocked over two tourists, studying a map as he lunged toward the train's door—the tips of his fingers pinched by the closing door. Martin banged on the door. "Open this goddamn door!" he hollered, discomfiting the by-standers who waited for the next train. The motorman ducked his head and ignored Martin. When he looked over his shoulder, he saw the two detectives at the turnstile. They had a hard time as they heaved their bulks over the metal bar. In the meantime, the train rollicked from the station.

He darted back and forth along the train platform, trapped. Fusco managed to get over the turnstile and helped Ayala over. Now Martin had no choice but to jump off the platform and onto the train tracks.

He sprinted along the tracks, tripped, and almost fell onto the third rail, the rail charged with an electric current powering the trains. If he had touched that, he knew he would have sizzled like a beetle on one of those bug grillers people hang over the patio in the summer. Into the inky darkness of the tunnel he headed as his two pursuers stood on the platform, bending over and peering into the tunnel.

"Martin, c'mon back!" Ayala shouted. "You're gonna get yourself killed!" Neither detective had any intention of leaping into that rat-infested, dark, dank, damp, stinking hole with a dormant lightening bolt running down the middle of it. Fusco slapped his thigh in frustration.

Martin ran, not bothering to look over his shoulder to see if he were still being chased. The tunnel grew darker and narrower as the uptown and downtown lines diverged into separate tubes. The only lights were the small blue bulbs spaced every thirty yards along the wall. But then Martin stopped in wonder as droplets of gold appeared on the rails in front of him. A white light rose above the tracks...then another white light...two unblinking eyes coming toward him! Just then a rumbling noise began to build. The subway train was turning a corner and was coming at full-speed toward him!

The motorman sounded his horn, not because he saw Martin, but because regulations required that a horn sound as the train approached the station. Coming around the bend, the motorman would not be able to stop the train in time even if he did spot Martin.

Quickly, Martin looked back toward the station. He was at least fifty yards away...with no chance to make it all the way back there. The train would be on him in a matter of seconds so he did the only thing he could do—immediately fall flat between the rails. He pulled his arms as tight as he could against his sides and scrunched his body against the rail bed. With a flash and a roar, the train descended upon him like an angry dragon ready to gobble him in one bite. Martin shut his eyes and held his breath, sucking his body into itself as much as he could. The train's hot, greasy, iron underbelly rushed over him...clack, clack, clack, clack. The dragon's fifty, round, metal teeth chattered less than a foot on either side of his head...so loud he thought his eardrums might pop.

He lay as still as a corpse in a coffin, expecting some low-hanging piece of machinery to plow into him, tearing his body straight down the middle. Then suddenly, the train was gone, as short-lived as wind over a wheat field. Martin gasped with relief—the dragon had spit him back out. In disbelief, he ran his hands over his body that was still of one piece. He then raised his hands to his chest and folded them in prayer, "Thank you, dear God."

He then rose and staggered off the tracks where he fell against the near-by wall, hyperventilating. The small blue light cast just enough light for him to see a railing running along the wall. Amazed to find a catwalk there, he quickly lifted himself up and rolled over onto it.

After resting till his heartbeat had gotten somewhat back to normal, he then stood up and walked along the catwalk. The tunnel was now amazingly quiet except for the occasional rat that squeaked in surprise and scurried away as Martin approached. Finally he came to a metal ladder. In the darkness he was unable to see where the ladder ended, but climbed it anyway. On the last step of the ladder, he moved his hand along the wall and felt a lever. When he pulled on it and pushed, a door began to creak open. Suddenly Martin left the pitch-blackness of the subway tunnel and entered the Manhattan night, a night without darkness—bleached out, orange.

When he stumbled onto the street, the city's pungent air never smelt better. He stood there a moment and looked in each direction to make sure the coast was clear of the two detectives. He guessed they were probably waiting for him at the next station platform. Of course, he couldn't forget about his two Chinese admirers. They just might be slithering somewhere in his vicinity.

Just then a taxi turned the corner and Martin stepped into the street to hail it. "Can you take me all the way to Massapequa?" he asked the turbaned Sikh driver.

"Most certainly," was the answer.

Quickly getting in the back seat, Martin hunched down low. His head was spinning and numb...like it was filled with cotton balls. He held his hand out in front of him and watched it tremble just as the rails had, the moment before the subway pounced on him.

Pops. I have to see Pops and tell him all that has happened. Martin moaned out loud at the thought that Pops may have seen the late evening's newscast. *I should have called him before I fled my apartment.*

Traffic wasn't thick on the LIE that time of night, so it wasn't long before the taxi pulled onto Pop's s street. A sense of relief immediately calmed his heart, which, for the past hour, had been jumping around like a colt on a fine spring morning.

"It's the fourth house on the right," he instructed the driver. But then, Martin noticed something that gave him pause. A car was parked a couple of houses down from Pop's house. Two people sat in the car. "Slow down," he ordered the driver. The Impala had that nondescript look that made unmarked police cars so obvious. Martin ducked down and peered over the edge of the window as they drove by. He glimpsed at the driver but couldn't see much in the darkness. Did the guy look Asian? Martin thought maybe he did, but wasn't sure. Was paranoia causing him to see things? He couldn't afford to gamble, given that there was a chance that the car was either a cop car or part of Hu's fleet. In either case, he had to get the hell out of there.

"Driver, take me back to Manhattan."

The puzzled driver looked in the rearview mirror at Martin. "What?"

"Just get me back to the city and quick!"

Back in Manhattan, he had the taxi stop at a brownstone townhouse in the West Village. Martin paid the cab fare, walked up to the front door of the brownstone and rang the doorbell. After a minute, he pushed the doorbell again. Finally a light went on inside, and shone through the front window. He stood quite still for another few seconds, as he knew he was being examined through the peephole. Finally the door swung open and there was Mihra in a silk, burgundy-colored robe.

"Martin!" she said with a look of alarm as she let him in.

"I know it's late, Mihra, but it's an emergency."

"I saw the news tonight," she said as she led him into the den at the back of the townhouse. Flabbergasted, she turned and looked at him as they both sat on the sofa.

Martin shook his head in disbelief as he told Mihra everything he knew. How Hap had come to his apartment in a panic because he had seen Dick Moore dropped from his window. That Hap had told him he was to deliver Lodestar information to Jo Hu. Then he told her he had a sneaky suspicion that Hu had something to do with Moore's death...since Hu was supposed to have met Hap at his apartment building right about the time that Moore was sailing through the air. The fact that Hu evidently was engaged in espionage of some type, notwithstanding his pretext for wanting the classified information only for due diligence purposes, further cast him in a sinister light.

"You really think Jo Hu is a spy and a murderer?" Mihra asked.

"I don't know what I think anymore," Martin replied. "But I can tell you that two, armed Chinese goons jumped me outside my apartment earlier tonight and they wanted the Lodestar stuff. I guess that dumb shit, Hap told Hu he had given it to me. Anyway, that confirmed what I was thinking about Hu."

"Where's Hap?"

"I don't know. I haven't seen him since he left my apartment. He was going back to his place to call his lawyer."

"But what about that news story, Martin? I almost fainted when I saw it."

"Hey, so did I. I have no idea where that came from, Mihra. My guess is Jo Hu had something to do with that, too."

"I can see why," Mihra said. "He wanted the cops on your case to divert their attention from him.

"I guess it wasn't too smart of me running from them like that. It was like an instinct, though, to just get the hell away."

"You need to talk to the police, Martin. Tell them everything that happened, everything you know. You didn't do anything, so there's nothing to worry about."

"Yeah, I know. But first, I need to call a lawyer." Martin was worried, as he had never felt bleaker or blacker in his life. He was surprised at how natural his instinct to run from the police was. Of course he hadn't done anything wrong, but still he ran. A few years before, Martin had been stopped by two policemen while walking one evening through a neighborhood in Massapequa, a neighborhood three blocks from his. They fingered him as the perpetrator of a rash of burglaries and went so far as to put handcuffs on him. "What's your black coon-ass doing around here?" one of the cops had asked him. And no matter how expensive the threads he was wearing, or how far into the six figures his pay was, no matter how upright and law abiding and Republican conservative he strove to be, he would always flinch whenever he saw a white cop because he knew that cop would be wondering what his "black coon-ass" was doing out of the "hood" and in *his* white world. The memory was embedded in every fiber of his body.

"It's one thirty in the morning, Martin. Wait until the morning before you call anybody."

"Yeah." Martin let his head fall back upon the sofa and shut his eyes. "Oh man…" he sighed.

As Mihra studied him, she stroked her hand across his brow, furrowed with anxiety; he kept his eyes shut. She had never seen him weak like this, not the Martin who was always so resolute and determined, his voice firm and fast clipped and his leg jiggling while he talked about the way things should be.

Tonight he was in need, in need of her. And because she found that weakness beautiful, she leaned over and kissed him on the mouth; her lips brushed wet against his. At first, Martin kept his lips shut but then parted them to receive hers. When she breathed hard into his mouth, her breath was warm, pine nut and earth-scented. Her nose nuzzled against his as she ran her tongue along his upper lip, causing his lip to tingle. In return he flicked his tongue against her teeth and her hand moved to his cheek. She paused to take another breath and then drew his tongue full into her watering mouth, cooing as she did so.

When Martin looked into the deep green of her eyes, it reminded him of a lake near his grandmother's house where he had swum as a kid. It had been way back in the woods, under the shade of some beech trees. And in the springtime, after a refreshing rain, the sun would come out again and the lake caught a splash of sunlight that would turn it the deepest green.

She forced herself to break away from him. As she stood up and took his hand she said, "C'mon, let's go to the bedroom." Martin, now putty in her hands, did as he was told.

The bedroom was on the second floor, with large windows that looked out upon a small garden in the back. Martin glanced out the window and saw the gibbous moon peeking around the corner of a large apartment building—its dark side starkly limned against the sky. Then he turned and saw Mihra as she removed her robe. She wore nothing underneath and stood silently and naked before him. He walked to her and kissed her again. She unbuttoned his shirt, pulled it off then reached down and undid his belt. When she unzipped his pants, she felt his hardness and made a soft sound.

As one, they fell onto the bed while his hands and mouth covered her breasts; they were much more ample than her conservative wardrobe had let one believe. Her hand held his hardness and she gently moved her hand up and down—from the stem to the rosebud tip—up, down, over and over. He groaned and sucked on her nipples until they were pert; then moved one hand down to where her thighs joined—she was wet for him.

He then shifted her around so she lay on top of him with her vagina pressed against his mouth and let his tongue enter her soft fruit. Mihra thrust her pelvis while her mouth fell onto his erection. She moved her head up and down in the same, even rhythm that she combed her hair—long, even strokes. Her insides tightened every time he throbbed inside her mouth.

Then she changed her position so she could straddle him. She brought her knees up, centered onto him and very slowly lowered herself so that all of him slowly entered her. All of him slowly moved up inside her until he plunged his full shaft deep inside her and caused her to cry out.

Her hands squeezing his pectoral muscles, on her knees she rocked back and forth, up and down, her hair falling in her face, her mouth open, her eyes halfway closed. He reached up and cradled her breasts as they slightly swayed. The moon's quicksilver light spilled through the window and washed over their bodies as her body lapped against him like a gentle wave against a ship's hull. Back and forth, up and down, in and out. He felt the wave inside him, the ocean surge and subside. As she rocked on and on, she gradually increased the tempo. And the moon pulled, pulled the tide inside his gut and he began to forget about all that had happened that night. The tide swelled and the moon pulled until everything dissolved into nothingness. He forget it all, even Mihra, himself, everything merged into a blank intensity...faded into whiteout.

CRASH! Mihra stopped and as her eyes flew open, she jerked her head toward the sound. Martin also sprang up and they both focused their attentions on the sound. Then it came again as more glass was shattered from the sliding glass door to the garden. Martin leapt from the bed and frantically tried to get dressed.

Just then, Odd Job exploded through the closed bedroom door. As he quickly scanned the room deciding his next move, that couple of seconds gave Martin time to grab the large down comforter and throw it over his head. While Odd Job wrestled with the comforter, Mihra yanked the ceramic lamp from the bedside table, stood on the bed, and swung it down as hard as she could on Odd Job's covered head. A muffled moan sounded from underneath the comforter and Odd Job collapsed into a heap, shards of ceramic all around him.

Not waiting another second, Martin leapt over the slumbering Odd Job and ran for the bedroom door just as The Skinny One was running into the bedroom. Before The Skinny One had a chance to even blink, Martin threw a right cross that was as straight and hard as a flying telephone pole. He reeled backwards toward the stairway and then went flipping and flopping, head over heels all the way to the ground floor. Not waiting, Martin hurried out the front door. The black and white moon was still up—yen and yang hanging in the sky.

CHAPTER 17

YELLOW DOG BLUES

BLINDLY MARTIN RAN FROM MIHRA'S APARTMENT and out onto the street. The streets in the West Village were lined with quaint townhouses and gingko trees and it was so quiet that the only sound was the frantic scuffling of Martin's feet. He sprinted up the street, lit by the moon and the turn-of-the-century street lamps that the neighborhood association had installed. *Get away; get away,* was the only thought blaring inside his head.

A woman walking her schnauzer looked at him warily as he ran past, *Was that 0. J. Simpson?*

He ran so fast his lightweight, canvas jacket spread out behind him like wings. When he arrived at the intersection of Houston and West Broadway Streets, he finally stopped running because he knew a black man running down a crowded street would surely draw the attention of any civic-minded people and the cops in the vicinity. At the corner he stood and gasped for breath while his heart jackhammered inside his heaving chest. He glanced over his shoulder to see if he was being pursued and then walked briskly over to Bleecker Street and avoided West Broadway all together as it was still quite busy even though it was well past 2:00 a.m.

His shirt was soaked with sweat as he hurried to a pay phone. He dialed information, got Mihra's number and then dialed her number. Three rings and then a gruff voice said, 'Yeah?" The voice hit his eardrum like a rock against a mirror…it was Odd Job. All along he had assumed that Odd Job would have been on his trail, but this was a nightmare he hadn't envisioned...his two Chinese "pals" still at Mihra's...*alone* with Mihra.

"Where is she?"

Odd Job said something in a garbled mix of Chinese and English that Martin couldn't understand. Martin heard the voice of The Skinny One in the background and a fumbling noise as he grabbed the phone from Odd Job. "We haf yo frien," he shouted. "Ya get back wen you gif dogumens. You no gif dogumens, we keel. You caw powice, we keel. She dead fish. You hewa?"

Martin gripped the phone hard as he said, "You lay one hand on her and I'll..."

"Gul fo dogumens. No mo. Bye.

Martin smashed the phone receiver against the phone booth's Plexiglas window. He walked from the booth, not knowing where to go, not knowing what to do. Stunned, bewildered. He grabbed his spinning head with both hands and tried to concentrate. But all he could do was ask himself, *What am I going to do?*

As he walked his thoughts spiraled in his mind. *Maybe I should just go ahead and give the documents to Hu. But I would certainly be committing espionage...then I would have no excuse, no alibi...Open and shut case. But I have to protect Mihra. I can't worry about myself anymore. I should never have gone to her apartment...that was so stupid. I have to get Mihra out of harm's way. That is now my number one objective.*

I'll just go to my apartment, get those fucking papers out of the freezer, set up a meeting with Hu and—hold it! You can't go back to your apartment, you stupid idiot. The police will surely have it staked out and you'll get nabbed as soon as you get near that place. And if Hu and his boys get wind that the cops have you, they'll assume you spilled all the beans and they probably would carry out their threat to kill Mihra. Remember, to them, she would be one more piece of evidence, a witness, to corroborate your story. Shit!

Martin continued to walk and now the cool air had chilled him and he buttoned his jacket. He was too tired to think anymore but mechanically put one foot in front of the other. By the time he got to Washington Square, it was almost three a.m. and he was completely exhausted from lack of sleep and anxiety. At this wee hour, the square was empty, except for a bum or two so he sat down on a bench and wrapped his arms around himself.

Suddenly he was startled by a noise behind him and when he turned saw a homeless man with one arm in a sling standing over a garbage can and sticking his nose like a raccoon into an empty yogurt cup.

Martin lay lengthwise on the bench. And he thought, *So it all comes down to this...lying on a park bench in Washington Square in the dead of the night—after all the schooling, the straight A's, all the accommodating, the proving, the following the right path, after the black embarrassment and black pride, dreams deferred, the courage screwing up, the dogged determination. After all the out-of-sight slights, after Clarence Thomas and Colin Powell, presenting Martin Sallworth, the nigger who rose with the cream, without paying affirmative action any never-mind. After the MBA, the Wall Street walk, the money talk, the talking right, the moola worshipping, the showing off, the showing them how a black man can do whatever he puts his white mind to. The odd-man-out against the odds, after hailing taxis that never stop after dark, and after all the heroics and poetry, it all comes down to this: Tin cans tied to the tail of a yellow dog!*

Martin shut his eyes and lyrics from an old Robert Johnson, blues tune, "Hellhound on My Trail," faintly rummaged through his head. *I've got to keep moving/I've got to keep moving/blues falling down like hail/blues falling down like hail...*

He put his hands under his head and jackknifed his legs, yawned and smacked his lips. And then out-of-the-blue, his erstwhile hero, Langston Hughes, spoke a lullaby to him...

Did you ever go down to the river/Two a.m. midnight by your self/Sit down by the river/And wonder what you got left/Did you ever think about your mother/God bless her dead and gone/Did you ever think about your sweetheart/And wish she'd never been born...

And just before Martin's heavy breathing turned into a snore, he remembered Langston saying...*My old man died in a fine big house/My ma died in a shack/I wonder where I'm gonna die/Being neither white nor black...*

Poor Pops, what must he think about me now...must call him...must call. Tell me more, Langston...So we stand here/On the edge of Hell/In Harlem/And look out on the world/And wonder/What we're gonna do/In the face of/What we remember...

Let's go on out on a good note, Langston. Before the whiteout and the blackout fade...Reach up your hand/Dark boy/And take a star/Out of the little breath of oblivion...Okay...okay...

Martin heard a tapping...somebody tapping at the door...or rather he felt a tapping. Whatever, he had to get up and open the door. Like a jet plane lifting through the clouds, he struggled to pull himself out of a heavy sleep. Another tap. He opened an eye and saw a man-in-blue standing over him, one of New York's finest, who tapped his billyclub against the sole of Martin's shoe and said, "All right, you. Get yourself up off that bench."

Martin quickly sat up. He raked his hand through his hair and tried to wipe away his wrinkled dishevelment. The sun was just coming up and in the gray light the street-sweepers were already at work.

"What are you doing here, bub?"

Martin stammered but didn't know what to say. He kept his face lowered as much as he could so that the officer wouldn't have a direct view of the face that had appeared on Channel 24 news the night before.

"Let's see some ID."

Martin's mind scrambled for an excuse not to show his ID because if the policeman saw his name, he was sure he would recognize it from all the news reports.

"Officer, I don't have my wallet. I left it in my apartment. My name is Langston Hughes. I'm an English professor at NYU. Call there and they'll verify that."

The officer looked Martin over. "And so you was conducting a seminar here last night with all the winos, dope peddlers and pick-pockets, professor?"

"Look, I'm embarrassed to tell you why I'm here but I guess I'll have to. I had a nasty tiff with my wife last night and she kicked me out of the apartment. I live on Eighth Street, off of Fifth. Anyway, I came here just to get my head together but didn't mean to fall asleep on this bench, I can guarantee you that."

The officer studied Martin once again. Martin did his best not to appear nervous, but he was silently praying that the cop wouldn't recognize him.

"Okay, professor. But next time pick an ivory tower in which to cool your heels. This ain't no place for a professor after midnight. You're lucky you didn't get rolled or worse."

"I got that, officer. Believe me, you won't find me dozing here again.

"On your way then."

Martin made his way out of Washington Square and walked up Fifth Avenue. He stopped at the nearest pay phone and made a collect call to Massepequa.

"Hello."

"Pops, it's me."

"Martin? Martin, my god, where are you?"

"Pops, I can't tell you because somebody might be listening."

"You're right, they might have my phones tapped. Lord have mercy, I saw that news report last night and the paper this morning. I about had a heart attack. Martin, what is this all about?"

"Pops, I can't explain it all to you now. But listen to me. Listen to me good...none of it is true. I swear on mama's grave that none of it is true. Do you hear me?"

"Of course I hear you, son. And I never believed it to begin with. But I been worried sick. But you oughta go ahead and turn yourself in to the police. You're innocent, you have nothing to fear."

"Pops, maybe I should have in the beginning. But I panicked when I saw that news report. Now it's too late."

"It's never too late, Martin."

Martin didn't want to tell Pops that Hu's Chinese flunkies were holding Mihra hostage.

"Why don't you come stay with me...at least until this thing blows over, I mean."

"Can't do that. I think they have your place staked out."

"Who does?"

Martin didn't know whether to say the police or Hu's boys and regretted letting that slip out. "The...ah...people who are after me. But listen, Pops, I'll figure something out. Really I will. Don't worry, okay."

"Where you gonna go? You got a lawyer? Call Clifton Adams, he's a lawyer friend of mine in the city."

"I might do that, Pops. But I gotta run. I'll figure something out. Don't worry about me."

"Call me tomorrow, Martin. Tell me where you are and what you're gonna do. Will you do that for me?"

"Of course."

"In the meantime, I'll be praying. Be careful, son. You know I love you."

"I'll call again as soon as I get where I'm going."

Immediately after hanging up the phone, Martin realized he had no idea *where* he would be going. He knew he couldn't go to his apartment, or to Pops or Mihra's. And if he went to any of his other friends, he would only be implicating them, exposing them to a charge of harboring a fugitive, aiding and abetting.

Now falsely accused, pursued by both the good guys and the bad guys, he had nowhere to turn and was totally at a loss as to what would be his best choice of action. Everything he once was had been flailed away, the skin of his identity stripped away. Martin Stallworth, the shining example, had died and gone to someplace besides heaven. Snatched up like a boneless soul on Judgment Day and the devil had the hindmost. Suddenly he felt completely raw, naked and vulnerable.

Just as he was about to sit on the curb along Fifth Avenue and place both hands to his face and weep with despair, a thought occurred to him—it came with a saving grace. *There is someone I can run to…of course, why didn't I think of him before? I'll head straight there.*

This sudden optimism about a possible sanctuary caused Martin to remember his appetite. He hadn't had a thing to eat in over twelve hours so he went to the nearest deli to get an egg and ham sandwich and a large coffee. While he stood in line, he automatically glanced at the newspaper rack. His heart literally skipped a couple of beats when he saw The New York Post. There, on the front page, was his face underneath the headline: **BOSS GETS TOSSED Two Wall Streeters Suspected of Throwing Boss out Twelfth-story Window!**

Quickly Martin lowered his head and furtively looked out of the corner of his eyes at the two other people who waited in line. They didn't seem to have noticed that a "celebrity" stood in front of them. Martin quickly paid for his breakfast and exited.

Outside on the sidewalk, a man was just opening a kiosk selling tourist souvenirs. Martin purchased a Yankee baseball cap and a cheap pair of sunglasses with stems fashioned after the World Trade Towers. After donning his disguise, his stomach quit churning long enough for him to gobble down his breakfast while he walked to the nearest subway stop. He had to get to his sanctuary.

He made his way to the Lexington Avenue subway stop and boarded an Uptown number 4. The subway platform was crowded, as people leaned over to peer beyond the shoulder of the person leaning over in front of them—all anticipating the coming train. Martin was barely able to squeeze onto the next train and felt better that the car was so crowded because, paradoxically, the more compressed the passengers were the less chance he would be noticed. And once again, Langston's words came to him: *Subway Rush Hour/Mingled breath and smell/So close mingled/Black and white/So near/No room to fear.*

Damn, what is it all of sudden with these Langston Hughes recitations, Martin wondered. He hadn't read the poet in years; these spontaneous invocations of his words were beginning to spook Martin, like Langston Hughs' ghost was haunting him…tagging along behind.

The subway car got less crowded the further uptown the train traveled. Martin got off at the Yankee Stadium stop because the area around the stadium was one of the few places in the Bronx where a person might find a cab, usually a gypsy cab but a cab nonetheless.

It wasn't but a few minutes later that one came careening around the corner, a huffing and puffing 1989 Lincoln Town Car. A cardboard placard with the word TAXI inscribed in Magic Marker occupied the top right corner of the windshield. Martin hailed it and when he hopped in the back, directed the driver to the Malcolm X Memorial Community Housing Center. "Okay, mon," said the Jamaican driver as he gunned the engine.

Martin laid his head back as his neck had a crick from sleeping on that wooden park bench. His body was coated with a film so oily that he felt he was merging with the greasy seat through osmosis. What he would have paid at that moment for just a toothbrush and toothpaste.

The taxi traveled several blocks north. Some neighborhoods were mostly Latino, with storefronts and signs in Spanish. Other sections were African-American. The Latino neighborhoods exuded mania, a barely contained mayhem, dogs and children wild in the streets, beat-up cars running red lights. The black sections were more subdued, somber, depressed, small knots of men standing at ramshackle corners, looking tired and unsure. And randomly alternating between the Latino and Black sections were stretches of dilapidated and abandoned buildings. In a pathetic effort at "sprucing up" a few of these boarded-up and wasted buildings, the City of New York had painted over the plywood such things as: blue window curtains, flower pots and smiling people leaning over window sills.

After going a couple of miles, the taxi came to a large area of nothing but weed-tufted rubble, the ten-acre site of an urban renewal effort that had never got past the demolition phase. Across the cleared ground, Martin could see the Malcolm X Memorial Community Housing Center, otherwise known as "The Malcolm X."

No towers loomed there as this project was built in the early seventies when public officials took it on faith that the root-cause of the crime and destruction afflicting public housing was the architecture. "Do away with those cold, impersonal, intimidating, inhibiting towers and the natural goodness of the public housing denizens would shine forth," they reasoned.

The project was originally called the John Lindsey Housing Project, named after the former mayor of New York. But a few years ago, after the Spike Lee movie, "Malcolm X," had made a splash, they changed the name.

The taxi drove to the project and turned down a side street off the main drag. *Things always look different from the inside out than they do from the outside in,* Martin reflected. He had seen projects like this scores of times before, giving them no more thought than he would brown smudges against the sky; never thinking he would be thankful to go inside one. Now that he was among them and the taxi drove more slowly, he could see that these "projects" stretched for acres.

"Where to, brother mon?" the driver asked Martin.

"Right here's all right."

After getting out of the cab, Martin stood and examined his whereabouts. When he saw on a building across the street the graffiti, **HELL TO THE SEEZERS,** spray painted in big, red, looping letters, he knew he was at the right place. *What to do next, now that he was here?* was the question he asked himself.

He saw a group of kids gathered at the corner, waiting for the school bus. He walked to the bus stop and approached a boy who looked older than the rest, a teenager with a tall, lanky frame that his weight was trying to catch up to.

"Hey," Martin said to him. The boy responded with a suspicious sizing up.

"Can I ask you something?" Martin asked.

The boy looked askance at Martin in his Yankee cap and Twin Towers sunglasses and asked, "You a roller, man? Cause if you are, I wanna see a badge."

"I'm not a cop, undercover or otherwise. I'm looking for somebody, that's all. Lives around here."

"Who's that?"

"Somebody who runs with the Seezers."

The boy shuffled his feet and looked away. "Shit, the Seezers. I don't know nothin' 'bout no Seezers."

Martin pulled a twenty-dollar bill from his pocket and held it up to the boy. "I really need to find this person. I need to know where the Seezers hang."

The boy studied the twenty-dollar bill. "Go over to the Malcolm X. Building C, apartment 2F. Ask for Omar." Then he quickly took the twenty from Martin's fingers.

"Thanks," Martin said as he walked away.

"Yeah, nice doin' biz wicha. Thanks for the Andy Jack. See ya in the next life." He shoved the twenty all the way down into the crotch of his underwear, a place where he was sure the thugs at school wouldn't find it.

Martin walked through the projects, a collection of brown brick, two story buildings with plain concrete balconies. Run-of-the-mill, flat roof, government housing. One out of every four windows was boarded up. Sagging clotheslines in the back. No grass in the hardscrabble yard but only glints of broken bottles. A netless, bent hoop on a leaning rusty pole as sad as a dead child's bubble blower. The smell of raw sewage coming from somewhere. Music floating on the air, even this early in the morning. Martin imagined that music played nonstop here, all day, all night. Different strains of hip-hop and soul snaking around each other, beats bumping against each other. One sound, one lovesick falsetto voice fought through, singing slowly, "Why you don't love me, I'll never know why/Now that you won't see me, there's no sun in my sky..." A curl of distant, hollow sound twisting across the big empty space that was the heart of the project—that was all the love song was. Far away, rising from the horizon, were the glorious skyscrapers of money-land Manhattan, promising nothing to the people here.

When Martin arrived at building C, he walked up the stairwell, reeking of urine, to the second level and along the open breezeway until he came to the door of apartment 2F. He took a deep breath and knocked on the door. After a minute and no response, he knocked again.

Finally the door cracked open and a bloodshot eye peered through the small opening at Martin. The eye was set in a face the color of a paper bag but with dark freckles sprinkled across it. "What?" the face yelped in a high-pitched voice.

"You Omar?" Martin asked.

"You mean XJE? Omar don't go by Omar. XJE is who he is now."

"Whatever, are you him?"

The eye stared at Martin for a few seconds. "What biz you got with XJE?"

"I don't have any business with XJE. I'm looking for somebody he knows...somebody who goes by the name of 'Trex.' You know Trex?"

"Everybody around here knows Trex."

"Get the word to him that Martin Stallworth is looking for him." The eye looked Martin up and down. "And tell him I'll be hanging out at that diner I saw up the street from here. You know which one I'm talking about?"

"The Dew Drop In. Yeah, if I see him, I'll tell him."

"You do that."

Martin walked away and just before he descended the stairs, turned and saw the person who had been behind the door leaning across the threshold. His torso was bare and he had a teased-out Afro that made his head seem oversized and out of proportion to his slight frame.

He made his way through the complex, back to the street leading into it and headed toward the Dew Drop In, a diner/bar/lounge that he had spotted across from the big, cleared tract as the taxi had taken him to the Malcolm X. By now the children at the bus stop had all vanished and his step quickened as he anticipated meeting Trex, as he was called in this neighborhood. Martin fully expected Trex would provide him some shelter until he could decide what to do next. What he needed most was a place where he could lay low for a day or two until his head cleared and he could figure out how to rescue Mihra. Then once he did that, he could then try and figure out how to rescue himself.

Just after he passed the bus stop, Martin saw a beige vehicle tear around the corner of the next street. He stopped and stared in wonder at the auto that was as wide as two regular cars and rode about two feet off the ground. Finally he recognized it as a Hummer. Intrigued, he watched as it speeded toward him, somewhat surprised a Hummer would be in such a neighborhood as this.

The car then swerved and jumped the curb in front of Martin. Startled, he leaped back as the Hummer skidded to a halt. The driver charged from the vehicle, not even bothering to turn off the engine off. He was wearing nothing but draw-string pants and one of those big, rainbow colored, crocheted, reggae caps. Martin then saw the freckles and realized this person coming toward him was Omar XJE. The two riders accompanying Omar also jumped out of the vehicle but his attention was so focused on Omar that Martin didn't notice the two circling behind him.

"Okay, Jasper, so you wanna meet Trex?" Omar shouted in mid-stride.

Omar was smiling wide, showing his two eye-teeth that were turned outward like fangs and shining with gold caps. Martin smiled back but before he could even utter say a word, Omar got within a foot of him and threw a right uppercut into his stomach. Every wisp of breath left him and he bent over and then fell to his knees. The world then whited-out as one of Omar's partners came up behind him and threw a pillowcase over his head.

Gasping for breath, Martin felt himself being lifted from the ground and hauled to the Hummer, into which he was unceremoniously dumped. Omar's two friends held Martin down as the Hummer rumbled back onto the street and sped away.

Martin was too disorientated to even wonder whether his captors worked for Hu or were bounty hunters working for the NYPD. All he knew was that he had been finally caught.

CHAPTER 18

BACK AT THE FACTORY

TERRY BARKER SAT AT HIS DESK, GLUMLY STARING off into space. The dark circles under his eyes evidenced his grief over the passing of his mentor, dare we say hero, Richard C. Moore. Moore had been the one who had ushered him into this business just after he had graduated—okay—attended, Long Island State University. It was the biggest break of his life and Richard C. had nurtured and guided him up toward the pinnacle on which he now glumly sat—head trader for the Whorman Skeller high-yield desk.

He and Dick had had an affinity for each other from the very beginning. They shared the same interests, like hunting, fishing, sailing, cigars, vintage wines and all the other clichés in which all Wall Street people are required to become accomplished. Once a year, in late fall, they would trek off to Montana to hunt elk on the cold, barren prairie land—just the two of them, shivering at night in pup tents and then rising before dawn to walk miles, hoping to catch a glimpse of an elk. Also they had shared the same sense of humor, which Barker thought of as "jocular" while others may have called it bullying.

We were so in tune with each other that on some days we even wore, without planning it, the same exact outfit to work, the same suit, shirt and tie. It was almost strange, in a cool, kind of way, he thought, *but, of course, those knucklehead salesmen always had a good chuckle whenever we inadvertently came to work looking like twins.*

Barker directed a glare toward the sales pit. *Yea, I knew they had resented Moore because he was so successful and powerful, because he was tough on them—demanded a lot from them. But I never thought they would go so far as to...as to murder him!* Barker shook his head and seethed. *You can never put anything past a bond salesman! Of course, when it came to Hap—nothing was unimaginable—I knew that fucker was a stark raving loony tune.*

The big shocker to Terry was that Marty was involved. Marty was okay, for the most part—maybe a little full of himself and cocksure at times. "Uppity" was a word that sometimes came to Barker's mind. And when Barker had heard that Marty wrote poetry, he couldn't help but speculate about his sexual orientation. But he felt he was basically a good guy—Black or not.

Look at them over there, Barker said to himself as he continued to observe the sales group, *they're as thick as thieves, happier than pigs in shit now that their leader, the brother that he had never had, the father figure to him, to all of them, was dead.* A phrase from the psychology class in college was on the tip of his tongue. *Oedipus complex, that was it. Who knows,* he thought to himself, *maybe they were all in on it. Maybe they're all off the reservation. Like those bad kids in Lord of the Flies.*

Maybe even I'm next on their hit list. I wouldn't put anything past them—just a nest of vipers.

"I wonder what he looked like?" Lori asked.

"Who?" Libby asked.

"Moore, who else? I was just wondering what he looked like after he hit the sidewalk. I've never seen anybody fall twelve stories. I mean, did he splatter or just bounce?"

Libby rolled her eyes at how crude Lori could sometimes be but Lyle was eager to paint a picture. "I tell you what you do, Lori. You go to the supermarket and find yourself the biggest pumpkin you can. Then take it up to the top of your apartment building and drop it. That should give you some idea how Moore's head looked after Hap pushed him out that window." Lyle joggled his head and smirked with self-pleasure.

"You mean Hap *and* Marty," Lori added. "It still boggles my mind about Marty. Hap, yeah, okay, maybe. Meshugge, Hap is. But Marty?"

Actually, when Lori first heard the news on Channel 24 the night before, she immediately reflected on what her Uncle Harvey always said about the shwartzer, "The lost tribe of Ham they are. A black cloud follows them wherever they go." She could still see him sitting in their kitchen, stuffing himself with pickled herring and becoming increasingly apoplectic about the shwartzer postman who had moved into the neighborhood. "The children aren't safe...keep the women indoors...lock up the silverware."

"You think you know somebody but you never really know, do you?" Libby opined. She was tempted to extemporize on her theory that Martin was acting out a kind of mini-slave rebellion, that he was naturally susceptible to a generations-old need to exact revenge for the crimes inflicted on his ancestors by the white race. The urge to kill the master was in the blood, a programmed genetic code with which all blacks were wired.

Moore represented the plantation owner, the white master and by killing Moore, Martin was actually freeing himself from the four hundred year old baggage with which all African-Americans, particularly black males, were burdened.

She was even tempted to state her opinion that given the repression that African-Americans have suffered, who's to say that Martin was wrong in killing Moore. What, after all, is right or wrong when one subsumes those antiquated concepts within the context of a racist power matrix? She was tempted, but didn't as her comments would only be wasted on this audience.

"Yeah, it's a shame, Marty seemed like a pretty decent guy," Lyle said, while really thinking, *Who can really be surprised by what some nigger might do. Hell, they kill each other at the drop of a hat, so what's so shocking that one of them kills their honkey boss. So Marty spoke good English and came off like a white person. He still had that wild baboon in him like they all do.*

Skeets, who had been quietly listening, finally spoke up, "Marty didn't kill anybody. And I don't think Hap, as crazy as he is, did either."

His three colleagues were surprised by Skeets' declaration. Lyle thought to himself, *If anyone would be quick to suspect a black guy of some crime, it would be a product of the Old South like Skeets. His forefathers, after all had fought a war to keep the darkies locked up.*

Instead Lyle asked, "But how can you say that, Skeets? You've seen the news reports."

"You think that jackass Warren Lush won't go out half-cocked with a half-baked story if it means getting a scoop? What are the facts? I haven't seen or heard any facts other than the police want to question Marty and Hap."

"But both Marty and Hap ran. That makes them look guilty, doesn't it?" Libby asked.

"Maybe, maybe not. Nobody's heard hide nor hair from Hap, so who knows what's going on in that scrambled brain of his. And the fact that Marty ran from the cops, well let me tell you, he wouldn't be the first innocent black man I ever saw run from the police, especially when the media's already tried and convicted him. The whole thing smells rotten and just plain doesn't make sense," Skeets stated.

"I'll tell you what I'll do, I'll bet fifty grand that that those two boys didn't murder nobody. Any takers?" he asked.

Lori, Libby and Lyle turned back to their desks, silenced by Skeets' challenge.

Chapter 19

Blood

Martin felt himself being hauled out of the Hummer. Each of his two escorts had him by an arm, bum-rushing him up a flight of steps.

"Take this stupid pillowcase off," Martin's muffled voice demanded. "I know exactly where we're going—Building C, apartment 2F!"

"You want me to pimp slap you, bitch," he heard Omar XJE's wound-up voice saying.

Martin heard the sound of a door being unlocked as he was ushered into apartment 2F. As the pillowcase was finally removed, a whiff of spoiled food and stale gangi smoke assailed his nose. With the shades tightly drawn over the window, the room was dim but he saw, against the far wall, a mattress on the bare floor, strewn with articles of clothing and other litter. A beat-up sofa with the springs showing through the torn upholstery was placed in front of a cabinet containing a 36 inch Sony TV and home entertainment system, including VCR and digital CD player and state-of-the-art Bose speakers.

"So who the fuck are you working for? The cops or Hu?" Martin snarled, getting right to the point. He had nothing to fear, having nothing left to lose.

Omar, sitting on the sofa with one of the helpmates who had accompanied him in the Hummer, screwed up his face. "Who's fucking Hu?"

"So are you bounty hunters for the police then?" Martin angrily asked.

Omar burst out laughing. "You are a crazy whacked nigga. Hey, Raze, you hear that? We be bounty hunters. Why don't you turn me in and I'll turn you in and we be rich?"

Martin turned and saw the person addressed as Raze leaning against a wooden kitchen table and holding the pillowcase. Raze didn't laugh or respond but just stared hard at Martin. And even though he didn't smile, Martin could see between his thick, parted lips a row of lustrous gold caps, from which a toothpick protruded. His head was covered with a blue bandanna knotted in front, reminding Martin of Aunt Jemima. He wore a black t-shirt with **EVERLAST** in big white letters across the front. His baggy hip-hop blue jeans slid halfway down his ass so that the TOMMY HILFINGER label on his jockey underwear was prominently displayed. The jeans pooled around his untied, tan Timberlands. He wasn't decorated with the usual B-boy accoutrements, the earrings, diamond nose stud, the diamond infested platinum Rolex or a gold basket weave necklace. His face was unadorned, except for the thin scraggly goatee and a scar as thick as a caterpillar running from behind his right ear to the middle of his throat.

The ice in Raze's black eyes made Martin slightly uncomfortable, but he wasn't about to show it. "Look, you little pickaninny," he said to Omar XJE, "I'll cut right to it. My name is Martin Stallworth and my brother is Henry Stallowrth. Evidently you know him by the silly street name, Trex. So I think the last thing you wanna be doing is fucking with Trex's brother. Now where is he?"

Omar grinned as he said, "He's standing right behind ya, Poindexter." Martin turned. Standing in the entryway that led from the front door to this room was a black man behind a pair of etiole Ray-Bans and wearing a black wool parka with Sean John's white signature gracing the left breast. In his right hand he held a leather leash attached to a heavy chain collar, around the thick neck of brindled pit bull.

"Hello, Henry," Martin said grimly, with the faintest hope in his voice.

Henry didn't say anything but walked past Martin, slightly brushing against him as he passed.

Dookie, the homey sitting next to Omar and wearing cheap wrap-around shades and a dark knit cap pulled down to his eyes to hide the fact that he was all of sixteen, leaped up to offer his seat to da man himself, Trex.

Omar looked at Henry and guffawed. "You frontin' me, Trex? You never tole me you had a bubba."

"Once I thought I did, but not anymore, Omar," he matter-of-factly replied.

Omar grimaced. "C'mon, Trex, you know what I go by now. It's XJE."

"Omar, man, I can't keep up with all your name changes. Last month it was Trey Sheek and before that it was Jail-O. Why don't you go back to what they use to call you in high school, Flap Jaws?"

"Why you wanna go by a car name anyhow?" asked Dookie, who had moved from the sofa to the mattress. "How 'bout namin' yo'sef Mercedes?"

"Listen here, little sugar britches, I'm sleek and powerful and I know how to pounce on pussy like nobody's bidness. Sometimes super sweet, sometimes super freak—like a Jag. Hey, maybe that oughta be my handle...Jag."

"Give it up, Omar," Dookie said.

"Hey, you dis me again and I'm gonna slap down your roody pooh candy ass in broad daylight right in front of yo momma!"

Martin stood in the middle of the room, holding his left arm, listening to the banter and completely ignored by Henry, Omar and Dookie, as if he were invisible. Raze, though, continued to stare a hole through him.

"I seen him," Raze muttered.

"What you say, Raze?" Omar asked.

"I say I seen this joker before. His face in the paper today. Killed somebody."

"Shit, yeah, now I recognize you," Omar squealed. "Saw you on TV news last night. Threw your boss out the window. Aiight! Big up with that!"

"So they're after you for murder, huh?" Henry asked casually. Martin had the feeling that Henry had known all along about the news reports.

"I didn't kill anybody."

"Trex, your bro's a loc'd-out G. But he don't look the case. He looks a little too bougie."

Martin guessed that "bougie" was short for bourgeoisie.

"Yeah, his shit's off the hinges, ain't it?" Henry responded as he patted the sofa cushion and said, "C'mon, Buster" to the pit bull, who jumped up into his master's lap.

"Funny, how the tables turn," Henry continued, as he patted Buster's head. "What goes around sure comes around, don't it? He used to be Mr. Straight-laced, Mr. All-American, and a Goody-Two-Shoes. Worked for Ronald Reagan's campaign, if you can dig that. The word 'oreo' has his picture next to it in the dictionary. Always making the grade, making his parents proud. What would Mama think about you now, Martin, my brother?"

"She would think that her son is in trouble and needs his brother's help," Martin steely replied.

"Oh, and what would she have thought when you jumped me at her funeral? Huh? And you got the nerve to slink in here and ask for my help, without so much as giving me my props, after not talking to me for five years, after embarrassing me in front of my friends and family. What did you call me at Mama's funeral? 'A no-account drug dealer' or something like that, wasn't it?

"Well you go back to Wall Street and Uncle Tom one of those rich white dicks you sold your soul to...but you can't go back to them cause now they won't have nothing to do with your murdering, nigger ass. You were gonna prove to them that a black man could be just as stuck-up, stiff, stuffy and money-grubbing as any of them. But now look at you. You ain't no Sidney Poitier talking mutual funds at some cocktail party. Guess who ain't coming to dinner now? You one of us again. Ha! Just another punk gansta thug running from the law. Get the fuck outta here, Martin!"

Martin stood in the middle of the room, the center of Henry and his gang's collective disdain. Even Buster seemed to eye him with contempt. Martin nodded his head. "Okay," he said as he turned and walked toward the front door.

"Hold it," Henry suddenly ordered.

Martin stopped and looked at him.

"What's that on your hand there? That ring?"

Martin looked at the ring and said, "Pops gave it to me. The ring they gave him at the Olympic Trials."

He looked at Henry and Henry looked at him for a few seconds. "I thought I recognized it," Henry finally said. "Yeah, you always were the apple of Pop's eye," he added, without the ironic edge in his voice. 'I got his name but you got his pride. How's the old man doing anyway?"

"He was doing a lot better until he saw my face on the 11:00 news last night." Once again he turned to leave.

"Stay right there, Martin," Henry commanded. "Hang here for a minute. Raze, Omar, Dookie, ya'll split."

All three rose and did as told. As he was leaving, Omar said to Martin, "Trex sorta smudged your shine, didn't he? Welcome to the 'hood,' Poindexter." He chuckled as he left.

"What did you come to me for, Martin? What do you think a thug like me can do to keep the cops off your ass?"

"It's not the cops I'm most worried about. The people who put me in this spot want my hide too."

"Who's that."

"It's too much to explain."

"Listen, jackass, you come in here and fuck my world upside down and ask me to help you. I wanna know what's going down. So plant your butt and spill."

Martin grimaced, all too familiar with that big brother, imperious tone. But he sat on the mattress and recounted to his brother how Hap had come to his apartment, all in a panic after seeing Dick Moore fall from his window; how Hap had the Lodestar documents and how he intended to give them to Hu; how he, Martin, had taken the documents from Hap and hid them in his refrigerator and then the news report a couple of hours later. He told how he had run until he ended up at Mihra's apartment and described the break-in and that now Mihra was being held hostage until he handed over the Lodestar papers. "They told me if I went to the police they would kill her," Martin concluded. A long groan/sigh signified the end of his story. Hearing himself tell it, Martin found it hard to believe it had all really happened to him.

Henry studied Martin. He shook his head. "Humph" was all he said.

"Henry, I don't need anything from you but a place to stay for a day or two—until I can figure out what to do. You made it clear how you feel about me; so believe me, I don't plan to hang around long." Martin didn't mention that he also thought he would be protected from Hu's goons here on the Seezer's turf.

Henry rubbed Buster's head and stared at the floor while Martin sat before him, like a supplicant before a prince. "C'mon, let's go," he said to Martin finally.

When they exited the apartment, Omar and Raze were standing in the breezeway outside. "I'm heading over to my place," Henry said to them. "Ya'll hold down the fort till I get back."

"Hey, bubba," Omar said to Martin, "don't take that punch in the stomach personal. My thing is if you're gonna be a monkey, be a gorilla. Dig?" Omar's round, too close together eyes went wide and wild.

Martin and Henry walked around the corner to the back parking lot, Buster leading the way, and approached Henry's Mercedes Benz 600, stealth black, tinted and kitted out. It looked as out of place in that parking lot as an M-1 tank.

Henry unlocked the car doors with his keypad clicker. Buster hopped in the back seat but stuck his blockhead between the front seats, smiling so that his tongue lolled from his mouth. Henry started the car and turned on the CD player. Martin was pleased but not too surprised that instead of some hip-hop, gangsta rap, misty Miles Davis flowed from the four speakers. He remembered how Henry had been such a jazz freak in high school.

Henry drove south from the Malcolm X and after a couple of miles turned east on White Plains Road. "So how did you know where to find me," he asked Martin.

"Pops told me."

"How did he know?"

"I dunno." Martin didn't tell Henry that a buddy of Pops who worked as a cop for the Public Housing Authority had told him that his son was the Caesar of all the Seezers and was ruling an empire that encompassed the Malcolm X.

"How long you been—" Martin paused to find the right word, "been hanging at the Malcolm X?"

"Came here after I left home. What was that, eight, nine years ago? Moved in with a friend."

Martin remembered how Henry had left home just after he had finished high school. Just after Pops had discovered that ounce of powder in his closet, just after their mother had started chemotherapy. "Get out of this house!" Pops had screamed at Henry in the middle of the night, the night that Henry had left home for good. "You're no son of mine. No son of mine is a dope dealer. Get out!"

Pops stood at the doorway to the bedroom Henry and Martin shared, in only a T-shirt and underwear, saliva spraying from his mouth as he bellowed once more, "Get out!"

Henry interrupted Martin's reverie, "This here's my crib," as he turned onto a side street off White Plains Road. He pulled to the curb in front of a two story, red brick townhouse on a street lined with identical two-storied, red brick townhouses. The street was free of litter and the yards were all well kept. Not the sort of place one would expect to find the "lord of the Seezers."

They exited the car and the first thing Buster did was lift his leg to mark his turf. Martin noticed a kid sitting on the stoop in front of Henry's place. He wore a dark-blue nylon warm-up suit with the ubiquitous Nike checkmark on the front. A skintight stocking cap covered his shaved head.

"Yo, wazhapnin?" Henry said to him. Henry and the kid walked away from Martin and engaged in a brief conversation, during which Henry pulled a wad of bills from his pocket, peeled a few off and handed them to the kid.

"He watches my house while I'm away," Henry explained as he turned off the alarm system and set about the task of unlocking his front door. The barred front windows reminded Martin of a fancy jailhouse.

The interior of Henry's house was minimally but tastefully done. It lacked the gansta gilded trash and silver flash and could have been a layout in some House and Garden article…"Eligible Decor." They stepped into a foyer with newly laid marble tile on the floor and reset lights in the ceiling. A few paces up the hallway, the parquet wooden floors were freshly finished, and to the left was the kitchen.

New granite countertops, cherry wood cabinets, a block island with inlaid electric range and a sub-zero refrigerator.

"Nice kitchen," Martin remarked.

"Finally got the damn thing finished last month," Henry said. "Had to knock out a wall to expand it."

"You cook?"

"Hey, don't you remember the meals I'd throw down when Mama got too sick to cook? That mean Chicken Kiev I mastered?"

"Sure. I'm glad you never noticed me shoveling it to Midge under the table." Midge, was the family Pekinese.

Martin was glad to see a smile, as brief as lightening against a storm cloud, brighten Henry's face, occluded by the sunglasses.

They walked down three steps to the sunken den, a large room dominated by the arrangement of overstuffed sofa and chairs, all covered in white fabric. The eggshell white paint on the bare walls was fresh enough that Martin could still faintly smell the latex. The room's windows were all covered with white chenille drapes, but the array of track lighting, which Henry turned on with a clap of his hands, kept the room well lit. A chrome and glass cabinet was laden with a wide-screened TV and deluxe stereo, with a DVD sound system. The real leopard skin rug under the chrome and glass coffee table was the only off-the-run touch to the otherwise antiseptic decor.

They went across the room to the staircase and up to the second floor where Henry directed Martin into a room with nothing but a bed and a chest of drawers. "Here's a room you can stay in. Some sheets and a blanket are in the closet there. The bathroom's straight down the hall."

Martin nodded his head and then looked directly at Henry and said, "Thanks, man. I, uh…" he paused, searching for the right way to say that he owed him one.

"You can chill here a day or two. After that, you're on your own. Last thing I need is for the heat bustin' my ass trying to bust yours." Henry nipped in the bud whatever brotherly sentiment was about to blossom forth from Martin.

Henry walked down the hallway to another room as Martin sat on his bed and wondered what to do next. His first thought was to change the clothes that he had been wearing for eighteen straight hours. Although he was bigger than Henry, he figured that he might have some of that loose, hip-hop garb that he could fit into.

He walked down the hall to Henry's room and he saw the room was not very large and was mostly filled by the waterbed. But unlike the rest of the house, it had a personal touch. The room was, in fact, touched all over, and was cloyed with souvenirs, mementos and photographs.

A somewhat deflated basketball that Henry had kept after his high school team had won the Massapequa city championships sat in a glass case on the dresser. A blown-up poster of Bob Marley that Martin remembered from when Henry lived at home covered most of one wall. Five different chess sets from Henry's days of competing in the Nassau County public school tournaments were neatly arranged on the credenza.

In the corner was a two-foot high stack of vintage albums from Curtis Mayfield to Curtis Blow. And everywhere were photographs, a score of them. Some were the same family photographs that Martin had seen at Pops' house. Others were not so familiar, like the one of Henry, Omar and three other G's kickin' it at Jones Beach, the stem of a Colt 45 bottle stuck between Omar's golden fangs.

But for the most part, the-items in the room brought back to Martin the Henry he had grown up with. Not the Caesar of all Seezers, the ganster prince, but the brother who had taken the training wheels off Martin's first bike and had given him a push. The brother who had knelt over Martin as he had lain in the street after having been hit by a car that fortunately had only been going twenty miles an hour. Martin could still remember how briny Henry's tears had tasted as they had fallen onto his face. The brother who had beat-up the neighborhood bully who had for six straight mornings extorted Martin's lunch money on the school bus. The brother who had taught him how to kick a football, catch a baseball, shoot a basketball. The brother who had been walking next to him on a street in Massapequa when a carload of white kids had screeched to a halt just to hurl racial slurs and beer bottles at them. The car had chased Martin and Henry for over five blocks before they had finally lost it.

In that room, at that moment, his brother had come back to Martin, pinched from a time warp, the memory of him immediate and fleshed-out. And then he saw it. "Wow, look at that!" he exclaimed. On the dresser was a framed photo of Henry and him, Henry's arm around his shoulder, after they had won the city summer league's two-on-two basketball tournament. They had beaten fifteen different teams to take first prize—one of the proudest, happiest moments in Martin's life.

Martin, without giving any thought to it, strode across the room to pick the photograph up. As he did, he saw the Glock 9 that had been stashed behind it. Martin stared at it as if he had seen a coiled rattlesnake. The handgun snuffed his trip down Memory Lane. He immediately set the picture down.

"Whadaya want?" Henry brusquely asked.

"I was wondering if you had an extra set of clothes I might fit into." Martin was suddenly feeling as deflated as the basketball in the glass case.

Henry rummaged in his closet. "Here, try these," he said as he handed Martin a blue sweat suit. Martin took the clothes and went to the other room and changed into them. He then lay on the bed. Weariness hugged his head.

He tried to forget the Glock 9 because seeing it had made him realize that his brother was now a total stranger. And then for no reason at all, he remembered the first time he had ever flown a kite. He remembered Henry's face, his snaggle-toothed smile because he had lost his two front teeth, as Henry had watched the kite flutter and flap as it took to the April wind like some exotic, princely bird that really didn't want to leave the two boys. It had been orange and red against the blue of the sky.

"Run, Martin, run!" Henry had shouted. "Let the string unwind. Don't look back. Help the wind!"

And then the string had gone taut and the cross sticks had bent and Martin had jumped high in the air as if the kite were pulling him with it—like a proud, magic bird spreading itself to the wind.

And when Martin had finally stopped, Henry had hurried to him. Martin vividly remembered his brother's puckish grin, his little nose turning up, his eyes as brown and dancing as their mother's and the small indenture between his eyes, where a lump of sugar could be placed and it would stay there. Henry had hugged his brother and Martin had kissed that place between his brother's eyes.

And the kite had suddenly dipped once, shuddered and then zoomed into the sun. The string had zipped through Martin's fingers, stinging them—Martin remembered that.

And then Martin was with the kite, as high as the kite, the cross sticks against his chest, the string the only thing still connecting him to this earth.

He had fallen sound asleep.

CHAPTER 20

RED NUT

HE OPENED ONE EYE JUST IN TIME TO SEE THE digital clock click to 3:38 p.m. He was surprised he had slept for over three hours. Then he yawned, stretched his calf muscles, pointed his toes, smacked his lips and rubbed his eyes. When he rose, he walked over to the window and swept aside the drapes that covered it in order to raise the window and let the fresh air come wafting through the guard bars. A wind chime clinked from the backyard next door. He lay back down on the bed and watched the phantom play of late afternoon light and shadow as it wandered across the ceiling—and thought about Mihra.

He sat up on the edge of the bed and as he rubbed his foot, he idly stared out the window at the bright spears of grass and a puffy milkweed—still thinking of Mihra. In the recesses of his mind he noted a birdbath was in the backyard, probably placed there by the prior occupant of the house. It was made of stone and in the shape of a naughty Cupid and surrounded by irises as stern as schoolmarms. As he continued his daydreaming, a fat little robin hopped into the bath and dunked five or six times. A spasm of wet feathers sent rainbow colored water droplets high over its head.

As picturesque as the early spring scene out the window was, Martin wasn't really seeing it because his thoughts were of Mihra.

One of his considerations was that maybe the thing to do was meet with Hu, explain what had happened to him and tell him that he had placed the Lodestar stuff in his refrigerator freezer but that the police might have searched his apartment and found them.

Yes, maybe the thing to do was just be completely up-front with the guy and make it clear that neither I nor Mihra had anything to do with any of this and posed no threat to him. Since Hap told me the address where Hu worked the last time I saw him...speaking of Hap, where in the hell could he be? Martin wondered. *In jail? Anyway, I can't worry about Hap as I have Mihra to worry about now.*

Okay, so I meet with Hu and tell him the truth. Would that really do any good? Martin asked himself. *Wouldn't Hu think that Mihra and I knew too much and try to erase us? Hu would know that the only way I could get myself off the hook about Moore's death would be to tell the police what I knew about Hap, Lodestar, and Hu.*

It then dawned on Martin that Hu was pursing him not only for Lodestar but also to insure that Martin told no tales—and the only way to insure that was to make sure he was dead. Martin shook his head, feeling absolutely powerless against Hu—he had no counter, no way to fight back. What added to his feeling of helplessness was that he couldn't seek help from the police and he alone was no match for Hu and his minions. Hu had all the cards, including the queen of hearts—Mihra.

Then, suddenly, an idea so obvious, so dumb and simple that it made perfect sense, almost slapped Martin in the face. The idea jolted him and caused him to jump up from the bed. He had a way to fight Hu; he **did** have a force to counteract Hu's. Help was almost literally staring him in the face and was all around him—The Seezers, one of the meanest, most notorious gangs in The Big "Rotten" Apple.

What if I met with Hu and a few of the Seezers were there as back up? Probably Raze and two or three more like him should do the trick. In fact, why not take it a step further and say to Hu, "Listen, motherfucker, if you don't let Mihra go, I'm gonna let my comrades here turn you into a nice big bowl of chop suey." But would Henry go along with his idea? Would he let me "borrow" his posse for a showdown with Hu?

Then Martin had an idea, an even better idea. Quickly he sprang from the bed all excited. *Forget the truth. Forget the threats, go to Hu and...*Before Martin could completely finish his thought, he heard somebody enter the apartment.

"Yo!" the person yelled.

When he left the bedroom and entered the den, he encountered Omar who anxiously asked him, "Where's Trex?" Now Omar wasn't wearing a hat and his Afro had been tightly braided into rows of small zigzags traversing his skull. The ends dangled down the back of his neck.

"I dunno," Martin answered. "Hey, man, I dig the do."

"I don't have time to exchange wid yo, dickrider. I need Trex."

"He's not here and I don't know where he went," Martin responded."

"Shit!" Omar hollered as he swung his arm through the air in frustration. "Where'd everybody go? Raze gone. Dookie gone. Bullethead dispear. Damn, is some kinda thug holiday goin' on?"

Omar let out another loud and long, "sheeeit!" and shook his head as he scratched the back of it. Then his eyeballs slowly rotated up until they locked onto Martin. "I guess that leaves you, Poindexter. C'mon wid me, man. I need yo help."

"What the fuck you talking about?"

"Don't get bugged. I need you for sumptin'. I need for you to ride shotgun while I make a drop-off."

"You're outta your mind if you think I'm going anywhere with you."

"C'mon, bro. I'll return the favor. You never know when you might need me." That last comment struck a chord since Martin knew he might very well need Omar and his crew if he was going to confront Hu. Give and ye shall receive. "What is it you want me to do?" Martin asked.

"Just ride with me, that's all."

"Where to?"

"I gotta go back to the Malcolm X. Drop sumptin' off. Take a minute."

Martin considered for a moment. "All right."

"Aiight! Let's go."

When they left Henry's house and walked toward the Hummer, a group of neighborhood urchins had gathered around it, awestruck. "Get your turd hands off my ride, you little chili pimps," Omar yelled.

"Hey, where you get them purple gators?" one of the boys asked Omar, referring to his crocodile shoes.

"Out of yo mamma's pussy, that's where." Omar raised his hand in a threatening manner and the pack scattered.

Once in the vehicle, Omar cranked up the tunes. A raspy-voiced rapper waxed rhapsodic about his "hoochie." "Still in the pussy/Then acted like it slipped out/ She said/'Pardon the puddle'/Spread open her cheeks/pushed hard in her butthole/Wasn't a bad date at all."

"Can you turn that shit off," Martin said in disgust.

"What you talkin' 'bout, Poindexter? That's mad ill. Kid Capone, my personal fave. Ghetto fabulous!"

After Martin reached over and turned off the music, Omar said, "You are crazy mean…but you did say you dug my braids, didn't you?" Omar smiled, causing his freckles to jump over the oily hillocks of his cheeks.

"Oh yeah, really dig it," Martin answered with a turned down mouth.

"Got the job done at the Magical Hands. I highly recommend it for gettin' flossy. Got their own pomade for finger waves. There's three things you don't ever change: mechanics, doctors and beauticians."

"You really are on the cutting edge, aren't you?" Martin said sourly.

"You damn right! I'm so ahead of my time, my parents haven't even met."

Martin couldn't repress a grin, however hard he tried to twist it into a sneer.

"I'm so wise, I'm gonna tell you what the three C's to love and happiness are. You wanna know?"

"Would it matter if I said no?"

"Them three C's be Cuban cigars, cell phones and Cristal. You got those, man, then you know you be spankin' ill-matic."

"Just cut the crap, okay? And tell me where we're going and what we're doing."

"I tole you already. We're goin' to make a drop-off at the Malcolm X."

"Drop what off? Dope?"

"Yeah. What you think I am, the Avon Lady?"

"Where is it?"

"It's in the back. Under the seat."

"Goddamn, what if the cops pull us over?"

"Why in the fuck do ya think I'm only goin' thirty miles an hour? The only reason I'm a be pulled over by the rollers is a DWB."

"What's a DWB?"

"Drivin' While Black."

Martin finally succumbed and let the chuckles flow out of his mouth. "No, you're not conspicuous at all in this modern-day pimp mobile."

"Don't you worry your pretty head about that. Cops on this beat know who I am and who the Seezers be. They also know who butters their bread. They paid good to leave us alone, as long we don't cap civilians or nutin' like that."

The Hummer finally turned into the Malcolm X and meandered through streets that seemed gray and scruffy even in springtime. Omar pulled to the curb.

"All right, Poindexter, here's the script. That's where the drop-off gonna happen, that apartment yonder, number ninety-eight on the door. See it?" Omar pointed to an apartment about thirty yards across the way. Number ninety-eight was easy to spot because it was the only one that had daffodils and tulips planted in front, unlikely as that was.

"The mack daddy we're dealin' wit goes by the handle, 'Red Nut.'"

"All you jokers gotta have a name, don't you?

"I knew the boy in high school. Real name's Dewayne. But he'd pull a gun on you if you call him that. Took up Red Nut after doin' his bid at Riker's.

"Now here's how it's gonna go down, Poindexter. I'll go in first, just to make sure everything be cool and all lined up. You keep your eye on the window and when you see me wave, you come on with the powder. And..."

"Hold it!" Martin exclaimed. "What's this bullshit about me going in? I just came along for the ride, remember? I don't wanna be involved in any way with any transaction. You understand?"

"Hey man, all I need is for you to bring the shit in when I'm ready to cut the deal. You can stand there and watch me work. Just be an innocent sucker. But I don't want to go walkin' in with the suitcase unless I know for sure they got their dough and ready to deal. Plus, I gotta let 'em know who you is since they haven't seen your boot-ugly face before. Red Nut gets spooked easy. Now c'mon, that ain't too much to ask of you to just mule one for me?"

"Okay," Martin muttered with acute irritation. "But you're gonna owe me big-time after this one, chump."

Omar then moved into the back of the Hummer and lifted up the back seat, where a stainless steel suitcase was hidden. He brought it up and put it in Martin's lap. "Now, when I give the signal from the window, you come on with the shit. Got it?"

"Yeah, yeah..."

Omar then reached over Martin's lap to open the glove compartment. "Here, you're gonna need this," he said as he held out a handgun, a Smith and Wesson six-shooter, police issue, to Martin. "Careful, Poindexter, 'cause it's already loaded."

Martin threw his hands up and let them fall hard on the suitcase in his lap. His face screwed up in aggravation. "Now why in the fuck am I gonna need that?"

"Take it, man, for your own good. This thing should go down smooth but you never know what might happen. Now, take it."

Reluctantly, Martin took the gun. It felt heavy, cold—a thing unto itself—magical and mean.

"Okay, now be watchin' for me from the window." Omar then exited the Hummer and pimp-strolled to apartment ninety-eight.

Martin trained his eye on the window. He clicked his teeth together and tapped the barrel of the gun against the metal case. The metallic rhythm and clicking teeth only made him more anxious. The tension from watching and waiting invigorated him, reminding him of the times when he was trying to execute a big bond trade. *What in the hell is Omar doing in there?* he wondered, tapping and clicking even faster now.

Finally, Omar's head appeared in the window and he waved Martin to come. "There's my cue," Martin said as he shoved the gun through his belt on the right side of his back, got a good grip on the suitcase, took a deep breath and calmly left the vehicle.

He walked to the apartment with an exaggerated confidence, as if he were strolling across the Whorman Skeller trading floor. "Yo, pizza boy! Over here" came from one of the balconies. "Hey, Stymie, what ya deliverin'? You fuckin' slum hustler!" Martin moved the suitcase over to his left hand so he could reach for his gun if he had to.

When he reached the patio porch and rapped once on the door, he breathed easier, even admired the tulips and noticed that someone had taken the time to paint the metal lounge furniture a hopeful blue and a lively green—even the bicycle chains that fastened the furniture to the brick wall were painted!

Maybe they were thugs, but at least they made a stab at the gloom squatting on every other apartment patio, Martin was thinking when the sound of what he thought was gunfire nearby distracted him. Expecting a bullet to whiz past his ear any second, he was relieved when the door finally opened.

Out of the skillet and into the fire. A black man, straddling a chair turned backwards, was the first thing he saw. The red leather suit, a tuxedo with tails, and the bright red skunk streak running down the center of his head blocked Martin's view. Then Martin moved his eyes to the eight-inch, serrated hunting knife in the man's hand, the tip of which was just a flick-of-the-wrist from piercing the scrawny neck of Omar, who was kneeling in front of Red Nut, and whose other hand gripped Omar's sweating forehead. Omar's eyes were bugged out, hopping from the knife at his throat to Martin and then back to the knife.

And then BAM! Martin was kissing the coarse wool of a hook rug. Someone or something had jumped him from behind and slammed him to the floor. Suddenly screaming and shouting erupted from all four corners of the room as a cockroach hurriedly sauntered past Martin's busted and bleeding nose.

"Five-O, man! Five-O!" he heard someone shouting. "Got a goddamned po-lice gun!"

Whatever it was that had its knee against his back pulled his wrists behind him. Then he felt something cold and tight around his wrists and heard the click of handcuffs.

"Yo, man, he ain't no narc!" he heard Omar shouting. "Leave the dude alone."

Martin's neck then pulled the rest of his body from the floor. "Mu' fockin' pig," sounded in his ear; the mouth speaking close, hot and wet.

When Martin was slung by the neck over in front of the chair, it gave him an opportunity to more closely observe Red Nut. His long wavy hair was shiny black except for the red coxcomb and fell past his shoulders. From his chin hung a small billygoat wisp of hair. Next he realized that Red Nut wasn't wearing a shirt under his leather tuxedo jacket, and a cravat of solid gold drooped over the tiny carpet-knots of fuzz covering his curving pecks. A pinpoint diamond dollar sign was stuck on his nose, while a gold dollar sign swung from his ear and still another one ran the entire length of his right-hand knuckles. To complete the outfit, Red Nut wore cherry-red tinted, round, old-fashioned, wire-rimmed glasses.

As Red Nut looked Martin over, Martin tasted blood dripping from his nose and over his lip and heard Omar say over and over, "I'm tellin' ya, the man's not a roller!"

Red Nut mumbled something and the only word he understood was, "wire." The thing behind Martin then came around to his front and then he saw that the cold, hard point against his neck had been the end of an A-K 47 barrel—it was being held by a black kid wearing a black stocking hose, fashioned into a skull-cap. Then the kid slowly and deliberately unzipped Martin's pants with one hand while the other held the gun barrel to his face. Somehow he managed to pull Martin's sweat pants, jockey underwear and all, to his ankles. The he ran his fingers up around and under Martin's sweatshirt and then down under his nuts.

Martin glanced toward Omar and almost darkly quipped to him, "At least we're keeping our chins up—a knife stuck under yours and an A-K 47 under mine," but held his tongue. The boy finished his frisk of Martin by ramming a finger up Martin's butthole, just to make sure nothing was hidden up there.

At this point, an elderly black lady, her gray hair pulled back, and wearing glasses with one stem missing, wobbled into the room.

"Get out of my house!" she hoarsely screamed. Her earth tone skin changed color when she saw Martin standing there with an A-K 47 fixed on him. Martin was too shocked to be embarrassed about being bottomless.

"I don't want no killin' in my house!" she hollered. Red Nut grunted and some boy wearing a shower cap came from somewhere and grabbed hold of the lady, who began screaming even louder, "Help! Help!" as she reached for a picture of a young man in a Navy uniform on the wall and smashed it against her attacker's head, the shower cap his only protection against the blow. Red Nut chuckled and then the boy raised a hand and slapped the old woman across the head hard enough that her head swiveled and her bun came undone.

"Help! Police! Help!" she kept yelling but now with a much weaker voice. The boy whacked her hard against the face again, her face going blank and her glasses flying onto the sofa over which she had placed a lace doily.

"Goddamn you, you little son-of-a-bitch!" Martin yelled, his vocal chord pushing against the gun barrel. The old lady might have tottered over except that the kid gripped her neck and drug her out of sight and there was silence.

The attention turned back to Martin as Omar said, his voice full of exasperation, "Check his wallet. He's not police, I'm tellin' ya."

Red Nut pointed toward Martin's pants and Martin's escort bent down, riffled through the pockets until he found Martin's wallet and tossed it to Red Nut, who flapped it open so that the kite's tail of credit cards unfurled. After throwing out all its contents, including credit card receipts and a hundred and fifty dollars cash, he studied Martin through the thick, tinted lens of his glasses, his refracted eyes larger than plums.

"Trex never gonna forgive you for fuckin' with his brother," Omar said, his eyes turning up toward Red Nut behind him.

"What you say," Red Nut said, looking down at Omar.

"The cat you're messin' with is Trex's brother. Check the last name on the driver's license there. Stallworth. That's Trex's name, too. You're fuckin' up bad, Red Nut."

The mention of Trex must have made an impression because Red Nut finally waved his hand, signaling Martin's bodyguard to un-handcuff him. With his hands now free, Martin immediately pulled up his pants then wiped the back of his wrist against his upper lip where his blood was now cascading over it in a steady flow.

Red Nut put his blade away and let Omar go. Quickly, Omar darted past Martin to the suitcase, which everyone seemed to have forgot about during the ruckus.

Casually, Red Nut picked up Martin's gun, popped open the chamber and emptied all the bullets into his hand before he tossed it to Martin, saying, "Der's ya pea shooter. I ain't no pistol teef." Martin took it and fell back onto the sofa, lightheaded and cross-eyed dizzy from gazing down the barrel of an assault rifle.

Omar, now all business, knelt on the floor and opened the suitcase. Inside were thirty or so see-through plastic packets filled with tiny crystals that sparkled under the light—perfect little bombs waiting to go off inside some rotten-toothed, drooling addict's head.

Omar took one of the ounces and tossed it over to Red Nut who didn't even think about catching it but looked at it on the floor where it had landed, glancing at it carelessly like it was a dove that had fallen dead from the sky.

"Check out the boy," he said to the shower-capped kid, who scampered to retrieve the heroin. The kid opened the baggie, touched the powder, tasted it, smelt it, and rubbed a pinch between his fingers. His teachers at school had probably never seen such concentration on his scornful face. Then he pulled a little bottle from his black, nylon jacket with **CHRIS ROCK DOES THE APOLLO** emblazoned in large, red letters on the back. He dropped a pinch into the bottle and watched the color of the liquid as it changed color. Next he held the bottle up for Red Nut to see and nodded his head. After which, he hustled to a closet, wheeled out scales like the ones you weigh cargo on, took the suitcase from Omar and turned it upside down over the scale, dumping out all the packets.

After peering at the number on the meter, he said to Red Nut, "It's about right—maybe just a little short." He wrapped his arms around himself, nodded his head and smiled smugly, pleased at how good he had gotten at telling good shit from bad shit.

Red Nut sucked through his teeth for a moment, his head balanced on his interlocking hands, the apex of the triangle formed by his arms resting on the chair back. "Give ya se'teen for it," he said to Omar as if even that were too much.

But Martin noticed how Red Nut's right leg jiggled, a sign that he was anxious for a deal. Even though Martin was new to the trade, he would have wagered that Red Nut had already pre-sold every single one of those ounces for twice what he was offering to buy them.

"No way," Martin shouted before Omar could respond to Red Nut's offer. "We want twenty-three." Martin nonchalantly flicked with his fingers a string of blood that had come from his leaky nose. He had pulled the number, twenty-three thousand out of thin air, his price having less rational basis than Red Nut's. But Martin was steady enough now to recognize a play when he saw one.

Red Nut turned and glared at Martin, as if Martin had just called his mother a ho bitch, voodoo witch.

"You funny, man. Who you s'posed to be, Eddie Murphy?" His leg was really jiggling now.

Fast on the uptake, Omar said, "Twenty-three, Red Nut. This shit's premium import. Hardly stepped on. Cut with lactose and no baby laxative."

"Shit, you crazy. You disin' me, bitch. I ain't ne'er paid dat much for powder. Most I e'er paid be twenty, uncut."

Well good, Martin thought, *now we got a floor under the price; we know that he'll at least pay twenty.*

"I tell you what, Omar," Martin said as he contemplated a corner of the ceiling and scratched his head, "the more I think about it, there's nothing on the street near this good. We better offer it at twenty-five and not a penny less."

Red Nut leaped from his chair and kicked it over on the way up. "You fuckin' wid me, nigga? Trex ain't ne'er grift me dat hard," he said as he faced Martin, both fists clenched, his teeth biting down on his bottom lip. His two peons tensed up and got poised tight.

Martin reached for a pack of cigarettes lying on the coffee table and popped one into his mouth, even though he didn't smoke. "Anybody got a light?"

"Shit on you, mutherfucka!" Red Nut bellowed as he swiped the cigarette from Martin's mouth. He hovered over Martin, a red-hot heat flash frozen in a black storm cloud. Not the least bit intimidated, or intent on not appearing so, Martin jumped to his feet and stuck his face right back in Red Nut's while Red Nut's two lieutenants waited for their cue to bring the house down. Omar inched closer to the door, apparently thinking that Martin had carried the profit motive a little too far. A neighborhood dog barking in three quarter time was the only sound for half a minute.

But Martin stuck to his guns, or in this case, his hunch that Red Nut was bluffing. Martin just knew that Red Nut was going to cave, he could feel it and he was looking forward to that; especially after Red Nut had bloodied his nose and made him stand there with his pecker hanging out for all to see. Now he meant to return the favor and take Red Nut's pants off, so to speak. "Take it or leave it," Martin said. "That's the deal."

"Take it or leave it, huh? I'm gonna leave it, all right, leave you in your grave, trick daddy!" said Red Nut as his head bobbed back and forth in time with each word that he spat out.

"Well, I guess that does it then," Martin responded and pushed past Red Nut and strolled over to the plastic bags still stacked on the scales. Red Nut's curses pelted Martin's ear rapid fire. "Cum suckin', pig footed, honkey talkin', pussy lickin…"

Ignoring the tirade, Martin calmly crouched down and began packing the bags back into the suitcase. Omar ran over to help him while the two kids fidgeted and shifted their feet as they watched Martin and waited for the word to lullaby Martin's ass. Martin was counting on the magic word "Trex" to ward off Red Nut's threats.

By the time he and Omar had filled half the suitcase, Red Nut had fallen silent. He paced back and forth as he twisted his lips and watched them stow away his lucre. Finally, it happened. "Okay, man, look here. I'll pony up to twenty. But that's it. Take it or leave it, like you like to say."

Martin stopped packing and looked up at him. Martin exhaled heavily, shook his head and said, "You know, this shit's just too good to give away like that and I..."

Red Nut spun on his heels and swatted at an invisible butterfly over his head, his long hair and coattails swirling about. He raked his hand across the kitchen counter behind him and scattered the tea set the old lady had placed there, his gold bracelets jingle-jangling as he did so. After the clitter-clatter and jingle-jangling shatter ended, Red Nut reached his hand toward Martin, his feet spread wide, his red streak spouting sweat beads and his bare chest was heaving. He could have been a soul singer, begging love from the girls in the front row.

"Let me tell ya, I needs that fuckin' boy," he said as his long, gold heavy fingers twisted the air in front of him. "But I can't pay no twenty-five, see? Just can't. You at twenty-five, me at twenty. What say we split it? Call it twenty-two fifty?"

Martin stood up and looked directly at him. "Twenty-three and you're done." He had come full circle back to his original price, just as he always knew he would.

Red Nut's body, rigid with anticipation as if he were about to leap into the air, fell loose, his head turning down and a "sheeee" whisked from his mouth. Then he raised a hand to the boys behind him and said, his head still down and his eyes shut, "Give the mutherfucka the money. Give the doggone man what he wants." Then he angled his head slightly and looked at Martin out of the corner of his eyes. He didn't utter a word but only shook his head back and forth.

The one wearing the shower cap exited into another room and returned carrying a brown paper sack and shoved it at Martin, snarling.

The old lady followed him into the room, shuffling absent-mindedly in her bedroom slippers and softly mumbling, "Anybody seen my dang specs? I knows I put 'em down somewheres here." A mean looking welt had formed on the side of her face and her wooly hair hung wild around her shoulders. Omar picked her glasses up off the couch and handed them to her.

"Got ya dough, now go," Red Nut said he slouched in his chair, his legs sticking straight out and his back to Martin. He sucked through his teeth and ran his fingers over the ridges of his gold collar.

"I'm gonna count it first," Martin said. Red Nut snickered at the ridiculous notion that he might cheat. Martin emptied the sack of hundred-dollar-bill blocks. There were ten bills in each block. And sure enough, he counted only twenty-two blocks. "You're short a G," he said to Red Nut.

Red Nut turned in his chair toward Martin. "Short, huh?" A smile displayed his teeth, as white as coconut meat. He stayed that way for too long which almost convinced Martin that he was going to tell him to kiss his ass as he reached into an inside pocket of his tux.

The bastard's not only going to call my bluff but blow me away too, Martin thought, sure that a handgun was in that pocket. Martin was a fraction of a second away from either hauling ass or having a heart attack. But instead of a gun, Red Nut pulled out the twenty-third stack and tossed it at Martin's feet.

Martin peeled two hundred dollar bills from it, then wadded one of the hundred dollar bills, put it into his mouth and chewed it like it was flank steak, all the while staring at Red Nut as his pretty grin melted away. The two boys gaped at Martin like he was crazy. "Look at that! Eatin' that money like a billygoat."

Even Omar, who had been replacing the ounces with the stacks of money in the suitcase, stopped to gawk at Martin. Then Martin spit the slobbery, balled-up bill into his hand and, after examining it, flung it at the two budding gangsters. They both folded their arms up and hopped away from the moist dough, like it was ostrich shit.

Red Nut pouted at Martin. "Yeah, you a cool jerk, man, a circus clown. Put you on TV. Make a million quick."

Omar handed Martin the loot and they headed out, not rushing but not wasting any time either. But before they split, Martin leaned over to the doddering old woman on the couch, lifted her hand and folded her fingers around the other hundred-dollar bill that he had taken from the stack.

She looked past Martin, as if nothing mattered because they all had been saved or damned by then anyway.

"I think I'm a gonna plant me some more flowers," she said aloud but not to Martin or anybody else. "Shasta daisy, candytuft, wee willie, marigolds. Wait to next year, though. Be a better year—Lord help us."

CHAPTER 21

ONE OF THE BOYS

OMAR SHOUTED ONCE THEY WERE BACK IN THE Hummer, "Man that shit was off the hinges! You was fiendin' in there, mad cool!" Omar was amazed and smiling, his eyes shining like a child's on Christmas morning. But Martin noticed Omar's hand trembled as he put the key in the ignition. "I thought Red Nut was gonna dust me and you for sure." He shook his head so that his hanging braids swung back and forth across his neck.

"C'mon, Omar, let's get the hell outta here before Red Nut changes his mind," Martin urged. He hadn't taken his eyes off door number ninety-eight the whole time since they had walked to the Hummer.

"And eatin' money like that, what was that about?" Omar asked as the Hummer lurched from the curb. His voice squeaked with delight.

"They call it 'bread,' don't they?" Martin answered, mad cool.

"C'mon, quit giggin' me," Omar almost begged.

"Just wanted to make sure it wasn't counterfeit. I saw Richard Roundtree do it in a movie once and thought it was kinda neat," Martin explained as he rolled down the window to let in the cool air. The sun was setting and the purple-bottomed clouds were blushing a dusky pink. Martin stuck his elbow out the window and set the seat as far back as it would go and gazed at the after-work bustle on White Plains Road. He had just one-upped a thug and he had his pants back on...as close to equanimity as he had been in many days.

"And you should have seen the look on Red Nut's face when you said twenty-three. You played that chump like a flute."

"Wasn't anything to it," Martin replied as he lay back against his seat. He thought how scalping a few grand from a punk like Red Nut was easy compared to getting a bond trade out of a skinflint like Owen Brosky.

"All I can tell you is your brother's gonna be happy with how you scored this deal. Trex told me he'd take nineteen for it."

"Glad I could help," Martin answered but his voice lacked the irony it would have had, say, five hours ago if he had been congratulated for helping his brother unload some product.

Martin was feeling like a champ again. Running in panic from his apartment after that news report, less than a day ago, now seemed like another lifetime. It very well might have been if the little rascal with the A-K 47 had gotten an itchy trigger finger.

But Martin fell out of his lazy-dazy tranquility when he suddenly remembered Mihra. He pulled a lever causing his seat to snap to attention and wondered if he should approach Omar about giving him assistance in confronting Hu. But no, a little more bonding was in order first, he decided.

"Speaking of my brother, how long you been running with him?"

"Trex? Oh shit, I guess about two years now."

"So how did Henry, Trex I mean, get started in this racquet anyway?"

"Oh, man, Trex a natural when it come to biz. He moved in Malcolm X I guess about seven years ago. Started out as a look-out, worked his way up to mulin', and before long he was scorin' the deal."

"Wasn't somebody already working that turf?"

"Dog! Check that out!" Omar exclaimed as he directed his attention toward a honey-bee-baby strolling down the avenue. "She a tootsie-roll in pumps!"

"Didn't Trex have to take that turf away from somebody?" Martin asked again.

"Sure. Tony P. was runnin' the show back then but he weren't no playa. He just a sissy-slut. Didn't take Trex long to bump him off."

"Bump him off? Did Henry kill the guy?" Martin asked tentatively.

"No, Trex didn't kill him. Trex never kilt anybody."

"But he had somebody do it for him?"

"He sic Raze on him. I don't know what happened. All I know is that Tony P. ain't around no more. Departed to parts unknown."

Martin's face chilled and his insides shrunk at the thought that Henry might have had somebody murdered.

Omar sensed the uneasiness in Martin's silence and said, "Look, let me tell ya, your bubba plays the game as clean as a body can play it. He don't even touch the stuff hisself. He stays pure when it comes to that. He won't even deliver it, don't like to even see it. And yeah, sometimes he's gotta make a point to somebody. But he always let Raze or Bullethead or one of those g's handle that part of it."

"But he's more than happy to sell shit to any taker, right?"

"Yeah, he's a bidnessman. There's a demand, so somebody has to be the supplier. I'm a bidnessman, too. We all bidnessmen the same way Al Capone was. Shit, what was he doin' but sellin' booze that some do-gooders didn't want nobody to have. The same thing with our product. I'm always lookin' for a new way to make some scratch. If I could figure out a how to buy white gold and make my friends think it was platinum, I'd do it. I'm schemin' right now on a way to buy liquor with food stamps. If I can pull that off, I'll make a bundle."

"Businessmen?" Martin said with a sneer. "I think thugs is more like it."

"Hell, yeah, we thugs. Don't give me no bougie sap rap, okay, Poindexter."

"You ever kill anybody, Omar?"

"Nope. Cause he who kills usually gets killed. If somebody dis me, I'll take em on hard, mess em up good. I ain't leavin' till I gets even. Might get thrown in the poky for it, but I stop when it comes to cappin' a dude. I'd rather be judged by twelve than buried by six, if you smell what I'm cookin'?

"Ooowee! Look at that flossy bitch," Omar said as he spotted another dame. "Let me tell ya, Poindexter, money might make the world go around, but pussy rules it."

They drove back to Henry's place and the homey outside guarding the crib nodded at Omar, who, as a trusted lieutenant, had a key to the house. They entered the house and made their way to the den where Omar went to the wet bar. "Got somethin' for you to try, Poindexter." A minute later he walked over to Martin with some kind of concoction in his hand. "Try this," he said as he handed the drink to him.

Martin took a sip and his face scrunched together. "What is this crap?"

"Wild Irish Rose with Ginseng. Why didn't the folks who invented crack think of this?"

Omar then went to the home entertainment system and soon a loud eruption of sound followed. A hip-hop classic called "Ho Dough," the refrain of which was: "Bitch better have my money..." followed by a swhooshing popping noise meant to sound like a fist hitting a face. Omar, wearing an oversized, starched denim shirt meant to look like prison garb down to the number stenciled on the shirt pocket, shifted his shoulders to the beat.

"Time to get down!" he shouted above the din and reached for what appeared to be a cigar humidor on the bookcase. But instead of a cigar, he pulled out a plastic pipe and vial. He lit up a rock and took a toke. The column of smoke hurried from his mouth as fast as it had gone in. "Ahhh....

"Now I'm gonna load one up for you, Poindexter. Celebrate your score on Red Nut."

Martin had tried cocaine, or dummy dust as he called it, a few times before. He was, after all, a Wall Street yuppie and occasionally taking drugs like coke and ecstasy was par for the course. But the effect on him had been far from bliss. He had felt ridiculous leaning over a mirror and seeing a rolled C-note jammed up his nostril. Martin was too much in control to ever enjoy the abandonment that drugs induced.

"C'mon, man, it won't bite ya," Omar exhorted as he held the pipe in Martin's face. "You tighter than a teenage twat. C'mon, it don't bite...only kisses," he insisted with a goofy, giddy smile plastered on his face.

Martin considered for a moment and then surprised himself by saying, "Gimme that damn pipe."

"Aiight! Now here, put your finger over that hole there," Omar instructed as he leaned over and positioned the pipe in Martin's hand. Omar's fingers felt rough and damp, like oak bark in March. "Now pull it in slow and easy."

Martin did as told and felt something like a scratching, hairy rodent had burrowed down his esophagus before his mouth exploded open with a hoarse pop. Omar laughed hysterically. Martin attempted it again, this time taking it in slower.

If someone had asked Martin at that moment why he had done something so stupid as to take a hit off a crack pipe, he probably couldn't have answered. Stress was an obvious reason. Anger. Anger at being falsely accused. Anger at having his name splattered all over the media for a murder he hadn't committed. Anger at himself for having stupidly exposed Mihra to danger. And now, anger that his brother was, to use that hackneyed media phrase, "a drug kingpin."

Mix a little anger and stress with a dash of self-pity and there you have it...a man who doesn't care anymore. *Fuck you!* was all he had to say to the world closing in and cornering him. *Fuck Jo Hu, fuck the police, fuck Henry, fuck Whorman Skeller, fuck grubbing for bond trades, fuck kissing the ass of all those nerdy white guys wearing glasses, fuck being a black shining example for all the cracker world to see, fuck the game, fuck the rules, fuck wealth, success, happiness. Fuck Langston Hughes. And finally, one big fuck you to Martin Luther Stallworth.*

That was why he drew in as deeply as he could the toxic smoke. And surprisingly, it felt great. All the stress, all the anger was blown away by the tornado of gray smoke funneling from his mouth. Everything seemed the same, yet nothing felt the same. The space between his ears expanded, became lighter, like a balloon filling with chilly helium. And the cranium balloon expanded until it lifted from the chair the tired body attached to it like a string. The music that had sounded terrible before, suddenly wasn't half bad. Martin stood up, twitching his shoulders and snapping his fingers, causing Omar to laugh and clap his hands. What had been closed before, now opened, all the private cul de sacs of his tissue. The scales left his eyes. Unlike a drowsy margarita high, this high awakened him, released energy locked up somewhere. And the energy converted to a purifying, clarifying light that left Martin and shellacked everything. Such a happy, gleaming light, but cool and sparse like the moon's.

Martin skated his feet and swung his arms, a slow and easy wind-up to a tap dance number. He then lifted his hands and twirled them over each other, dancing a modified boo-ga-loo that gradually became shadow boxing. "Fuck Jo Hu," he murmured to himself as he threw a right cross, his hips turning all the way into it. He danced to the music, punched to the beat, smiling like a man who had nothing left to lose.

"Hey, Omar, load me up one more. One more, that's all I need."

"Yeah sure," Omar said, spreading his golden gap smile. "'Just one more...' that's what they all say." And so they shared another toke and then another.

It wasn't long before both Martin and Omar had reached the zenith of giddy garrulousness. Now any topic was fair game for conversation. "Hey, Poindexter, lemme ask you somethin'. How come you end up peddlin' bonds on Wall Street and your brother's peddlin' dope on Main Street. Ya'll suck from the same tit, growed up in the same house, didn't you? How come you so bougie and Trex so street? You a bond daddy and Trex a smack daddy? How come that?"

Martin thought for a moment. "The simple reason is that Henry was a mama's boy."

Omar turned his head quizzically and stared at Martin while his brain digested that nugget. He then burst out laughing. "Oh yeah, that's a good one. Trex a mama's boy." He held out his hand for Martin to slap palms.

Although Martin laughed along with Omar, he remembered how devastated Henry was after their mother had discovered she had cancer, the mother who had especially doted on Henry from the day he had plopped out of her womb. Henry had never been the same from the moment Pops, with tears in his eyes, had told his two sons that their mama had a "problem." Henry had his difficulties staying between the straight and narrow even before then, had never been an angel, but his mother had been the only reason, as far as Martin could see, that he had tried to be good. And then that reason had been eaten alive slowly before their very eyes.

*Speak of the devil and up he pops...*Martin thought as into the room marched Henry Trex along with Raze and two other members of the Seezers, and Buster trotting along beside him. At that very moment, Martin had the crack pipe stuck in his mouth, ready to take another hit.

"What the fuck's going on here?" Henry asked, glowering from behind his ever-present Ray-bans. He clapped his hands and the track lighting shone forth. One light beam hit Martin directly in the face, causing him to squint.

Omar jumped from the sofa and onto his feet.

"We're partying down, bro!" Martin shouted, standing with the loaded pipe still in his hand, in the spotlight. DMX was on the system with "An Ode to Hoochie Hole" blaring away. Henry walked to the DVD player and turned the music off before he strode over to Martin and slapped the pipe out of his hand. The pipe flew through the air and shattered against the wall.

"Hey, what's with that?" Martin yelled.

Henry then turned to Omar, who was cowering as if he were trying to hide within himself. Henry's hand reached for Omar's throat and locked onto it and Omar's freckles seemed to expand and his eyes bug out. He gargled words that couldn't quite get out of his constricted throat as his hands took hold of Henry's wrist, trying to wrench himself free from the grip. Henry's wiry build belied his strength.

"What do you think you're doing turning my brother onto that shit?" Henry asked, his teeth clenched. He worried Omar's head back and forth with one hand and then slung Omar onto the floor. "You little punk, trying to hook my brother on that shit!"

Omar began crawling on all fours and Martin attempted to interject, "Henry, he didn't do anything..."

"You shut the fuck up," Henry hollered, cutting Martin short. He then kicked Omar in the rump as he continued to crawl. "Don't you ever get that shit around my brother ever again!" Key words were accented by respective kicks in the ass. Raze and the other two Seezers doubled-over with giggles, which they tried to stifle with their hands over their mouths.

Omar finally reached the steps leading to the sunken den, hopped to his feet and ran.

"Get your butt to your room," Henry ordered Martin, as if they were back in high school and their mother was in the hospital and Pops was at work and Henry had dominion over the household.

Martin, flummoxed by the dope and Henry's surprise attack, spluttered an incoherent remark and then shambled back to his room and fell onto his bed.

Damn Henry still thinking he can order me around like that, he thought to himself as he stared at the ceiling. *Who in the hell does Henry think he is?*

Martin lay there waiting to come down, wanting to come down as he was dead tired but oh, so terribly, terribly wide-awake. The cocaine would not let him sleep so he lay supine and clenched his hands like a patient receiving shock treatment. His heart was palpitating, his nerve endings quivering and his head was throbbing. As he was clenching his teeth, he was worrying he might have screwed up any chance of Henry helping him with Hu.

And he thought about Mihra and moaned aloud as an avalanche of ugly thoughts crashed down upon him. *My god, what have I done to her?* he thought as he tossed and turned onto his side and hoped that his thoughts, like the colors inside a kaleidoscope, would rearrange themselves if he shifted his body.

Now there was no more pretending. Now he knew it and couldn't ignore it. But there was no joy in the knowing and his grip tightened even further. His life had always been a matter of rising expectations, upward mobility, infinite promise, and eternal reward. Always-perpetual improvement. Never a moment's doubt, hardly a pinch of pain. Living according to a grand plan. The black guy who could mix with the crème-de-le-crème without apologies or insecurities or with even a chip on his shoulder. But now there were no more lies or faking cockiness. For the first time in his short existence, he faced a futureless future—one without beginnings or endings. No way out. No place to hide. He ground his teeth even more. Oh, how he yearned for sleep!

Once, again, he thought about Mihra and what he had inadvertently done to her. And he thought about Pops and what he believed he had done to him. And he thought about Henry and somehow blamed himself for what Henry had become. Suddenly, his chest heaved and his ribcage protruded like a set of horns as he held in his breath. A plaintive wail sounded, made even more pitiful by its smallness. An eerie, disembodied sound, like a note in a whale tune, dying among the quiet of the evening. And along with the wail came a single tear, breaking, clear, and warm. It swirled around the socket of his eye, traced the slope of his cheek, careened past the corner of his mouth, and hurried over his chin and down his shuddering throat...then the darkness came.

Martin woke and automatically glanced at the digital cock. 2:13 a.m. But what had awakened him? A sound had awakened him. Carefully he listened and heard it again. The grinding sound seemed to be coming from down the hallway. After he heard it again, Martin recognized it was someone retching. He rose from the bed, looked out the door of his room toward the bathroom down the hall and saw the bathroom door was open and the light was on. He could see Henry on his knees with his head hanging over the toilet.

Martin walked toward the bathroom door. "What's the matter, Henry?"

Henry looked up from the commode. He didn't appear to be embarrassed about hugging the toilet; the look on his face only said, *Oh, it's you again.* He turned and sat on the floor, his arm resting on the toilet rim. Martin noticed blood trickling from Henry's mouth.

Henry closed his eyes as he rubbed them with his fingers and when he opened them again, Martin thought he was seeing the ghost of his mother, her spirit inhabiting Henry's shell and peering through his eyes. Those same, amber-colored, almond shaped eyes like hers.

The bathroom light was bright and the tile and chrome gleamed, causing Martin to remember how Henry had always been such a clean freak, a borderline obsessive compulsive.

Henry yawned before saying, "Ulcers. Bleeding ulcers. They get rowdy every once in awhile."

Martin leaned against the doorjamb and commented, "Must be from stress, huh? You got some blood on your chin, by the way."

Henry wiped the blood away with a piece of toilet paper. "Stress? Now why would I be under any stress?" he asked, ironically.

"I know next to nothing about how you live your life," Martin answered, "but I can see enough to know that it's not a walk through the park."

Henry snickered, "Yeah..." Without his sunglasses on and his entourage behind him, sprawled on the bathroom floor, to Martin he seemed much older and more tired beyond his thirty-one years.

At that moment, Martin felt a pang of sorrow for his brother. "Why you doing this, Henry? How did you end up like this?"

Henry looked at Martin and laughed. He laughed until he clutched his sides and began choking—then leaned his head over the toilet and again spit out blood.

After recovering himself, he sat back against the wall and took a couple of deep breaths. "Why am I doing this? Same reason you're doing what you're doing, whatever it is you do. What is it you do anyway?"

"Sell high-yield bonds." Martin almost added that that was what he once had done for a living, anyway.

"What they call junk, right? Why they call it that? Cause it's just another way for some slick white dudes to rip each other off. You're peddling junk for money and I'm peddling feel-good for money. You're in a racquet and I'm in a racquet, so get off your damn horse. You're no better than me," said Henry to his brother.

"What the hell are you spieling, Henry? How can you compare what I do with selling poison to your own people, kids and all, like you do? You're full of shit!"

"I don't sell anything to any kids. And if I find that anybody with the Seezers is, then that punk's outta here quick with a lotta lumps on his head."

"It's still shit that ruins people's lives."

"Listen, Martin, these people around here don't have any lives to ruin. They don't have anything to live for. And that ain't my fault. Most of them don't have jobs and those that do, well, those jobs really ain't worth having. Their mothers are skanks and their daddies unknown. When dusk comes around here, you go inside cause when the stars come out so do the bullets. So why take away their only chance to get away from it all for a little while? That's all I'm doing, giving them a free, first-class ticket to some resort island for a couple of hours or so. That's all they got. And if I don't give it to them, I can damn guarantee you somebody else will."

"Henry, you're better than that. You were raised better. You were meant for something better."

"Well nigger, what was you meant for? To be sucking on a crack pipe like I caught you doing a little while ago?"

"Hey, didn't you just tell me that that stuff is just a free, first-class ticket to Club Feel Good? So why did you throw a damn hissy-fit like you did?"

"Cause you're my brother," Henry answered, straightforward.

"A brother who hasn't spoken to you in five years. So why do you give a shit?" Martin wanted to know.

"Cause I used to look up to you, that's why." Henry then paused, as if even he, himself, were surprised by his answer.

Martin shifted uncomfortably in the doorway.

Henry coughed and put his fist to his mouth to keep the blood from coming up. "Look, brother, I'm gonna be straight up with you about this." He paused before continuing. "I mean you were everything, Martin. So damn smart in school. A great athlete. Mr. Popularity. It almost made me sick sometimes. But still, I was proud of you too.

"And so when I see you toking off that pipe with Omar, it was sorta like seeing someone take a prized trophy that you had since you was a kid and smashing it to pieces. You're too good for that shit, Martin. That's why I went off. Am I making any sense? It's late and I'm sick and maybe I'm babbling too much. I'll be sorry in the morning for what I'm saying."

"I get what you're saying, Henry."

For the first time, Martin's thoughts coalesced into an understanding of his older brother. *Henry had never been a good student. He had a reading problem—"A Perceptual Motor Problem," the psychologist had finally called it. And so growing up, he had always lingered in the shadow of his younger brother's academic achievements.*

And Pops had never held back in his public exultations about Martin's accomplishments. On the other hand, Pops had constantly rode Henry, not accepting the psychologist's explanation for his academic failure. That, to Pops, had been like admitting that his son was mentally handicapped or retarded. "You're just not trying hard enough," had been his constant refrain. "You got a bad attitude, boy." Maybe because Henry was the oldest, maybe because he had Pop's name, whatever the reason, Pops had always come down extra hard on Henry. And just before Henry had finally left home, the confrontations had become more heated, uglier, even verging on violence.

"But deep down, you probably resented that that trophy wasn't yours, didn't you, Henry?" Martin softly asked.

"Meaning it was yours to claim?"

"Yeah. You really hated my guts, didn't you?"

"Look man, my head was really twisted back then. I was flunking in school and thinking I was stupid. Pops was constantly breathing down my neck, sticking his face in mine and asking me why I couldn't be like you. Nah, I didn't hate you. It just made me more determined to be a success in something—in anything. I knew it wasn't gonna be in academics or straight business cause there was no way I was gonna play second fiddle to you…so I found my own gig. Found something I was really good at. And here I am. Just look at me…successful beyond my wildest dreams! Leaning over a toilet, puking up blood.

"So now I'll ask you what you asked me, Martin. How did you end up like this? How did you end up peddling paper on Wall Street? You were better than that."

"I guess the same reason you gave me. One word…money."

"You were gonna be a journalist or something like that, weren't you? A teacher maybe? You were so into poetry and stuff like that. You won all those writing awards. You had it, man, a gift."

Martin's heart sank with the suspicion that he had squandered that gift, had blown it and had missed his calling. More than once, recently, he had recollected that scene his first year in college, in the American Lit class. He recalled the professor, Mr. Joshua Ehrenprice, calling out names as he handed papers back to the class.

Mr. Ehrenprice, despite being one of the more renowned professors at the university, had managed to be an excellent teacher. New England-Boston-Cambridge reeked from him, and it wasn't surprising that he was an expert on the subject of Robert Lowell. He even looked somewhat like Lowell—long gray-white wisps of hair combed straight back, the black horn-rimmed glasses, the sleek brow and pointed nose, all held up by a gray turtleneck or thin, elegant tie.

He remembered that when Mr. Ehrenprice had called out, "Martin Stallworth," he had paused and studied this student as the latter had strolled up to retrieve his paper, "The Influence of Spirituals on the Poetry of Gwendolyn Brooks." And as the professor had handed the paper to Martin, he had asked if he could speak with him after class. Martin had done as asked and dutifully waited while Mr. Ehrenprice chatted amiably and patiently with one student after another, each one eagerly awaiting the chance to impress the professor with a witticism or astute remark.

Finally, he had turned to the last student still standing there. "Mr. Stallworth, I was greatly impressed with your paper."

Martin had shifted his feet, nodded his head, and looked down. "Thank you."

"May I ask your age, Mr. Stallworth?"

"Eighteen."

Mr. Ehrenprice considered for a moment. "I am astounded that an eighteen-year-old wrote that paper." Martin had nodded again, averting his eyes toward the paper in his hand as if expecting it to do the speaking for him. For a second, he had wondered if he was being accused of plagiarism.

"I know it's way off in the future, but have you any plans upon graduation?" Mr. Ehrenprice had kindly asked.

"Not really," Martin had said.

"Well, I suggest you do something with your writing."

"That would be nice," Martin had inexplicably muttered.

"Fine. I look forward to hearing and reading more from you, Mr. Stallworth."
Martin had then turned and left the room, a little embarrassed yet very proud.

"I tell you what your problem is, baby brother," Henry continued, interrupting another one of Martin's brief, self-torture sessions of "what-ifs." "It's Pride because you were told by Pops and everybody else so many times how you could do anything you wanted that you got where you believed them. You really did think that you could be a poet, a writer, or whatever and at the same time be Mr. Bad on Wall Street, making a ton of jack—being all things to everybody all the time. And so, you didn't make a real commitment to anything, did you? You never went full out on any one gig. And now, here you are having risked nothing and have ended up with nothing."

Martin winced. "Shit, Henry, you're coming down hard on me, man."

"Just being straight up with you, bro. But you're still young. You're back at zero. Not too late to figure it out and start again."

"Man, I got some more immediate problems than worrying about my future. I got to get Mihra out of this."

"Yeah, that's a hard case, Martin." Henry leaned his head back against the wall and closed his eyes.

"Henry, can you help me?"

Henry opened his eyes and he and Martin stared at each other for several seconds.

"As a brother, Henry," he added, hesitantly."

"What is it you want me to do?" Henry asked. Martin sat down on the edge of the bathtub and began to tell Henry his plan.

CHAPTER 22

DEUS EX MACHINA

AS THE WINDOW-TINTED SILVER SHADOW EXITED the garage underneath the office building at 48th and Third, Jo Hu was sprawled in the back, reading Barron's. Just as the car turned left onto Third Avenue, Odd Job, who was accompanying Hu in the back, shouted to the driver, "Stop!"

"What's going on?" Hu asked.

"Stallworth!" Odd Job answered as he lowered the left side window. "I think I saw him back there," he said to Hu in Cantonese. "Back at that corner."

"You're kidding," Hu replied, startled.

Odd Job craned his head out the window. "Yeah, that's him."

"Now isn't that interesting," Hu mused aloud. "Back up to that corner," he ordered the driver.

When the car stopped at the corner, Hu leaned across Odd Job and said through the window, "Dr. Stallworth, I presume?"

"The one and only," Martin coolly responded.

"And I bet that you're standing here because you want to talk with me?"

"Could be."

"Then why don't you hop in the car with us and we'll discuss whatever you want."

"Yeah, right. No, instead, why don't *you* hop out of that Rolls and we'll take a stroll down Third Avenue."

Hu considered for a moment and then said, "Okay." Odd Job opened the door and got out of the car, prepared to go with Hu.

"Tell your orangutan there to stay put," Martin said to Hu.

Hu said something in Chinese to Odd Job, who slunk back into the car.

"And tell him no funny business, like getting on his cell phone and calling in some goons to come bust me up. Look around and you can see I got my own reinforcements."

Hu surveyed the scene. Standing in the building's outside alcove, slumped against the polished granite wall amidst a small group of cigarette smokers was Raze. Raze, wearing a skully and a red leather letter jacket, looked hard at Hu and flashed him a gang high sign. With his pinkie and index fingers sticking out on his right hand, he then tapped them against his heart three times.

When Hu turned to his left, Omar was leaning on a parking meter and smiling so that his gold fangs glistened in the sun. And to his right, Hu saw Henry, standing erect in a black trench coat, his feet spread and his hands behind his back, inconspicuously conspicuous in the middle of the sidewalk among the flow of passersby. He made no facial expression toward Hu but still looked menacing behind his signature sunglasses.

"Friends of mine," Martin said with a smile, "from a fine organization you may have heard of, called The Seezers."

Hu chewed on that bit of information for a second or two and then leaned toward the car window and spoke briefly to Odd Job.

"Shall we?" Martin said to Hu as he bowed and twirled his hand out.

"Let's walk and talk," Hu said. And so they proceeded up Third Avenue, escorted by Henry, Omar and Raze as the Rolls Royce glided slowly along the curb beside them.

"So you and your friends been hanging out at this corner all day?" Hu asked.

"Nah. I called your secretary. Told her I was an investor in your fund. I'll do my fake Chinese accent for you some time. Then I sweet-talked her into telling me that you had a 3:30 p.m. meeting outside the office. So we planted ourselves here about 3:00 p.m. and I took a chance that when you drove out you'd recognize me from all the news reports."

"Okay, so we're here. Good. I'm glad we've finally met. I've been wondering over the past couple of days when I'd hear from you."

"Where' s Mihra?" Martin immediately spat out.

"Ah, don't worry about her, she's in fine hands," Hu answered with mock solicitude.

They stopped at a corner when the light turned red and Martin said, "Let her go, Hu."

Hu smirked. "You are the one who has the key to let her free, my friend."

"I'm not your fucking friend."

Hu's face then turned from charming to chilled. "You know what I want. Now get it to me and I'll give you back the girl. It's that simple."

The light changed and Martin, Hu and their following entourage proceeded.

"All the shit going on and you think it's that easy for me to get Lodestar to you?"

"There's an old Chinese proverb, 'You only catch big fish in choppy waters.' Yeah, things are dicey right now, but I want that fish."

Hu, who had been looking straight ahead the whole while he talked to Martin, suddenly stopped and looked directly at him. "Don't you understand, slick? I don't really give a damn about Lodestar, and I certainly don't get any kicks out of holding your girlfriend for ransom. But there are some people who really, really do want that information. I don't have any idea why they want it. But I do know they're the kind of people who don't like excuses. And when they don't get what they want, then they get mad and somebody gets hurt. So, before they hurt me, I'm going to hurt you and your girlfriend. Or you give me what I want, I give them what they want, and then you get what you want. After that, we all go on our merry little ways."

Martin didn't say anything for half a minute as they continued up the avenue. "So where do you wanna meet to do this?" he finally asked.

Hu looked at him quizzically. "Do what?"

"The exchange. The documents for Mihra. Let's do it tomorrow, get it over and done with. I've got them. Where's the best place to meet?"

Hu turned and did something he rarely did, smile brightly and unabashedly, without irony or hidden intentions, his face scrunching itself up so that his eyes turned into slits, like a man whose neck had just slipped through the noose.

The Hummer cruised west across the Cross Bronx Expressway. Crowded in the vehicle were Martin, Henry, Omar, Raze and two other sleezer Seezars who nobody even bothered to introduce. An Ole Dirty Bastard joint was playing on the car CD player

They made their way through the usual creepy-crawly Bronx traffic until reaching the western side of Manhattan where they exited onto Henry Hudson Parkway. The passengers in the vehicle all gazed straight ahead, glazed in the eyes and brain, slumped in their seats and not uttering a word—like soldiers on a mission, a mission unlike any other on which they had been.

The scenery changed as they drove along the bluffs overlooking the Hudson River and the view got scenic all of a sudden, sort of un-Manhattan the further up the island they went, more green, budding cottonwood, ash and birch forcing pathways over the stone walls above the parkway. The buildings beyond the greenbelt were mostly well-kept brownstones instead of the usual high-rises or office buildings.

They exited the parkway and entered a woodsy park where the road wound up a steep hill full of crags, boulders and thick with foliage and strangling vines. Martin, sitting in the front seat, grew increasingly nervous as they continued up the hill until reaching a gray, stone building halfway overgrown with ivy. It looked rather medieval with its red, tile roof and lancet windows.

As Henry parked the vehicle, Martin unnecessarily said, "This must be the place."

"Hell, man, what is this, a damn church?" Omar asked.

"It's called 'The Cloisters,'" Martin condescended to answer.

"What's a damned cloisters?" Omar wanted to know.

"A place where nuns live," Henry answered.

"Dog, it don't seem right we're doing this deal at some kinda holy joint," Omar protested as he suddenly got righteous.

"Holy…ain't nothin' that no more," Raze muttered from the back seat.

"This place isn't a church or a real cloisters, it's a public museum," Martin said. "So shut your trap, Omar."

When Martin and Hu had discussed the day before where to meet to swap Mihra for Lodestar, Hu had insisted that the place be public. A glimpse of Martin's cohorts had made him wary of any place that might give them an opportunity to jump him. Martin had also agreed, as he certainly didn't want to meet on Hu's turf. The meeting place had to be on neutral ground and public enough to prevent anybody on either side from getting trigger-happy.

Martin had had an inspiration and suggested The Cloisters, a place he had visited often while at Columbia, which was just down the road from there. He had told Hu, "It's public but since it's at the tip of the island and off the beaten path, there's less chance of a bunch of cops hanging around."

Hu had nodded, thought a bit, and then said, "Agreed."

Martin had also insisted that Hu be there as further insurance against any monkey business and had pointed out if things didn't go as planned, the bad publicity wouldn't be good for a mover and shaker like him.

Henry then turned and faced everyone in the back of the Hummer. "Okay, here's how it's going down. Martin's gonna go inside here and meet some chump who's gonna lead him to the girl. I'm gonna trail behind Martin. Omar, you see that exit up front there? You hang out there. Raze, you follow three minutes behind me, but you stay put at the front entrance. You oughta have a straight view of the exit where Omar'll be from where you are."

Then he directed the other two to take their positions on a knoll, about thirty yards beyond the exit where Omar would be stationed. "Hug those trees there so you won't be noticed," he instructed the two.

"Now, Martin is gonna lead the dude who has the girl, and whoever else might be with him, to the exit where Omar'll be. And that's when we move in, when we see Martin walk out that door. But don't move until you see the girl with him. Everybody hear that?" Everybody in back nodded their heads.

Henry continued, "Now listen, they might have their own G's planted all around here, too and thinking exactly like we're thinking. So keep your eyes open for any slant-eyed characters and don't get wild unless you have to. We don't want nobody to get hurt, if we can help it. All we wanna do is grab the chick and get the hell outta here as fast as we can. Okay, everybody loaded?"

At that prompt, all four in the back raised their Glocks. "Chic-click, chic-click, chic-click, chic-click," sounded in unison as they simultaneously loaded their clips.

Henry then looked at Martin. "Martin, you got you piece?" Martin felt in his parka pocket for the same Smith and Wesson six-shooter that Omar had given him. He nodded yes, still amazed that he was carrying heat and wondering whether he really had the guts to use it.

Henry then returned to the crew in the back. "So we all singing the same song, on the same page?" Again, nods from all around. "I'm gonna park this muther down the road, at the bend back there. This thing be too easy to spot in the main parking lot. So that's where we all will meet up. No matter what happens, get back to the Hummer." The four all piled out and as unobtrusively as possible, slunk to their assigned posts.

Then Henry looked at his watch and murmured, "Right on time." Then in a low voice to Martin he said, "All right, bro, it's show time."

Martin took a deep breath and opened the door. Under his arm he had a small satchel. But before leaving, he looked at his hand and the ring that Pops had given him for his birthday. He twisted the ring off his finger and turned to Henry, "I want you to have this, in case something happens."

Henry frowned at the ring. "Whatcha talking 'bout? C'mon man, ain't nothing like that gonna happen. It's not like we're storming the beaches of Iwo Jima or something. Don't look so glum, like your number's up. Worst comes to worst, we gotta show our pistols, show a little muscle, scare the shit out 'em so they hand over your friend. That's all that's gonna happen. Lighten up, brother."

"Please take it Henry. I owe you and it's the only thing I got that's worth giving."

Henry sighed and turned his head, "Okay…" He took the ring and slid it on his finger. "You know Pops would be pissed as hell you giving me his ring."

"He wouldn't have any problem with it, if he knew how you were saving my ass."

"I haven't saved anybody anything yet. Get going, Martin. Hu's waiting for you."

After Martin got out of the vehicle, Henry then turned the Hummer around and drove back down the road to park in a less conspicuous place.

Nervousness caused Martin to stretch his legs and curve his torso back until he could see the blue-sky overhead, paled by the thinnest cover of cloud or pollution. Birds chirped the praises of spring and the moist breath of new life caressed his face. *A fine day to commit espionage,* he thought. Actually, he wouldn't be committing espionage since the satchel contained no top-secret documents but sheets of blank typing paper. If everything went according to plan, Hu wouldn't know that until after the Seezers had descended upon him and Mihra was safe in his arms. Martin reached into his jacket pocket and felt the handgun.

Martin trudged slowly and steadily up the hill, following a flow of people, many of who had cameras around their necks. He found himself humming "The Old Rugged Cross," which was his mother's favorite gospel, as he walked.

Past the heavy wooden doors of the entrance was a long hallway, cool and bare, the rough limestone floor slightly inclined. The hallway led up to an atrium with a rib-vaulted, stone ceiling and a large rosette window. Gregorian chants were being piped in from somewhere and a lady at a wooden booth was handing out clip-on metal buttons for six dollars apiece. A security guard stood nearby. *Is he just a little too thorough in checking me out?* paranoia made Martin wonder. Then he reached into his jacket pocket for his wallet, careful not to pull out the gun instead, and handed the lady six dollars. He glanced at the guard, lowered his eyes and walked on.

Although Martin had told Hu *he* would show up alone, he had allowed Hu to have one person accompany him. This person was to meet Martin at the gardens in the center of the complex wearing a Cincinnati Red's baseball cap so that he would be easy to spot in Yankees/Mets land. He would give Martin a signal by tipping the bill of his cap several times, as if he were telling Martin to steal third. When Martin saw that, he was supposed to go up to him and say, "The days are getting longer." The contact would reply, "Winter's over." Then Martin would follow the gentlemen to one of the less trafficked areas of the cloisters, where Hu and Mihra would be.

As Martin walked on, in search of the gardens, the Gregorian chants soothed him with their voices rising and falling, trailing off and surging back, ghostly and holy. He entered a room with white plaster walls, stone windows and a wooden roof. On the wall to his right was a gilded wood altarpiece depicting Virgin and Child standing on an upturned crescent moon. And he thought, *What if Hu tries something funny, pulls a gun on me, what will I do then?*

In front of him, four walnut-wood women mourned a deposed Christ. Five-hundred year old paint poured from the ugly gash under Christ's rib cage.

As he continued to walk through more rooms filled with saints, angels, wiseman and virgins, the monks continued to send their souls up through the PA system. Finally, Martin saw the garden through the arched doorway.

The garden actually occupied a courtyard that was divided into quarters by walkways. Each quarter of the garden had a small tree and its own set of flowers, such as grape hyacinth, crocus, Christ's eyes, narcissus, and Madonna lilies—bees buzzed. The walkways all led to the center of the garden where stood a pink marble fountain surrounded by white daffodils.

When Martin looked, there, leaning against the bowl of the gurgling fountain was an Asian man wearing a Cincinnati Red's baseball cap and he stood straight when he saw Martin walking through the arcade that was covered by a low-slung tile roof. There were four or five tourists strolling about the garden so Martin continued walking through the arcade, all the while staring at Cincinnati Red.

The contact stared back at Martin, turning in place as his eyes followed Martin and several times reached for the bill of his cap…each time tugging on it harder.

Martin finally stopped at one of the walkways leading to the fountain where a hellish beast with a whole human leg in its mouth squatted at the base of the arcade column beside Martin. As he walked to the fountain, a bell from the finch-infested tower tolled eleven times, almost one time for each step he took. He held the satchel across his chest so that it would be clearly visible to the contact. "The days are getting longer," he said to the pig-faced man with the moustache that barely covered his harelip.

As the bees buzzed, the man's harelip wiggled into a grin as he responded, "Yes, winter is over." Then he nodded his head sideways toward the museum and walked in that direction with Martin following.

They passed through a room where a dozen or more tapestries hung beneath the sixty-foot ceiling and a unicorn took center stage in each tapestry. Martin noticed one where men on horseback were driving huge spears into the pure white hide of a unicorn as it gored a snarling hound with its swiveled horn. Another canine had its fangs buried in the unicorn's hindquarters, blood from the wound dripping onto a yellow rose underneath.

Soon they descended down a narrow, winding stairway into a small chapel. The room was about sixty-feet deep and thirty-feet wide. At the rounded end of the chapel were three stained glass windows, roughly twenty-feet high. The sun shining through the glass scattered the light into colors of ruby red, garnet red, sapphire blue, amber and green.

The stained light surprised Martin—he could have been inside a kaleidoscope looking out. Set about the room were several stone sarcophagi containing the dusty bones and hair of dead personages. Three of these glorified coffins occupied the middle of the room and six lined the walls. The Gregorian chants gently gliding over Martin's head were now more spooky than soothing.

He continued to follow Cincinnati Red toward the back of the chapel. They passed by the stone figure of some long-gone knight laid out over his entombed remains, his shield lying over him and his sword at his side. The chain mail of his armor had been intricately chiseled. His hands were folded in prayer and a forever smile was on his face, as if he were certain that God would congratulate him for all those Saracens he had butchered.

Then Martin saw them, standing off to the side, within the shadows of a small alcove. Mihra was standing next to Hu and above them were windows whose panes displayed scenes from the New Testament—The Annunciation, The Adoration of the Magi, and The Agony in the Garden. One pane celebrated Christ kicking down the door to Hell; his foot pressing down on a harried, ash-colored demon with big pointed ears and a long snout.

Hu and Mihra stood there, side by side, like a grim bride and groom ready to say their vows. Martin's heartbeat accelerated, upon seeing Mihra and knowing that he was so close to setting her free. Suddenly, Mihra's face suddenly went from grim to horrified, "Behind you, Martin!" she shouted before Hu could manage to put his hand over her mouth.

Martin turned and saw that his escort was pointing at him for some reason. Then, in a split second, he noticed that the finger pointing at him was extra round and black, as if he were wearing an ebony ring around his fingertip. And in another nanosecond, he realized it wasn't a finger pointing at him but the shortened barrel of a silencer attached to a gun aimed right between his eyes.

In the passing of still another millisecond, before Martin had time to completely digest the fact that this person was about to splatter his brains all over the reclining knight's smiling face and before he fully comprehended that the ringing in his ears was from a loud clapping noise coming from the other end of the room, the gunman grabbed his shoulder and spun on his heels, raising his gun into the air as if he were suddenly in the mood to do a Greek dance.

Then, a smile, or maybe it was a grimace, spread across Cincinnati Red's face and his raised gun fired, the bullet spitting through the silencer. Chirst before Pilate popped and smithereens of green colors tinkled to the ground as the unabashed sunlight instantly pushed through the opening. The gunman then twirled into the wall and slithered behind a sarcophagus.

Martin turned and saw that Hu and Mihra were crouched behind the statue of a cardinal whose his nose had been shaved off. He turned once again at the sound of a voice coming from the same direction that the loud clapping noise had come from. The voice somehow penetrated his shocked and thick-as-clay consciousness as it commanded, "Hit the floor, Martin. Get your ass to the floor."

Martin quickly crouched at the other end of the sarcophagus from his would-be assassin. He turned himself around and saw Henry peeking from the portal that opened into this room of death. The spitting-hissing noise sounded again, coming from behind Martin and over his head. A big chunk of stone disintegrated from a pilaster that Henry was hiding behind.

Martin slumped lower as he saw Henry peer again and raise his automatic and fire two, quick shots near him. The first shot hit Saint Margaret of Antioch, lying over the sarcophagus directly in front of him, and she lost her nose that was too big anyway. The second shot made a ricocheting sound and Martin heard another shatter of sacred glass.

Just then Martin remembered he was carrying a gun in his pocket. *You damn idiot,* he scolded himself as he reached for the pistol and turned himself around to face the gunman less than three feet away. Martin peeked over the top of the sarcophagus and when his assailant rose to fire another shot at Henry, Martin raised his gun, aimed and quickly squeezed the trigger twice, "CLICK. CLICK." The gun didn't fire, as the gun chamber was empty—because Martin had left the bullets in his jacket pocket!

The gunman ducked back down. From the other end of the sarcophagus, Martin heard a snicker and mumbled Chinese that probably translated into, "What a dumb ass." Martin could picture him grinning, his harelip bunching together like a caterpillar hunching up a stalk.

As Martin frantically inserted the bullets into his pistol chamber, he looked up just in time to see Henry's body lift into the air as if it were on a pulley. In amazement he watched Henry float toward him, his Glock spitting fire, an angel of vengeance.

Henry clambered over the first sarcophagus and scampered onto the second one housing Saint Margaret. "Muthafucka!" he yelled as he straddled the top of the sarcophagus and, gripping the gun with both hands, squeezed off another round. Martin balled up and wrapped his arms around his head as discharged shell cases clinked and ricocheting bullets kaplinked in his ear.

The next thing Martin knew, someone had him by the shoulder. He looked up and saw Henry hovering over him. The sudden quiet was deafening. *Could it be that Henry was shaking him out of a nightmare?* he dazedly wondered.

"C'mon, Hu and the girl just split," Henry informed him as he lifted Martin to his feet. Cincinnati Red was hunched over the knight with the blissful smile. His baseball cap had fallen from his pitch-black hair that was sprinkled with tiny shards of colored glass. His head was turned at a neck-breaking angle toward the tall windows. Blank eyes stared in disbelief at Christ bearing His cross up a skull-shaped hill and his forehead bore a perfect, red oval, like a Hindu mark, where the bullet had entered. A rapidly expanding pool of blood drained from his ear and seeped onto the sepulchral stone, quickly turning the knight a rich red.

Not wasting any more time, Martin and Henry chased after Hu and Mihra. As they hurried through more rooms, beatific virgin smiles, babes with two chubby fingers pointed heavenwards, blood and wounds, stone men of sorrow, without noses, without hands, flashed before Martin's eyes. By the time they saw Hu and Mihra bolting through an exit, the screams of a hysterical woman in the sarcophagus room were ruining many a tourist's morning. "Police! Somebody call the police!"

Martin and Henry sprinted toward the exit that Hu and Mihra had just left, which also just happened to be the exit where Omar was stationed. And when Martin and Henry finally burst through the exit door, they saw Omar with his gun drawn and pointed right at Hu's head. "Give her up!" Omar was shouting and the two Seezers stationed in the copse of trees were running down the knoll toward Omar. A quick thought zipped through Martin's mind as he watched them on his way to Mirha, *They look so young that they could be mistaken for two playful boys racing each other.*

Martin rushed toward Mihra, grabbed her arm and pulled her away from Hu and she fell sobbing against his chest. As he hugged Mihra to him, he saw over her shoulder Hu standing quite still and smiling mysteriously.

Then heard Henry mutter, "Oh, shit!"

As Martin looked around, he saw, converging upon them from all points, half a dozen of Hu's henchman, led by Odd Job, a semi-automatic Beretta in his hand. Two of his buddies were carrying Uzi's and one a sawed-off shotgun.

"What do we do, Henry?" Martin shouted and saw a rare moment of confusion and fear disrupt Henry's face.

And so they stood there, an asymmetrical choreography of a dozen men pointing their fully loaded automatic weapons at each other, all frozen in their positions, a cacophony of bellowed and shrieked threats in at least two different languages drowning out the chirping robins. And at the every center of this poised crossfire were Martin and Mihra, holding each other for dear life.

Jo Hu turned toward Martin and revealed the .44 Magnum he had hidden underneath his black sweater. When he began screaming at Martin, he sounded like a threatened, bluffing gorilla and took two steps toward Martin and Mihra.

Automatically, Martin turned sideways so that his body was between Mihra and Hu and gripped his gun harder—his trigger-finger as tense as a drawn bowstring. "Back off or I'll blow your fucking head off!" Martin yelled.

But Hu now acted like a wild, wounded animal, going berserk and screaming, his mouth wide-opened and his eyes unblinking.

Martin was sure that he would be forced to shoot this madman. But then he remembered the satchel still in his hand that was pressed against Mihra. While holding the gun in one hand, he held out the satchel with the other and shouted, "Lodestar!"

Suddenly Hu stopped screaming, his face collapsed and he seemed stunned with the remembrance of what all this commotion had been about in the first place...*Lodestar!*

Then, while everyone kept their guns trained on each other, Hu's screaming was replaced by hyperventilating pants and he deliberately reached out and took the satchel from Martin.

But Martin's trigger finger didn't relax, for he knew that as soon as Hu looked into the satchel and discovered no Lodestar documents, but only blank typing paper, then that would be the last straw that would shatter Hu's proverbial camel's back and they would all be drug into a bloody, gruesome mess.

At the very moment that Hu was about to open the satchel, four Mercury Ford Sables came speeding up the road. The cars came bounding over the curb, veering onto the grass and fishtailing as they sped down to the knoll. Everybody's attention was now being diverted from the person on whom they had trained their gun and stared in wonder at the cars rumbling toward them.

The autos skidded to a halt on the slick grass and out jumped a platoon of men in suits and ties. They unholstered their handguns as they ran. "FBI!" one of the men shouted. "Drop your weapons!"

And so, another dimension was added to the bizarre standoff. Now, sixteen more men aimed guns at men who aimed guns at men who aimed guns. Martin looked at Henry who looked at him and then they both looked at Hu. The expression on all three faces silently asked the same unspoken question, *Who invited them?*

Martin almost whimsically smiled at the notion of a new headline in the New York Post, "Armageddon in a Nunnery!"

Chapter 23

One Year Later

EIGHT O'CLOCK MONDAY MORNING FOUND MARTIN bumping down Houston Street in a yellow taxi. His long lost, and newly found friend, Langston, had something to say about Monday mornings:

> No use in going
> Downtown to work today,
> It's eight,
> I'm late-
> And it's marked down that-a-way.
>
> Saturday and Sunday's
> Fun to sport around.
> But no use denying-
> Monday'll get you down.
>
> That old blue Monday
> Will surely get you down.

He stared out the taxi at the light spring rain spritzing the streets. The Village was still drowsy. And then he remembered something…"Mihra, I forgot to tell you, some lady from Water Works called yesterday and said she had found a porcelain sink like you wanted for the downstairs vanity."

Mihra, sitting across from Martin and staring out the window said, "Good."

"Now what's that gonna cost?" Martin asked.

"About five hundred."

Martin nodded, "Not too bad. I can't believe it but we might just stay within budget."

Martin and Mihra had figured that seventy-five thousand dollars would get her brownstone to where she wanted it and to where he wanted it as well. Martin was footing the bill in gratitude for Mihra letting him move in with her. The seventy-five grand was the end of the stash he had accumulated while at Whorman Skeller, but Martin thought, *Good riddance to the last trace of my former life.*

"And that kitchen job is really looking good," he continued. "Those corian counter tops look great with the cabinets, don't you think?"

Mihra still looked out the window and barely managed to say, "Uh-huh..."

Martin studied her for a moment then asked, "What's up, babe? You've been mopey all morning."

Mihra sighed and forlornly shook her head. "I missed my period this month."

"Yeah, well, what's wrong with that? No mess, no PMS, right?"

Mihra looked at Martin incredulously. "Are all men so clueless, Martin? What it means is that I may be pregnant!"

Martin's face fell blank and he emitted a noise that was a cross between a mew and a moan, and then asked, "You're kidding?"

"No, I'm not kidding. I ran out and got a pregnancy test kit while you were getting ready but I didn't have time to do it yet."

Martin put his hand to his head. "Oh man..." And after a minute or two of silence, he said, "You know we'll have to get married real quick if you're pregnant."

Mihra shrugged. "What's the rush? What is it, like, a third of babies born today are born out of wedlock?"

"Mihra, we are not having our child born illegit. I'm not living up, or rather living down to that old black male stereotype of the irresponsible impregnator who—

"Okay, all right, Martin, enough already," Mihra said, cutting him off. She knew how he could orate on the topic of "Ideals for Black African-American Males and Ideas for Their Improvement." What had once been a topic for dinner conversation was gradually turning into a crusade for Martin, who, she thought, was sounding more and more like a modern-day Booker T. Washington. But it was too early in the morning for a stem-winder.

"And what about your parents?" he asked. "Particularly your old man? Man, is he gonna bug out. He'll go on a jihad if he finds out you're pregnant and not married."

"What does it matter what he thinks? He's already practically disowned me for shacking up with a man—especially a black man. Besides, if I'm pregnant and it's a boy and he can have a grandson, he'll be willing to forgive a lot of things. But if it's a girl, well…who knows…"

"Mihra, if it's a boy and it's a bastard, to use the term I'm sure he'll use, then shame and anger is all he'll feel."

"Martin, I think I know my father better than you, okay."

"All I'm saying is that if you are pregnant, we're getting married and quick."

"How dare you issue orders to me about things of such importance, Martin. You got a lot of nerve!"

Martin tossed his hands up and let them fall dejectedly onto his lap and they went back to staring out of their respective windows.

"Listen to us," Mihra said in a softer tone. "We're arguing like we've been married for years."

"Nah, we have too much sex to be mistaken for a married couple," Martin said with a leering grin.

Mihra laughed and took hold of Martin's hand. "That's why we're in this predicament. That night you jumped me in the kitchen and threw me on the table. I didn't even have time to put my diaphragm in. Look, there's no point in us getting all worked up until I find out whether I'm pregnant or not. Okay, sugar bear? I'll do the test as soon as we get to the studio."

The taxi turned off Houston and onto Mott and then into a small parking lot in front of a two-story building. Occupying the building was Inner Ear Sound Studio, jointly owned and managed by Martin and Henry Stallowrth and Mihra Klahabani.

Martin and Mihra exited the taxi and walked up the steps to the locked front door. After Martin pushed the door buzzer and identified himself on the intercom, he and Mihra walked through the foyer and into the reception room, where a young, black woman handed Martin a bunch of pink message slips. "Tommy Mottola called and asked that you call him back at 3:00 p.m. today for a conference call with some Sony suits."

"I'm going back to my office to check what we got scheduled for sessions today," Mihra called as she exited the room. Martin coughed nervously, knowing that Mihra was really going to do her pregnancy test.

"And also somebody from Hard Copy called and said they'd be here in fifteen minutes for the interview," the secretary continued.

Martin slapped his forehead. "Damn, I forgot all about that. Is Henry in yet? Maybe he could do the interview instead."

"Henry's back in the studio, working on something. But the Hard Copy producer said they specifically wanted to interview you."

"Oh, man..." Martin groaned. *How many more of these interviews could he stand? Hadn't the public seen and read enough about him?*

It seemed that every major newspaper had reported how he had single-handedly busted the biggest espionage ring in recent memory. Okay, the truth was that the FBI had been tracking Hu a long time before he had entered the picture. And *The New York Times* reported that the Feds had been following through wiretaps and an informant, the whole saga—all the way from Hap delivering the Lodestar files to Mihra's kidnapping

But they hadn't intervened, even when Martin had been publicly accused of murdering Moore or when Hap had been "shorted" or when an innocent victim like Mihra had been kidnapped. Martin still went dizzy with rage whenever he considered how careless the US government had been with his, Mihra's and Hap's lives.

The FBI's excuse for not acting was that they didn't want to blow the chance to catch Hu red-handed. And when they had heard about the meeting at The Cloisters, they had planned to stake out the place and be ready in full force for the bust. But they had gotten caught in the mid-town Manhattan gridlock and so had shown up at the scene about forty-five minutes later than they had intended. A minute later and they would have found a few more candidates for the sarcophagus room.

And whether it was on Good Morning America, Dateline, the Larry King Show, or People Magazine, Martin would try to downplay his role by saying, "All I wanted was to clear myself as a murder suspect and free my girlfriend. I really hadn't set out to expose a spy ring..." he would try to explain. But nobody wanted to hear that. The story was too compelling with—spying, murder, an internationally known rogue trader as villain, and the coup de grace, a young black man as the all-American hero. All just what the media was always praying for, another news story to rival that of Princess Di's death.

And the story had gotten even better now that the American hero and his brother, whose shooting of "Cincinnati Red" had been cleared as self-defense, and girlfriend had bought a recording studio and started their own hip-hop label.

(Fortunately, none of the puffery, infotainment stories had questioned where Martin had gotten the million plus dollars that this enterprise required. The real answer was that it had come from the lucre that Henry had amassed as the erstwhile drug lord, Trex.)

And now, Hard Copy wanted to do one more, follow-up story on the American hero and his life as a "recording impresario."

Martin walked into the next room, which served as a lounge. Sprawled about on the couch and floor were the members of Biz-E-G's, the first act Inner Ear had signed. They were a group that Henry, as the de facto talent scout for the label, had discovered playing at the Tunnel one Sunday night. The boys were now all comatose, having pulled an all-night recording session. Their brand of hip-hop was gangsta-flavored. Seeing one of the thugs asleep on the floor, Martin for an instant imagined a chalk outline drawn around his body.

Adjacent to the lounge was one of the two sound rooms. At the control panel was Henry and a couple of engineers. A rapper was on the other side of the glass spewing at the mike. And standing behind Henry was none other than Pops.

"Hey, what you doing here?" Martin said to Pops as he entered the sound room. Buster ambled up to Martin for a pat on his blockhead.

"Layin' some tracks," he answered over the rapper's cadences resounding in the room.

Henry turned from the control board and said, "Pops found this kid at his gym. The kid heard about us on BET and did a number for Pops. I'll tell you what; the kid's rhythmic. We might wanna work some with him, Pops." Henry held his hand—the hand bearing Pops' ring—back over his shoulder for Pops to slap.

"Yeah, I tell you what," Pops said, "the little man throws a riff about as good as he does a left hook. He's a little buck wild is his only problem."

Martin was glad to see that Pops and Henry were talking again. Pops had come to the studio for the first time about three months ago, "Just to check it out." But he wouldn't come until Martin had convinced him that Henry had given up slinging 'caine. "I see Annie Belle every time I see that boy," he had murmured to Martin.

Martin's secretary then entered the room to tell him that Kolonel Kaos was on the line. Martin left the sound room and took the call in his small adjoining office.

"Wazhapnin?" the Kolonel asked.

"You're what's happening," Martin assured him. "We got you scheduled for the session at 3:30 p.m. today—you better not miss it like you did last time."

Kolonel Kaos was one of several rap artists whom Martin was working with on a project that he had conceived and developed. He was taking poetry from well-known African-American writers and transposing it into a hip-hop context. Most of the major names had signed onto the project and Martin was almost done putting down the tracks except for Kolonel Kaos's number. The poem he was to rap was Ishmael Reed's, "Oakland Blues."

"You got your lines down?" Martin asked.

"Man, I been trying to slip into this thing but some of it ain't jivin'. I mean these first four lines are outta the groove, 'Well it's six o'clock in Oakland/and the sun is full of wine/I say, it's six o'clock in Oakland and the sun is red with wine…' Now why does the man have to go repeatin' hisself? You know what I'm saying? Why don't you save yourself some tape and let me chunk the first two lines?"

"Listen, uh…" (Martin paused, never knowing what to call him. Was he really supposed to address him as Kolonel?) "Listen, you just read it the way it's written. This isn't like ripping off James Brown or Tower of Power for a sample. I had to pay good money for permission to use this poem. So instead of me asking Ishmael Reed to change his work to please you, you're gonna have to take it as is. You got me?"

"Man, I don't know. This really ain't my bag, you diggin? My stuff is a little more grimey and crimey. This ain't hip-hop, it's more hip-pop. You really think niggas out there are gonna listen to this?"

Martin was about to say, *That yes, he did think there were plenty of blacks who were proud of their literary heritage and who would want to hear it on this CD.* And as evidence of that, Martin could have pointed to the rumors that this project, dubbed the "Caged Bird," had put him on the candidate list for a NAACP Black Image Award.

Martin had nixed that, however, when during his Larry King appearance he had described the NAACP as, "…peopled by political dinosaurs, who were trapped in a 1960's mindset that thought the only way black people could get anything was if white people gave it to them." The next day, Martin got a call from an NAACP representative, who said, "Maybe you heard, Mr. Stallworth, some rumors floating around that you're up for a Black Image Award. I'm just calling to tell you that there is about as much chance of that as a Klansman going to heaven."

But Martin didn't say any of that to the Kolonel. What he did say was, "Look man, if you don't wanna do this gig, just tell me. It's no sweat off my back. Smallie Ballies has been begging me to get on this CD. So if you bail out that leaves a slot open for him."

"Smallie Ballies, man you gotta be pullin' my pud! That little mac rimes like's got a dry-backed turd in his mouth. He's a whacked out crack head nigga to boot. He'd cornhole a cat for a bowl. I saw him shufflin' down Lenox just week, leaving a trail of drool behind him like a slug. Tried to kill his manager five different times I hear, but always too fucked-up to aim straight. Smallie Ballies? Gimme a break!"

"So you'll be here at 3:30 p.m. with your lines down then?"

"Book it, Dan-O."

Martin's secretary's voice then came over the intercom informing him that Mr. Skeets Daniel was on line five.

"Yo, Skeets!"

"Marty, my man. How's my soul bro doin'?"

"Juggling, Skeets, juggling. How's retirement treating you?"

"Nothin' too strange or wonderful. Myrtle Beach is what it is. Chasin' a lot of birdies on and off the golf course."

"I bet you are."

"Hey, I called just to thank you for that generous contribution you made to the scholarship fund we set up in Hap's name."

"No problem."

"It still chafes my ass that Boston College wouldn't go for it. I guess all those news reports made Hap sound like he was a spy or something but you and I know better. I'm just glad his high school took it. I guess a little ole catholic school in South Boston can always use some bread…Hey, you hear about Lori Putterman?"

"No, what happened?"

"Oh man, you're not gonna believe this. She got arrested last week."

"For what?"

"Kickbacks. Evidently she'd been doing some quid pro quo business with that ole bond hag, Gloria Shanks. They came onto the trading floor and handcuffed her right there, for everybody to see."

"Poor Lori."

"I hear she put up a wicked fight and tried to make a run for it. They chased her all around the trading floor and everybody was applauding and cheering. And when they finally caught her, she kicked and screamed like she was being put on the last boat to Hades. Supposedly broke one of the agent's nose with the toe of her Ferragamo."

"How long do you think she'll get?"

"Well, if they convict her, she could get 2-3. But I don't think it'll get that far. She'll end up copin' a plea. Probably have to rat on Shanks, who probably is the one who finked on her in the first place."

"I hope it works out for her."

"Somebody'll probably be calling you for a contribution to help pay her legal bills. They already hit me up."

"Damn, working on Whorman Skeller's high-yield desk is expensive, huh?"

"Not to mention unhealthy."

"Hey, whatever happened to Libby? I haven't heard a thing about her since I left..."

"She got married."

"Who was the victim?"

"That Don Languano fella. Rich son-of-a-bitch. Gave her the money to open up a Body Shop. Can you believe it?"

"There's not much anymore I wouldn't believe."

"And you know who they made head of the high-yield desk to take Moore's spot?"

"No, who?"

"Lyle Shiner."

"Oh, you're joking."

"Proves that old adage, the shit floats to the top on Wall Street."

"The guy's a survivor, I'll give him that. Did that fucking Lodestar deal ever get done?"

"Nope. It finally got pulled."

"I guess with all that was happening, there was no chance of it getting done."

"No, not really. I think it could have gotten done. It's funny, but all that publicity actually generated some interest in the deal."

"What was the problem then?"

"That dickhead Kinkaid went and sold the company to ATT. Pulled the rug right out from under us. Evidently, he had been negotiating the sale of the company the whole time he was trying to do the bond deal. Guess he wanted to see which deal, the sale or the bond financing, was better for him. In the end, selling was the way he went."

Martin's stomach went queasy. "God, you mean all that hell we went through was for nothing? A total waste of time and lives, was moot, just a sham because Kinkaid was trying to sell the company the whole time? I'm feeling sick, Skeets."

"That's high finance for you, Marty."

Just then there was a knock on the door and a chubby guy with a Prince Valiant hairdo stuck his head into Martin's office, ignored the fact he was on the phone and asked, "You ready for make-up?"

"Skeets, I gotta run, some guy here's asking me if I want some make-up?"

"Watch your rear, son. I'll talk at you soon."

Martin said to "Prince Valiant," "Makeup? What are you talking about?"

"Debbie Norville takes at least an hour to get done, so I need to start on you now if we're going to stay on schedule," he answered with the expected lisp.

"Oh yeah, that interview. Okay, let's go."

The makeup artist set up a portable vanity stand next to Martin's desk. "Okay, let's start with a little mascara..." Armed with an eye stencil and smelling like a wilted lily, he leaned his bulk over Martin's chest. "Now look into my eyes," he said, just a little too breathlessly.

Martin was saved from that by Mihra entering the room. "Hello, sweets," he said to her.

"Well, I hope you know the words to Rock-a-bye baby," she said with a shrug and a huge, lopsided smile.

THE END

0-595-27682-2